"I don't mess around for sport," Lainey whispered. "When I kiss someone it means something."

Brad leaned toward her intimately, looking sexy as hell. Every bit the intimidating bachelor he'd been on TV. "Maybe that's the problem," he returned, grasping her by the shoulders. "Whenever I've kissed someone, it's never once meant anything close to what it should."

"What are you trying to say?" Lainey murmured, wishing she didn't recall quite so vividly how passionately he'd kissed, or how tenderly he'd held her in his arms.

His gaze drifted over her. "It's high time my kisses *did* mean something."

He took her into his arms and kissed her deeply. She clung to him, kissing him back. Sensations swirled through her as his hands moved down her spine, working their magic.

The kiss turned sweeter, more tender. "Brad…we really shouldn't do—"

"Do what?" he prompted lazily, kissing her again.

"This," Lainey said, kissing him back.

When he finally let her go, she was so dizzy she could barely stand.

Dear Reader,

There is fiction, and there is real life, and when the two come together these days it is called "reality TV." Like many of you, I have watched programs dealing with survival, business and home decorating. But it's the programs about romance that fascinate me the most. Can someone really find the love of their life on a semiscripted TV show? Or is it all about the money and achieving fifteen minutes of fame?

I don't know the answer to those questions, but I do know it was a heck of a lot of fun creating my own reality television show, *Bachelor Bliss*, and imagining what would happen if the ultimate Texas cowboy/ladies' man, Brad McCabe, somehow got roped into signing up to appear on one.

I figured he wouldn't find romance there. That would come later—after the experience of chasing fame and fortune had wreaked havoc on his life.

And I knew it wouldn't be easy, either. True love never is. Which is why I paired Brad with an old high school classmate he had barely known existed. Someone with ambition of her own—*journalistic* ambition. For a private guy like Brad, that's a worst-case scenario.

How did it all end? Well, to find that out, you'll have to turn the page....

I hope you enjoy reading this romantic comedy as much as I enjoyed writing it. If you'd like to know more about this and other books, I invite you to visit my Web site at www.cathygillenthacker.com.

Happy reading!

Cathy Gillen Thacker

THE ULTIMATE TEXAS BACHELOR

Cathy Gillen Thacker

HARLEQUIN®

TORONTO • NEW YORK • LONDON
AMSTERDAM • PARIS • SYDNEY • HAMBURG
STOCKHOLM • ATHENS • TOKYO • MILAN • MADRID
PRAGUE • WARSAW • BUDAPEST • AUCKLAND

ISBN 0-373-75084-6

THE ULTIMATE TEXAS BACHELOR

Copyright © 2005 by Cathy Gillen Thacker.

This edition published by arrangement with Harlequin Books S.A.

® and TM are trademarks of the publisher. Trademarks indicated with ® are registered in the United States Patent and Trademark Office, the Canadian Trade Marks Office and in other countries.

www.eHarlequin.com

Printed in U.S.A.

This book is dedicated to Joshua Douglas Gerhardt,
ultimate flirt and total heartbreaker.
Welcome to the family, little one.

Chapter One

"Come on, Lainey. Have a heart! You can't leave us like this!" Lewis McCabe declared as he pushed his eyeglasses farther up on the bridge of his nose.

Aside from the fact she was here under false pretenses—which she had quickly decided she couldn't go through with, anyway—Lainey Carrington didn't see how she could stay, either. The Lazy M ranch house looked like a college dorm room had exploded on moving day. Lewis needed a lot more than the live-in housekeeper he had been advertising for, to bring order to this mess.

Lainey studied the nerdiest—and most technologically brilliant—of Sam and Kate McCabe's five grown sons and wondered how anyone so rich could still be so out of step with popular culture. Where had he gotten those clothes, anyway? From some 1980s-style shop?

"What do you mean *us?*" she asked suspiciously. Was Lewis married? If so, she hadn't heard about it, but then her knowledge was spotty at best since she hadn't actually lived in Laramie, Texas, since she left home for college ten years ago.

The door behind Lainey opened. She turned—and darn near fainted at the sight of the man she had secretly come here to track down.

Not that she had expected the six-foot-three cowboy, with

the ruggedly handsome face and to-die-for body to actually be here. She had just hoped that Lewis would give her a clue where to look, so that she might help her friend Sybil Devine hunt the elusive Brad McCabe down and scrutinize the sexy Casanova celebrity in person.

"Brad, of course, who happens to be my business partner," Lewis McCabe explained.

"Actually, I'm more of a ranch manager," Brad McCabe corrected grimly, shooting an aggravated look at his younger brother. He knocked some of the mud off his scuffed, brown leather boots, then stepped into the interior of the sprawling half-century-old ranch house. "And I thought we had an agreement, Lewis, that you'd let me know when we were going to have company so I could avoid running into 'em."

Lewis shot Lainey an apologetic glance. "Don't mind him. He's been in a bad mood ever since he got done filming that reality TV show."

Lainey took the opportunity to gather a little background research. "Guess that didn't exactly have the happily-ever-after ending everyone expected it to have," she observed.

Brad's jaw set. Clearly, he did not want her sympathy. "You saw it?"

Obviously he wished she hadn't. Lainey shrugged, not about to admit just how riveted she'd been by the sight of Brad McCabe on her television screen. "I think everyone who knows you did."

"Not to mention most of America," Lewis chimed in.

Bachelor Bliss had pulled in very high ratings, especially at the end, when it had taken an unexpected twist. Which wasn't surprising, given how sexy Brad had looked walking out of the ocean in a pair of swim trunks that had left very little to the imagination. He'd been equally appealing on the back of a horse, riding into the mountains at sunset, or dressed in a tuxedo while enjoying a night on the town.

The only thing she hadn't liked was the sight of him kissing one pretty woman after another…and he had done an awful lot of that.

"You shouldn't have wasted your time watching such bull," Brad muttered, his scowl deepening as his voice dropped a self-deprecating notch. "And I know I shouldn't have wasted mine filming it."

Lainey agreed with him wholeheartedly there. Going on an artificially romantic TV show was no way to find a mate. "For what it's worth, I don't think they did right by you," Lainey said.

Brad's brow arched as if he dared her to go on.

Lainey gulped but held her ground. "The way they depicted you was not very flattering," she continued bravely, knowing that if she was going to convince him to open up to her, he was first going to have to realize she did indeed believe he had gotten a raw deal. And more importantly, that she wanted him to be able to tell his side of things. Which, to date, he had not done.

"Gee." His gaze clashed with hers. "You think?"

"I agree," Lewis put in genially, seeming not to notice the sparks arcing between Brad and Lainey. "Those producers did make you look like a womanizing jerk with the attention span of a flea."

Brad folded his arms over his chest, frustration coming off him in waves. "Maybe I *am* a womanizing jerk with the attention span of a flea," he said.

Somehow, Lainey didn't think so. For one thing, the McCabes—who were known for their honesty and integrity—would never have let him get away with that in real life. She knew he'd tried it as a kid, shortly after his family moved to Laramie, Texas, and had gotten reined in quickly, both by family and by the girls he had triple-timed. And for another thing, Brad had not appeared to be enjoying himself on the TV show as he tried to decide which of fifteen eligible women to take as his bride. Instead, he had seemed…

impatient with the entire process. Restless. Except when with Yvonne Rathbone, the flame-haired beauty he had eventually paired up with. Then, he had seemed genuinely lovestruck. Until the end, anyway.

"And maybe you're not," Lainey countered calmly.

Not that her opinion was widely shared. Thanks to the brouhaha that had followed the finale of the eight *Bachelor Bliss* episodes featuring Brad McCabe, he had been a fixture in gossip columns and celebrity magazines. Everyone wanted to know why Brad had done what he had, but Brad wasn't talking—at least not to the press.

And thus far, those close to him weren't talking, either.

It was Lainey's task to see what she could do about changing that, and letting the whole truth and nothing but the truth finally be known. Not that it looked to be easy.

She had heard from mutual acquaintances that Brad Mc-Cabe's experience as the sought-after bachelor on *Bachelor Bliss* had turned him not just into *persona non grata* where the entire viewing public was concerned, but also into a hardened cynic. Judging by the scowl on his face and the unwelcoming light in his eyes as he swept off his straw cowboy hat and ran his fingers through his gleaming dark brown hair, that assumption seemed to be true.

The Brad McCabe that Lainey recalled from her youth had been two years ahead of her in school, cheerful and charming as could be. He had been more city kid than cowboy back then. Full of charm and life, always ready with a wink and a smile and a witty remark.

Now, he appeared ready to bite her head off. His brother's, too, as Brad surveyed them both with shadowed, sable-brown eyes.

Lainey swallowed hard and tried not to notice how nicely the blue chambray shirt hugged his broad shoulders and molded to the sculpted muscles of his chest, before disappearing beneath the waistband of his worn, dark blue denim jeans.

"Not that I expected to see you out here, in any case," Lainey continued truthfully, forcing her eyes away from his rodeo belt buckle and gazing back up at his face. "Since word is you've been hiding out from just about everyone."

"I'm not hiding." Brad looked ready to kick some Texas butt. Hers, specifically. "I'm getting on with my life. And there are plenty of people in Laramie who know exactly where to find me."

Lainey shrugged as another shimmer of awareness sifted through her, weakening her knees. "The press can't seem to locate you."

"And that's exactly the way it's going to stay," Brad enunciated clearly, looking deep into her eyes. "I have nothing to say to them."

Which was a problem as far as Lainey was concerned, as she was currently trying to fulfill her long-held dream of becoming a reporter.

"Brad figures too much has been said about him as it is," Lewis confided to Lainey. Lewis tried to adapt some of his older brother's inherent cool as he slouched against a low wall of moving boxes, but instead he knocked several over. They tumbled to the scuffed wooden floor with a clatter. Lewis scrambled to pick them up while Brad, shaking his head in silent exasperation, leaned forward lazily to lend a hand. "The past is over," Lewis continued. "He's looking toward the future. Which is why he agreed to start up this ranch with me—"

"You have to pay in half to be a partner," Brad interrupted, looking irritated again. "I haven't done that. Therefore I'm the ranch manager." Brad turned back to Lainey. He looked her up and down suspiciously, from the top of her carefully coiffed chin-length blond hair, to her casual suede slides. "And you are…?"

It shouldn't have surprised Lainey Carrington that Brad McCabe didn't recognize her. Brad was two years older than she was. It had been a good ten years since they had run into each other in the halls of Laramie High School. And she hadn't been back to Laramie much in the last couple of years since her parents died.

She touched the strand of pearls around her neck. Wishing for some odd reason that she was wearing something other than the demure, pale blue sweater set and knee-length khaki skirt, she smiled. "I'm Lainey Carrington."

To Lainey's frustration, Brad still had no clue.

"When I was in high school I was known as Lainey Wilson," Lainey explained. "Greta Wilson McCabe, who runs the Lone Star Dance Hall—"

"Our aunt by marriage." Lewis beamed.

"Right." Lainey nodded. "Well, Greta's my cousin."

"Lainey was one of the princesses on the Homecoming Court, when she was a senior and I was a freshman," Lewis explained. "I remember because the dress you wore for the parade…"

Had caused quite a scandal. Lainey felt herself flush bright pink.

Brad looked at Lewis and lifted a brow, waiting for him to finish.

Lewis started stammering and staring at the toes of his Birkenstock sandals. Obviously, he wished he had never started the story.

Figuring she might as well own up to it—Brad McCabe was going to hear all about it later anyway—Lainey put in dryly, "Suffice it to say, the dress I chose for the festivities was a little too 'adult' for the occasion." She had picked it up at a secondhand shop in nearby San Angelo that was run by the Junior League. The black velvet dress had been beautiful, no doubt about it, and at ten dollars, quite a steal. But the plunging neckline, short clinging skirt and five-inch stiletto heels had been more suited for a sophisticated cocktail party than a high-school football game.

Lainey had known this, of course, even as she had accepted a dare from her friends to wear it. She had worked to disguise the deep V neckline, front and back, with an embroidered white-and-black silky evening wrap that she had worn with movie-star grandeur. Until a strong gust of Texas wind had ripped it off her shoulders and under the wheels of the junior-class float behind her.

And there she had been, her décolletage exposed nearly to the waist for all the world to see. A terribly embarrassed Lainey had had no choice but to finish the parade, sans wrap. When the floats had reached the stadium, the entire Homecoming Court had been whisked off the backs of their borrowed convertibles and onto the football field for the crowning ceremony during the pre-game festivities. The principal, seeing Lainey being walked across the field by a gawking football player, had been apoplectic, as had many of the other parents, at the amount of cleavage exposed. Lainey's equally ostentatiously dressed mother was the only one who hadn't thought it a big deal.

"You got suspended for violating the school dress code, didn't you?" Lewis asked.

Lainey nodded, her humiliation complete. She hadn't thought about any of this since Chip Carrington had taken her under his wing and made sure she knew what suitable attire was. Ten years had passed and she'd never worn anything the slightest bit risqué since.

Brad threaded his way through the boxes and furniture stacked here and there, and made his way into the kitchen. He pulled a soda can out of the refrigerator, seemed to think about offering one to Lainey, then didn't. Probably, she figured, because he didn't want to give her an excuse to linger.

She watched as he popped the top.

Wordlessly, Lewis walked over to the fridge and got out two cans of blackberry-flavored soda. Lewis brought one back to Lainey, still talking to Brad over his shoulder. "The reason you probably don't recall any of this is that you had already graduated from Laramie High School two years before, and gone on to…well…"

"Flunk out of college," Brad said, finishing yet another sentence Lewis never should have started.

Visibly embarrassed, Lewis pushed his glasses up on his nose again. He shoved a hand through his spiky, light brown hair. "Yeah. Guess you two have that in common, since you both were always in trouble back then."

Only because she hadn't had the guidance she needed, Lainey thought resentfully. "Well, not anymore," she said firmly. "I have an eight-year-old son now." She was a pillar of the community in the Highland Park area of Dallas. Or at least she had been, until she had agreed to drive out to the Lazy M Ranch, to see what she could find out for her friend, Sybil.

Brad and Lewis both glanced at her left hand, checking out the wedding and engagement rings she had recently stopped wearing. "I lost my husband, Chip Carrington, two years ago."

"Sorry to hear that," Lewis said.

Lainey nodded, even as she noticed the flash of sympathy in Brad's eyes that disappeared almost as quickly as it had appeared.

"That why you're looking for a job as a housekeeper?" Brad asked with a look of utter male supremacy.

Lainey didn't even want to consider what her blue-blooded in-laws, Bunny and Bart Carrington, would think about her taking a position as a domestic. Financially, she didn't need to, thanks to Chip's trust fund. Emotionally, intellectually…well, that was something else. She wasn't sure how much longer she could go on living a life that didn't even feel like her own. There were too many hours in a day, not nearly enough for her to do—and with her son, Petey, needing her less and less… Not that loneliness and boredom were any excuse for what Sybil had asked her to do, or offered in return,

Lainey chided herself. Even if such action was the gateway to the career she had always yearned for and had never had the opportunity to go for. At least not yet.

Aware Brad was waiting for her answer, she said, "I'm not here to apply for a job."

Suspicion hardened the ruggedly handsome features on Brad's face. "Then what are you doing all the way out here?"

Sybil had been right—this man had turned into quite a handful. "I was on my way back from Laramie and heard Lewis had bought a ranch out here. So I thought I would stop by and say hello."

"And yet you two were never friends," Brad stated suspiciously.

Lewis glowered at Brad, then turned back to Lainey. "I'm glad you stopped by and I'd be even happier if you'd agree to help me out here. Forget him." Lewis indicated Brad with a telling glare.

Brad stepped between Lainey and Lewis. He gave Lainey a slow, deliberate once-over that had Lainey's pulse racing before addressing Lewis again. "I'm merely pointing out I think it's mighty peculiar that Lainey here stopped by out of the blue. After what? Some ten years or so?"

"What are you insinuating?" Lainey asked coolly, her soda halfway to her mouth, not sure whether she was angrier with Brad or herself for getting into this predicament. Surely there was an easier story she could have started with to jump-start her career!

Brad flashed her a crocodile smile that didn't begin to reach his battle-hardened eyes. "That Lewis is not what you are in search of."

BRAD HAD BEEN HOPING—in direct contradiction to the knot in his gut—that Lainey Carrington's sudden appearance at the Lazy M had been innocent in nature. The look on her face, when he voiced his suspicion, told him it was anything but.

Yet another female he couldn't trust.

Why did that surprise him?

Was it her angelic beauty that had him wanting to believe he could trust her? Her fair, perfect skin and the ripe peach hue blushing across her high, elegant cheeks? The silky cap of neatly arranged honey-blond hair around her oval face? The straightness of her pert, slender nose and the determined set of her feminine chin? Or was it the enticing curve of her bow-shaped lips and the warmth in her long-lashed, forest green eyes? Brad couldn't say for sure what it was that attracted him to her so fiercely. All he knew was that he had been around beautiful women all his life and been chased by more than he could count, but none had stopped him dead in his tracks the way Lainey Wilson Carrington had. None had made his heart stall in his chest, to the point he felt frozen in time. Like this moment was something he would always remember.

Which was maybe why he should continue giving her a hard time. To keep the walls up and prevent himself from succumbing to such cornball sentiment. Brad gave her his kick-butt glare. "I'm still waiting for that explanation."

"Maybe you should back off," Lewis said, looking ready to rumble for the first time Brad could remember. That didn't surprise Brad—something about Lainey, some inherent sense of vulnerability, had brought out the knight in him, too, before he had come to his senses.

Lainey turned to Lewis with a reassuring smile. "I don't mind explaining what brought me here." She drew a breath and turned back to Brad. "I stopped by because I wanted to talk to Lewis about the computer-software video games his company puts out. I heard some of the companies used kids to focus-test new products before they are actually marketed and that Lewis had built a new facility in Laramie for his company, McCabe Computer Games. I wanted to know if it would be possible to have my eight-year-old son, Petey, participate in a trial of a new computer game. I thought it might be a fun thing for him to do this summer while school is out. But when I arrived and saw the chaos, and realized Lewis was in the process of interviewing household managers, I knew that it wasn't a good time to be stopping by after all."

Brad's gut told him that as truthful as Lainey was obviously trying to be, she was also leaving out some mighty important parts. The deliberate omissions were what concerned him most. "And you have no interest whatsoever in me," Brad surmised.

The color on her cheeks deepened self-consciously, even as her chin lifted a challenging notch. "Why on earth would I be interested in you?"

Brad answered her with a lazy shrug. "The same reason everyone else in America is. Because I am the villain du jour."

Lewis added, "You wouldn't believe how many people— folks the family hasn't heard from in years—have called up, wanting the inside scoop on what happened with Brad on that TV show."

Lainey flushed and didn't meet Brad's probing gaze. Another sign, Brad thought, that she was nosy as charged.

Lainey defended herself with an indignant toss of her head. "Believe me, I had no idea you were out here, Brad McCabe. Never mind in such a cantankerous mood!"

Not one to take an insult lying down, Brad narrowed his eyes at her. "What is that supposed to mean?" he demanded.

Lainey glared at him, sipped her drink, and didn't reply.

"I think that's pretty clear." Lewis stepped between Brad and Lainey. "She's telling you that you're rude."

Brad wasn't about to apologize for that, darn it all. "I don't want company," he announced bluntly. Hers or anyone else's."

Lewis arched his brow. "Fine by me. Then leave. 'Cause I want to talk Lainey into helping me out here."

Lainey sighed and tore her gaze from Brad's. "I told you, Lewis. I am not in the market for a job as a housekeeper. I need to be at home with my son this summer."

Lewis was undaunted. "Your son could come to work with you. Test out new games here at the ranch and at my company's new facility in Laramie. He'd have a blast!"

It was all Brad could do not to groan as Lainey hesitated, clearly tempted.

"I'm not asking for much. I just need help getting settled," Lewis continued persuasively. "All of my stuff unpacked and organized, along with Brad's."

Lainey tilted her head. "Your moving company should have offered that service."

"They said they'd unpack it for an extra fee," Lewis explained. "They also wanted me to tell the workers where to put everything. I couldn't do that because I don't know where it goes. I don't have time to think about stuff like that. Never mind figure out how to get a kitchen put together and all that."

Lainey looked at Brad as if expecting him to help. "Don't look at me," he said gruffly. "I've got my hands full trying to get the stable, pastures and barns ready to go."

Sighing, Lainey turned back to Lewis. "Don't you have a girlfriend who could help you?"

Lewis flushed beet-red and shook his head.

"What about your little sister or your stepmom?" Lainey insisted.

"They both think he should be doing it himself, and they're right," Brad said. "It's best to be self-sufficient."

"Spoken like a die-hard bachelor," she muttered just loud enough for them both to hear.

"The truth is," Lewis said, "Laurel and Kate probably would help me out, but Brad doesn't want them around right now. 'Cause they ask too many questions. You know…about how he's *feeling* and stuff."

Brad rubbed his jaw. "I think Lainey Carrington can do without the play-by-play."

"Well, it's the truth!" Lewis countered.

Brad's temper flared. "Sometimes the truth does not need to be told!"

"Sounds like you have a pretty complicated situation," Lainey told Lewis sympathetically.

"So will you help me out?" he asked eagerly. "I'll give you one hundred dollars an hour to help me get organized. Because that's what professional organizers charge. At a few weeks—let's say three—that would be twelve thousand dollars, give or take. If you decide you want to cook for us, I'll pay you for that, too."

To Brad's chagrin, Lainey seemed intrigued.

Lainey blinked. "What were you planning to pay a housekeeper?"

Lewis shrugged. "If she lived in, fifty thousand, with free room and board. Like I said, I'm planning to make the guest house into the housekeeper's quarters."

Lainey cast a look in the direction Lewis was pointing. Her soft lips pursed thoughtfully. "How much room does it have?"

It was all Brad could do not to groan out loud as his brilliant but clueless brother answered. "Eleven hundred square feet—a kitchen, living room, two bedrooms, one and a half baths."

"She already told you no," Brad interjected, knowing the last thing he needed was a nosy female underfoot. Lewis would be gone all day. It was Brad who would be here at the ranch, dealing with Lainey one-on-one, running into her every time he turned around!

Lainey scowled at Brad. "Excuse me. I don't believe either of us was talking to you."

Brad closed the distance between them, not stopping until they were nose to nose. "Well, I *am* talking to you. And let's be serious here." He paused to let his gaze drift over her in an insulting manner before returning to her green eyes. "A woman like you isn't cut out to live and work on a ranch." She was clearly pampered and city-chic. She even had pearls and earrings on. No woman on a ranch wore pearls and earrings and suede shoes with the heels and toes cut out. Plus, she had sensational legs! How was he supposed to get any work done when she was walking around in a skirt, showing them off?

Lainey folded her arms and leaned toward him. "Oh, for heaven's sake!" she scolded him fiercely, oblivious to the way her stance was lifting the soft curves of her breasts. "He isn't asking me to dig ditches!"

Brad frowned, refusing to let the alluring fragrance of her perfume distract him. With difficulty, he kept his gaze away from the fabric stretched across her breasts. He'd already had one glimpse of her shapely form, he didn't need another. "Those hands don't look like they've done any hard labor indoors, either," he continued.

Lainey released a long-suffering sigh. "I use hand cream," she explained as if to a moron, then turned back to Lewis, all smug self-confidence. "You say I can bring my son to work with me?"

This time Brad did groan out loud.

Lewis perked up. "Heck, yeah. You can even bunk in the guest cottage if you like. That way the two of you wouldn't have to drive back and forth to—"

"Highland Park."

Which was, Brad thought, one of the most exclusive neighborhoods in Dallas.

"This is the worst idea I've ever heard," Brad said, figuring the last thing they needed was some small-town-girl-turned-society-mama out here.

Lainey and Lewis turned to Brad. "No one asked you!" they declared in unison.

Lainey said to Lewis, "You understand it would only be for a few weeks?"

Lewis grinned, looking ridiculously slaphappy. "Unless I can talk you and your son into staying on permanently."

"You don't even know if she can cook!" Brad practically shouted.

Lewis shrugged. "If she doesn't, she can learn. Can't you, Lainey?"

Lainey took a long drink of her soda, then set the can down. "I certainly could. You've got a deal, Lewis. In the meantime, I've got to get back to Highland Park."

Which still wasn't saying if she did or did not know how to cook, Brad thought. Which in his view was an absolute necessity, since it was a twenty-minute drive to the nearest restaurant and the appeal of frozen dinners, sandwiches and prepackaged food—the only stuff he and his brother were capable of fixing—was already wearing mighty thin.

"But you'll be back?" Lewis asked anxiously.

"Oh, yes. Tomorrow." Lainey stared at Brad, all stubborn defiance. "First thing."

Chapter Two

"No."

"Excuse me?" Lainey stared at her sister-in-law, sure she hadn't heard right.

Bunny Carrington touched a hand to the glossy black chignon at her nape. "Bart and I cannot let you take Petey out to some godforsaken ranch for the next few weeks."

Bart, Bunny's henpecked attorney-husband, hadn't said anything thus far. But that wasn't surprising to Lainey. According to Lainey's late husband, Bart had traded away his say in most everything when he agreed to marry Bunny and take her last name of Carrington, instead of have her take his.

Like Lainey, Bart's roots were decidedly blue-collar. In marrying Bunny, he had married up. And now, twenty years and a pair of twin girls later, he was still letting Bunny run the show.

Lainey sat down on the edge of the plush, ultra-suede sofa in Bunny and Bart's family room. Through the plate-glass windows, she could see Petey romping in the lagoon-shaped pool with his eighteen-year-old cousins, Becca and Bonnie. Relieved he was not privy to any of this, Lainey stated calmly, "I think you misunderstood me. I wasn't asking your permission." Any more than she was asking their permission to work as a reporter. "I just wanted you to know where you could contact us."

Bunny glanced at Bart. He looked troubled, too, but not necessarily in agreement with his wife. Obviously, Bunny wanted Bart to say something.

Finally, the tall gangly man with the perpetually defeated expression on his face, cleared his throat. "I think what Bunny is trying to say here is that some changes may need to be made."

A chill ran down Lainey's spine. No one had to remind her that thanks to the terms of the trust Chip had set up for Petey, which Bunny oversaw, all of Lainey's finances were controlled by her sister-in-law. Which was another reason why it was so important she start making some money of her own—soon. "What kind of changes?" Lainey asked suspiciously.

"Bunny thinks that it's impractical for you to be incurring such steep mortgage payments every month."

It hadn't been Lainey's idea to have a ridiculously high mortgage payment every month. Chip was the one who had insisted they purchase a home in Highland Park. Lainey began to relax, ever so slightly. "I'm glad you brought this up," she said, relieved. "I've been wanting to sell the house. It is much too big for just Petey and me."

Not only was it an unnecessary expense, but also the home had too many memories of her and Chip. Lainey was finding it impossible to move on, when everywhere she went she saw and felt her late husband's presence. Lainey had loved her husband terribly. She saw Chip's good qualities in Petey every day. But now that she and Petey had gone through the mourning process, it was time to build a new life.

Lainey smiled at her in-laws. "Petey and I would be happy with something much smaller and less expensive. Which is why I've been thinking about relocating back to my hometown of Laramie, Texas."

Lainey had no family ties there any longer, since both her parents had passed on years ago, but Laramie was still as friendly and laid-back as ever. When she had driven out there earlier this morning, she had been surprised to discover how much it had felt like home.

Bunny and Bart regarded each other tensely.

"You misunderstand us," Bunny said finally. "Bart and I want you and Petey to move in here with us."

BRAD WAS ON HIS WAY OUT to the barn to begin unloading bundles of PVC pipe from his pickup when a familiar dark green SUV turned into the lane leading to the Lazy M ranch house. The vehicle zipped toward the parking area and stopped just short of the guest house. Seconds later, Lainey Carrington was stepping out of the driver's side.

She was wearing an open-necked hot-pink silk shirt with three-quarter sleeves, a trim black skirt that failed to reach her knees, and open-toed sandals that, like the rest of her outfit, were hardly suited for life on a working cattle ranch. Despite the eye-catching hue of her blouse, her outfit was conservative enough to be worn in a corporate setting. The way it hugged her slender curves was another matter indeed.... Just looking at her made Brad's mouth water.

The knowledge of his own desire made him frown. He had promised himself at the end of the TV show that he was swearing off all women for at least a year. It hadn't been a problem—until now. Unbeknownst to the producers who had hired him for *Bachelor Bliss*, his rep as a bed-hopping ladies' man was a hell of a lot more fiction than fact.

She went up to the ranch house door, rang the bell, pressed it again and again. Finally, she came back down the steps and looked toward the barn, where he was busy unloading the back of his pickup truck.

She got back in her vehicle, drove the short distance to where he was, and got out of her SUV again.

Apparently remembering all too well the way they had parted, Lainey gave Brad a cool glance. "Lewis around?"

she asked, stepping nearer in a drift of remarkably alluring perfume.

"Nope." Brad lifted one bundle onto his shoulder, then another.

She marched closer yet, her sexy shoes tapping across the blacktopped ranch driveway. She seemed to be spoiling for a fight. Although, not necessarily with him, Brad noted.

"Care to elaborate?" Lainey asked tightly.

"Nope." Carrying the bundles of pipe, Brad headed for the newly painted beige barn.

She skipped to keep up with his long strides. "Don't be such a—"

Curious as to what she would call him, Brad prompted, "What?"

"Donkey's rear end!"

He grinned. Somehow, he hadn't seen her cussing. At least not out loud. Not that her verbal imagery hadn't done the trick in getting her message across.

Lainey danced across his path, forcing him to detour around her. "Just tell me where he is and I'll leave you alone," she said.

Grimacing, Brad set the bundles down on the cement floor of the barn with a loud *clank*. Then he straightened to face her. "He went to Laramie, to work at his facility there."

Her expression fell and she took a step back. Sunlight poured down from the blue Texas sky, illuminating the honey-gold strands of her hair. "How long is he going to be gone?" she asked.

Brad shrugged, noting the flush of color across her cheeks, the mist of perspiration at her temples. "You'd have to ask Lewis, but he usually puts in a twelve-hour day, if not more." So did Brad.

Frustrated, Lainey raked her teeth across her lower lip. "I really need him here, to tell me where he wants me to get started."

Determined to be as ornery as possible, in hopes she would get ticked off and leave, Brad tipped back the brim of his hat and regarded her with an indifferent gaze. "You'll have to take that up with him."

To his disappointment, Lainey looked undeterred. "I guess I could go ahead and move my stuff into the guest house."

Brad looked back at the SUV. The rear seat was down and it looked packed to the gills with stuff. Even the front passenger seat was heaped with belongings. Brad frowned. "Where's your son?" Not that it mattered to him, but the other day, Lainey had sounded like her son Petey was a very important part of her life.

"Obviously, he's not with me today."

She didn't look happy about that. Which made Brad ask before he could stop himself, "Everything okay?"

Lainey folded her arms in front of her. "You really care?" she asked.

He shouldn't, Brad knew. Not if he was going to keep his distance from the lovely blonde.

"That's what I thought."

Suddenly, she looked near tears. Brad, who had never been much good in the comforting-others department, had an insane urge to take her in his arms. Instead, he remarked, even more matter-of-factly, "If you want to go around looking like you lost your best friend, that's your business."

Lainey swallowed hard, her eyes moistening. "How about if I go around looking like I am losing my only child, then?"

"What are you talking about?"

"Nothing." Lainey sighed and shoved her hands through her hair. "It's none of your business anyway."

"True enough." Brad was silent. What was going on here? It wasn't like him to get involved in anyone else's private business. He had enough trouble managing his own. "Still, if you want to talk…" he found himself saying.

Lainey's voice grew turbulent. "He's at the theme parks in central Florida with his two cousins, aunt and uncle."

"Why didn't you go?"

"Because I wasn't invited."

Ouch. "That was rude."

Lainey's slender shoulders stiffened. "I'm sure Bart and Bunny didn't mean anything by it. They thought I needed some time to myself."

She didn't *look* like she needed time to herself. Brad strode back to the pickup for another load. "When will they be back?"

Lainey remained in the shade of the barn. "The end of the week, which will give me enough time to get settled in and have everything ready for Petey here—so it's probably for the best, anyway."

She didn't look as if she believed that, Brad noted. Not that it was any of his affair.

"Is the guest house unlocked?" she asked.

Brad dropped the second load of pipe next to the first, then fished in his pocket for the key. He dug it out and handed it over, knowing the reason why Lewis had made himself scarce when Lainey would be moving in. Not that it was up to Brad to deliver the bad news to Lainey. It was her fault. She should have investigated further before taking the short-term job with his brother. "Lewis asked me to give this one to you."

"Thanks."

Years of ingrained training had Brad asking, albeit reluctantly, "Need any help unloading your SUV?"

"Nope." She swung away from him, and walked to her vehicle, spectacular legs flashing in the bright June sunlight. As he watched her go, Brad couldn't help but notice she looked more like a well-to-do suburbanite, out for a day of shopping, than a housekeeper or—what was it Lewis had called it—personal organizer?—about to embark on the massive task of making the Lazy M ranch house livable.

Telling himself to quit thinking about her and concentrate on the installation ahead, he continued unloading his pickup, laying pipe, sprinkler heads, fans and linear heat sensors on the cement floor of the freshly scrubbed-out barn. He was nearly done when he heard the first scream. Shrill and terrified sounding, it split the air with the intensity of an air-raid siren.

"What the…?" Brad dropped the box in his hand.

Another scream pierced the air, louder and longer than the last.

He took off at a run.

LAINEY WAS STILL SCREAMING when Brad charged through the open front door and found her crouched, still shaking and scared, atop the kitchen counter.

His expression went from panicked to amused in an instant.

"Look, I know the place is a mess, and you must feel frustrated as hell, but don't you think you're overdoing the drama just a tad?"

Lainey wished that were the case. Not that Brad didn't have a point. Perhaps she shouldn't have yelled like a banshee when she discovered the state of her quarters for the next few weeks.

Unbelievably, the guest cottage was in even worse shape than the Lazy M ranch house. Instead of being crowded with boxes, though, it was heaped with old furniture of various kinds and all sorts of odds and ends. In short, it looked the way many people's attics looked after being neglected a good ten, twenty or thirty years. But that wasn't why she'd been yelling her head off for the past two minutes.

"Follow your nose, cowboy!" She pointed to the source of the foul odor that had prompted her to head for the kitchen in the first place. "And get those…*creatures* out of here!"

"Huh?" His expression perplexed, Brad swaggered through the maze of belongings and stared down at the five exceedingly ugly creatures on the other side of the counter. "Armadillos?"

"Nine-banded armadillos." Lainey shuddered, not about to

admit how glad she had been to see Brad charging to her rescue. Not that she considered herself a damsel in distress, of course. "A whole family of them."

Brad braced his hands on his waist. "I can see that."

"I hope that's all of them, anyway!" Lainey shuddered again. She didn't know what she would do if she found other creatures in the guest house, as well. The four baby armadillos, weighing about five or six pounds each, were backed into the corner of the U-shaped kitchen, toward the sink. The mama—a behemoth the size of a terrier and a lot less friendly—was guarding the only way out.

Brad flashed her a bad-boy smile that was enough to make her stomach drop. "It is."

"How do you know? You just got here!" She was the one who had been crouching uncomfortably on the kitchen countertop, her skirt hiked up around her thighs, for what seemed like an eternity as she screamed for help.

Brad's glance slid from the floor, to her legs, and then to her face. "Because armadillos always have four identical offspring—every time," he told her in a husky voice that soon had her tingling all over. "They all come from the same egg, hence they are the same sex."

She couldn't believe she was talking reproduction with one of the sexiest bachelors alive. "Well then, let's hope Papa Armadillo isn't around here somewhere, too," she declared.

He shrugged his broad shoulders, unconcerned. "Oh, they never hang around for the birth. He probably took off months ago, shortly after, uh, getting her in the family way."

She felt herself flush. "Do we really need to be talking about the mating habits of armadillos right now?" she muttered, trying to no avail to bring the hem of her skirt down, just a little. Unfortunately, the fabric was too tight and she lacked maneuvering room.

"You brought it up. What did you do to rile Big Mama up, anyway?"

Telling herself Brad's scrutiny was not sexual in nature, Lainey explained, "I walked in and almost tripped over one of her babies. Next thing I knew, I was surrounded by scurrying…screeching…beasts." She shuddered again, recalling the panic that had ensued.

He reached over and gave her bare knee a warm, companionable squeeze. "Given the way you were screaming and leaped up here, they probably think the same thing about you."

Trying not to think about the way her skin was tingling from just that brief casual contact, Lainey frowned at him. "Very funny."

He folded his arms in front of him. "I suppose you want me to remove them."

Lainey rolled her eyes. He was enjoying her discomfiture and dragging this out on purpose! "Duh."

"Okay." Brad pivoted on his heel. "I'll be right back."

"Wait!" She reached out for his shirt, missed. "You can't leave me here!"

But of course he already had.

She looked back at the armadillos nervously. She hadn't seen one of them since she was a kid and living in rural Laramie. And she'd never viewed one this close. The mother had a pointed face and large pointy ears that stuck straight up. A hard brown shield covered the mama's shoulders, another her rump. Between the two were nine bands, hence the name. Her tail was long and tapering, sort of like a rat's tail, only this was completely covered with disgustingly bony rings. She had scattered yellowish hairs across her body, particularly around her face, and wicked-looking claws on all four of her feet. Lainey had no doubt Big Mama would fight to the death to protect her young—Lainey would, too.

She did not want to tangle with the animal.

What seemed like an eternity later, but was really only a couple of minutes, Brad strode back in, carrying a large metal animal cage and wearing heavy-duty elbow-length leather ranch gloves. "Just so you know," he warned her, eyes twinkling, "this probably isn't going to be pretty. Or quiet."

Unsure whether it was excitement or annoyance speeding up her heartbeat, Lainey said in a strangled voice, "Just get them out of here!"

Brad moved a couple of boxes to block any exit attempt the five armadillos might make, then waded into the kitchen, trap in hand. When the baby armadillos scattered, Big Mama ambled away from Brad and then broke out into an awkward run, slamming into the side of one cupboard, then another. For a while it was kind of like trying to catch a greased pig. As soon as Brad would get near Big Mama, she would head off in the other direction. Unperturbed, Brad stalked the mother armadillo calmly, until he finally had Big Mama cornered, then reached down and grabbed her swiftly by the base of the tail. Big Mama squawked in terror and spun wildly, but Brad held on and somehow managed to drop her into the metal trap and shut it again without getting scratched or bit. The other four babies were caught in the same manner. Once all five were in the trap, Brad locked the lid.

Lainey breathed a huge sigh of relief. She hadn't realized until that moment how glad she was to have Brad there, saving the day. "Now what?" she demanded.

"Depends." Brad gave her an assessing look. "You like armadillo meat?"

"You're kidding."

The corners of Brad's lips twitched as he said drolly, "Guess that's a no." Brad picked up the cage of animals and swaggered for the door.

"Tell me what you're going to do with them!" Lainey called after him, belatedly feeling just a tad sorry for the cornered creatures. She was sure, after thinking about it a moment, that they hadn't meant to intrude or scare her to death.

"You want to know?" Brad's dark brown eyes held a dare. "Come along and see!"

LAINEY THOUGHT ABOUT IT for a minute, then declined his invitation with a shake of her head. Accepting dares was what had always gotten her into trouble. It was enough of a risk just accepting a job here without disclosing what she hoped to gain for herself, and do for Brad in the end. "Thanks, anyway," she said.

"Suit yourself." He headed amiably out the door.

Lainey heard the sound of metal on metal as he put the cage into the back of his pickup, then he climbed behind the wheel and drove off.

When she was sure he and the "uninvited guests" were gone, she climbed down from her perch and started to explore. But no sooner had she cleared the kitchen than a sound near the door had her spooked again…and climbing right back up onto the kitchen counter. Surely Brad McCabe wouldn't be gone that long, she told herself.

Fifteen long minutes later, he returned. He pushed back the brim of his Stetson. "Any particular reason you're still sitting up there?" he asked with a curious lift of his brow.

Lainey was beginning to feel pretty darn foolish, but better safe than sorry…. "I thought I heard something over there."

Brad frowned. He seemed to know instinctively that she wasn't joking around. "Where?"

Lainey pointed toward the living room window she had opened soon after she arrived. She could handle just about anything except wild animals. Those scared the heck out of her.

Looking more bored than scared, Brad strode over to investigate. He reached the antique sideboard that blocked Lainey's view, stopped dead in his tracks. "Well, I see the problem," he said eventually, backing up slightly and rubbing his chin.

"What is it?" she demanded, feeling even more alarmed.

He leaned over. When he straightened he held a half-burned pillar candle in his hand. "What do you think? Look dangerous to you?"

Lainey regarded Brad skeptically, aware her knees were still shaking a little. "That's all it was?"

He glanced around, looking puzzled. "I don't see anything else over here. This, however, was on the floor, lying on its side."

"Why would it just fall off like that?" she asked suspiciously.

"The wind?" He set the candle on top of the sideboard and lazily made his way toward her.

Lainey's heartbeat kicked up a notch. "You're sure there are no more wild animals in here?"

"Well, I don't see or smell anything else," Brad drawled as he walked through the combination living room and dining room, past the kitchen and half bath, and through the back hall, where the two bedrooms and full bath were located. He returned to stand in front of her, grinning wickedly. "Now, are you going to continue sitting up there or are you going to get down so we both can get back to work?"

Swallowing hard around the sudden dryness in her throat, Lainey moved toward the edge of the counter. "First tell me what you did with the party of five," she countered curiously.

"I drove them to a distant pasture and turned them loose next to a stream."

Sounded good to her. "Are they going to come back?" she asked nervously.

He taunted her with an impudent smile. "After the way you were carrying on?"

She tossed her hair—something she hadn't done since high school. Maybe college. "I'm serious."

"It's doubtful." He regarded her, eyes alight with interest. "Since there are numerous places for them to burrow and there's plenty for them to eat where I let 'em loose."

Lainey scooted to the end of the counter. "What do they eat?"

"Grubs, earthworms, insects, sometimes berries and bird eggs. Not that I saw any bird's nests in the area."

Lainey realized there was no way to get down off the counter gracefully. She fervently hoped Brad would realize that and turn away—but he didn't. "How did the armadillos get in here in the first place?" she asked, carefully swinging her legs over the side of the counter.

Brad watched as her skirt slid higher than she would have liked.

Wordlessly, he reached for her. Hands on her waist, he lifted her down to the floor. He held on to her just long enough to steady her and make sure she had her balance. That was all it took for Lainey to feel a surge of desire more potent than anything she had ever felt.

She sucked in her breath, stepped back.

He stepped back, too, looking just as stung, as they struggled to claim the threads of the conversation.

"We were talking about how they got in here," Lainey prodded, trying to appear cool.

"Beats the heck out of me." He shrugged, the powerful muscles in his shoulders straining against the fabric of his shirt. "I didn't see any holes in the wall. The guest house sits on a cement slab, so they certainly didn't burrow through that."

Lainey bit her lip as she noticed the flush of sun on his face. And something else…something interesting…in his eyes. "And they're too big to come up through the plumbing," she said.

Clearly enjoying toying with her, he looked her over from head to toe. "They don't like water anyway."

So full of facts, he was practically an encyclopedia of Texas life. "So how *did* they get in here?" Lainey challenged. If he knew so much, he must know that.

"Must have walked in last night."

Lainey regarded Brad skeptically.

Reluctantly, he explained. "The place had a musty smell, so Lewis propped open both doors and a few windows to get a nice cross-ventilation going. It was after dark, and armadillos are generally nocturnal this time of year. Big Mama probably thought this looked like a good shelter, or maybe she was just foraging for food with her babies and got shut in here when Lewis closed up."

Lainey walked over to survey the place where the candle had fallen. She did not appreciate having the wits scared out of her for the second time that afternoon. How was she ever going to sleep in here tonight? "Well, don't open up the place to whatever might inadvertently wander in here again," she warned him haughtily.

Brad angled a thumb at his chest. "I didn't do it the first time."

Lainey swung around to face him, bumping her face on his shoulder in the process. "You weren't concerned about the musty smell?"

Once again, Brad put out a hand to steady her. "Why should I be when my brother already was?" he asked, his capable fingers radiating warmth through her shirt to her skin. "Besides, *I* didn't hire you to help us get organized."

"And why is that?" Lainey demanded tartly.

"I don't see any sense in paying someone for something you can do yourself."

Lainey pushed away the ridiculously romantic fantasies his nearness was evoking. "Except you two *haven't* done it yourselves," she pointed out.

"So?" he shot back. "We would have gotten around to it eventually."

She smirked, not about to let him get away with that whopper. "How long have you been living out here?" she asked.

He stepped toward her. "We closed on the property two weeks ago."

She felt a completely uncalled-for fluttering in her middle. "And continued to live in this chaos?"

He poked the brim of his cowboy hat up with maddening nonchalance. "Why not? Doesn't bother me any more than armadillos, field mice, snakes and porcupines do." He lifted a brow. "Course if *you're* not comfortable coming face-to-face with wild animals, *you* could always head on back to Dallas."

That sounded like a dare. Lainey stepped toward him this time, not caring that her move left them mere inches apart. "Excuse me?" She angled her head up at him.

"This is a ranch, you know." He leaned toward her ear and whispered conspiratorially, "Animals of all sorts are supposed to be all over the place."

It was the stalking males that worried Lainey.

"I know where I am, thank you very much!" Not that she would ever let herself fall prey to someone as demonstrably fickle as Brad McCabe. Even if she had always wondered just how ardently he could kiss....

"Good." He paused, gave her a self-assured, faintly baiting look. "'Cause for a moment there, you bein' so surprised and all, I was beginning to wonder just how much you remembered about life out in rural Texas."

"Enough," she replied sweetly, "to know a great big pile of horse bucky when I see or hear it."

"Excuse me?" He mocked her earlier reprimand to a tee.

Finally, for Lainey, everything fell into place. "I know what you've done here, Brad McCabe. And I am not amused," she told him heatedly. "Not in the least!"

Chapter Three

Well, that was good, Brad thought with no small trace of irony, because he sure as heck didn't have a clue what she was talking about.

"You planted those armadillos in here to chase me away!" Lainey declared with an indignant toss of her head.

"Now why would I go and do a darn fool thing like that?" he demanded right back, furious at being once again *erroneously* suspected of being the bad guy, and at the same time amused because she was so far off track in her assumption.

Lainey ran a hand through her tousled blond hair, pushing it off her face. "You made it abundantly clear yesterday afternoon that you did not want me here!"

Brad adapted a no-nonsense stance, legs braced apart, arms folded in front of him. He figured he would let her make a fool of herself first, then set her straight. "So?"

Lainey's green eyes glimmered hotly. "So I accepted Lewis's job offer anyway."

Brad released an exasperated breath. "An action I am sure you will quickly come to regret, if you haven't done so already."

"Well, these silly little hijinks of yours are not going to work!" She stomped closer yet.

Brad hooked his thumbs through the belt loops on either side of his fly and rocked back on his heels. "Sure about that?"

"I have just as much right to work on this ranch as anyone else."

"Maybe so. But can you handle it?" Brad stepped closer, purposefully invading her space, not stopping until he had backed her against the sideboard in the center of the room. "Can you handle me?" Not sure why he had started this, except somebody had to set her straight, Brad flattened a hand on either side of her, caging her between his arms, and leaned in close. "You know my rep." He let his glance drift lazily over her softly parted lips before returning, ever so deliberately, to her eyes. "I'm bad news with all the ladies."

To Brad's surprise and grudging respect, Lainey inhaled deeply and stoically stood her ground. "A fact that makes no difference whatsoever to me, since I am a widow."

And thereby off the market—perhaps forever—in her estimation. Not in Brad's. Lainey may well have felt she had already been there, done that, but he hadn't. And being around Lainey, even for a short period of time, had him thinking all sorts of crazy things. Like what it would be like to have her in his bed. Or his life. And not as a thorn in his side. But as a lover, confidante, friend.

Not that this was even a possibility, he reminded himself sternly.

He was in the business of getting her out of here as soon as possible. Before he got in over his head and she got hurt.

"Well, yee-haw."

She lifted a brow in wordless inquiry, her cheeks turning an even deeper pink.

He smirked in a way meant to infuriate. "If memory serves, a lot of young widows I've come across in this town have been hot to trot." And he was reputed to be randy as could be. If that combination didn't send her running…and get her safely and quickly off the Lazy M Ranch…he wasn't sure what would.

Unfortunately, Lainey wasn't taking his hint.

She lifted her chin, ice in her smile. "I am not in the least bit sex-starved, I assure you, Brad McCabe."

He felt a stab of jealousy as unexpected as it was intense. He hadn't heard anything about Lainey having a boyfriend. Nor had she mentioned that as a potential problem yesterday when Lewis had been talking to her about moving to the ranch for a couple of weeks—or longer. Surely if there was a man in Lainey's life important enough for her to bed, she would have wanted to run the possibility of her moving out here with "the most loathed bachelor in America" with her beloved, if only as a courtesy. Or, at the very least, asked Lewis if it would be all right if she had "visitors"—meaning a territory-staking male friend—at the ranch to see her while she was here. Instead, the only person she had seemed concerned enough about to mention was her eight-year-old son. Who was, coincidentally, also the person in her life most likely to prevent her from kicking up her heels and having a little fun.

Somehow, looking at the stiff way in which she was holding herself, and the defenses that were in high gear, Brad didn't think Lainey had been kissed in a good long while. Too long, actually.

"Yeah?" He leaned in even closer and lowered his mouth to hers, prepared to have a little fun. "Well, let's just put that declaration to the test."

Lainey hadn't thought Brad was really going to kiss her. She'd thought he was only trying to scare her off the ranch, and out of his way, by pretending to put the moves on her. But there was nothing feigned about the feel of his lips pressing against hers. Nothing fabricated about her reaction to the imprint of his tall, strong body pressed warmly against hers.

She hadn't felt this alive, this much a woman, since…well, she couldn't remember when. And though she repeatedly told herself she really had to stop this now, with every shift in pressure of his warm wonderful lips, every stroke and thrust and parry of his tongue, she felt herself sliding deeper and deeper into the mystery that was him. And heaven only knows what might have happened next, had she not heard a discreet feminine exclamation of dismay, and a throat clearing—loudly—behind them.

Lainey and Brad broke apart at the same time, and turned in the direction of the sound. Right away, Lainey recognized Brad's uncle, Travis McCabe, and his wife, Annie. The handsome couple had both owned ranches before they married some fifteen years ago—since then, the Rocking M Cattle Ranch and the Triple Diamond had been combined.

"Lainey! I don't know if you remember me," Annie Pierce McCabe said, stepping forward, looking much younger than her forty-five years.

They had never been friends—there was too much of an age difference—but Lainey had admired the moxie Annie had shown, creating a new life for herself and her three sons after her divorce. "Of course I do." Lainey accepted the slender, red-haired woman's welcome. Annie was one of Lainey's role models, and one of the reasons why Lainey had been thinking about moving back to Laramie permanently, once her job at the Lazy M was done. "I've been using your barbecue sauce since it first came out." Lainey smiled.

"She's famous for it, all right." Looking fit and strong as ever, Travis wrapped a hand affectionately around his diminutive wife's shoulder, then greeted Lainey, too.

"Travis…Annie." Brad nodded at them both.

"Brad." Travis glared at Brad in scolding fashion even as he shook Brad's hand.

"We came to help!" Annie said, in an effort to let them both off the hook.

But Lainey knew that unless they addressed the ardent clinch that Annie and Travis had just witnessed, it would be like trying to ignore the elephant in the middle of the room. She wrinkled her nose, pretending to misunderstand, while at the same time transferring her embarrassment—and the blame for the romantic fiasco—squarely where it belonged, onto Brad McCabe's handsome shoulders. "You knew Brad would be putting the moves on me?" Lainey asked their company innocently.

Brad gave Lainey a surly look that let her know he had expected her to get him back; he just hadn't known—until this moment—how she was going to do it. "Hey," he chided amiably, clapping a calloused hand across his broad chest. "I saved your life, sweetheart!"

Sweetheart. Why did that sound so good coming from those lips, even if it was in sarcasm, and not a true endearment? Determined to demonstrate she was not intimidated by Brad McCabe, no matter what he dished out, she stood her ground. "I hardly think that's the case, since those armadillos were not going to bite me."

Brad chuckled. "You never would have known that by the way you were screaming," he countered.

Lewis came in behind them, as eclectically dressed as always. "What did I miss?" he demanded, looking about as unsuited for ranch life as was possible.

"Nothing," Brad and Lainey said in unison, while Annie and Travis shook their heads and stifled grins.

Lewis frowned. "Doesn't look like nothing," he murmured.

"Your brother was harassing her," Travis explained helpfully.

"I thought I told you not to do that!" Lewis reprimanded Brad.

And just that quickly, the balance of power in the room shifted. Lewis hadn't meant to remind Brad that Lewis, not Brad, actually owned the Lazy M.

"Right. *Boss.*" Brad slapped his cowboy hat back on his head and stomped out. Travis shot a look at his wife, and then followed Brad.

"I—I didn't mean—" Lewis stammered, upset.

"I know you didn't and so does he," Annie said gently, before turning back to Lainey. "You remember my three older sons?"

"The triplets?"

"Teddy, Tyler and Trevor are twenty now. They're all working the ranch for the summer."

Lainey could hardly believe it. "They're in college now?"

"Yes. Tyler's planning to be a vet, Trevor a cattle rancher, and Teddy wants to breed horses. They all just finished their sophomore year at Texas A&M. They're on their way over. They're going to help us move furniture and try to make the guest house livable for you and Petey. Speaking of which, where is your son?"

Regret swept through Lainey. "Petey is on a trip with his relatives. He'll be joining me this weekend."

"Oh. Our two youngest boys will be so disappointed. Kurt is nine and Kyle is eight and they were so excited to hear there's going to be another guy roughly their own age, on the next ranch over."

Two boys came in. They were followed by three strapping young men who did indeed look all grown up. All five had rusty red hair and freckles, just like their mother. "They're bein' strict with us!" the taller boy, soon introduced as Kurt, said.

"Yeah, and that is not their job," his slightly smaller brother Kyle pointed out. "It's yours and Daddy's."

"They were headed for mischief," Teddy told his mother.

"If anyone would know it when we see it, it'd be us," Trevor grinned.

Tyler's eyes twinkled even as he claimed, "We weren't that bad."

Lewis and Annie groaned as Brad and Travis came back in. Lainey had been just a teenager when Annie and Travis's romance began, but even she remembered the triplets—who had been four at the time—had caused lots of havoc in the months and weeks before, during and after Annie and Travis had gotten together.

"Really?" Travis countered, his eyes twinkling, too. "Because I seem to remember, among other things, some 'flying' eggs…"

A chuckle resounded through the group at the memory. "All right, all right, maybe we were that mischievous, but we've grown up okay," Tyler claimed.

That they had, Lainey noted admiringly. It was clear all five of the brothers loved one another dearly. She had so wanted for Petey to experience the love and camaraderie of siblings, too. Instead, he was growing up an only child, just the way she had….

But there was no more time to think about that, because Annie had had enough of standing around. She clapped her hands together, looking every bit as anxious to get on with the "organizing" task ahead as Lainey was. "Okay, guys," Annie told the assembled crew, "now that we've got all of you here to do the heavy lifting, let's get busy and start moving this furniture where Lainey thinks it should go…."

"LET ME GET THIS STRAIGHT," Brad said early the next morning when Lainey came face-to-face with him and his brother in the Lazy M ranch house kitchen. "It's only your second day on the job and you already want time off?"

Lainey ignored Brad—who looked unbearably attractive in jeans, boots and an old chambray shirt—and spoke directly to her real boss, or at least the only person she planned to take any orders from. "I wouldn't ask if an old friend of mine weren't in Dallas today, on business." *With me.* "I haven't seen Sybil in a couple of years and she has enough time to have lunch with me. I'd really like to go."

Clearly aware he was annoying her, Brad looked her over, taking in the fit of her pale yellow, linen sheath dress, matching cardigan and shoes, before returning ever so slowly to her face. "Must be nice to be a dilettante," Brad mumbled under his breath, just loud enough for Lainey to hear.

"Better than a smart-mouth any day of the week," she muttered right back.

Lewis stepped between them. He looked annoyed at Brad, too. "Will you leave her alone before she quits on us?" Lewis demanded.

"So what?" Brad finished the second half of his orange juice in a single gulp. He set the glass down on the counter with a *thud*, as determined to rile Lainey as ever. He shrugged indifferently. "Then we'll simply hire someone else who will work more than one day in a row."

"Keep it up," Lainey told Brad, walking around Lewis to confront him, "and I'll be tempted to kick you in the shin." It would serve him right for kissing her the way he had, when she knew he hadn't meant it. And she, unfortunately for her, had.

"Not going to hurt much with those fancy sandals you're wearing," he said in a tone sexy enough to make her want to kiss him all over again. "And speaking of footwear…" He pretended to study her carefully. "This being a ranch—with free-roaming wildlife and all—"

Oh, brother. Like she was going to fall for that again. "Not to mention one very big and ornery beast," Lainey added sweetly, hoping to shame him into behaving.

"—don't you think it's time for you to start dressing a little more practically?"

Lainey had been thinking about it—until he mentioned it, anyway. Clothes that were just right in Dallas seemed a little too fancy here. Lainey had been dressing the way Chip had expected her to for so long, she had no idea how she would dress if it were up to her. Deciding she did not like the presumption in Brad's eyes, she said, "I suppose you'd like to see me in boots and jeans?" The question was, what would she like to see herself in?

"Depends on how much leg you intend to keep flashing. Yesterday, for instance, when you were climbing up on that kitchen counter, I could see…"

The heat of a self-conscious blush warming her face, Lainey headed for the door before she was tempted to smack Brad McCabe's ornery face. She couldn't believe he had kissed her, and she had kissed him back. What in the world had she been thinking, even letting him come to her rescue?

"When are you coming back?" Lewis asked hopefully, as he followed her to the back porch.

Lainey turned around and smiled at Lewis. He at least was truly one of the nicest guys she had ever met. "Later tonight. And don't worry. Beast or no—" she glared over Lewis's shoulder, at Brad "—I'll be here working the rest of the week."

LAINEY JOINED HER OLD FRIEND Sybil for lunch at The Mansion on Turtle Creek, and typically Sybil got right to the point. "Were you able to find out where Brad McCabe is right now?" she asked as soon as their iced teas had been served.

Lainey knew it would serve the Texas cowboy right if she were to put the most tenacious magazine editor in the country on his tail, but Lainey couldn't do it. And not just because of the way Annie and Travis's crew—and Brad and Lewis, too—had pitched in to help her begin the task of organizing the Lazy M Ranch and guest houses the previous afternoon.

Pure and simple, ratting out Brad would be the wrong thing to do. Even if doing so would help her old friend and former college roommate. "I have to tell you, Sybil, from what I learned, Brad McCabe is in no mood to be interviewed."

"So?" Sybil ran a hand through her short jet-black curls. "Be persuasive. Change his mind. You're a pretty single woman. He's supposed to love pretty single women."

One would certainly think so, given the way Brad had been portrayed on the reality TV show. "Even if I were able to get an interview with him—a feat which it is doubtful I'll be able to perform—I can almost guarantee you that he wouldn't answer a single question about what happened on *Bachelor Bliss*. Nor is he likely to agree to be photographed for *Personalities Magazine*."

Sybil frowned, disappointed but not defeated. She leaned across the table, looking as lithe and trendy as ever in her designer pantsuit. "I need that cover story, 'America's Most Loathed Bachelor,' if I am going to prove myself worthy of the editor-in-chief position."

Lainey knew Sybil was in hot competition with another senior editor for the post. The July first edition of the bimonthly celebrity magazine was Sybil's chance to prove herself. Her competition was working on the June fifteenth edition. Whoever had the highest sales would win the post. Lainey wanted Sybil to win, but she did not want to sacrifice the privacy of her family and friends to make it happen.

Even though, Lainey added sarcastically to herself, it would almost serve Brad right if she did expose his whereabouts. Where had he gotten off thinking he could haul her into his arms and kiss her as if there were no tomorrow? She wasn't one of the babes who had lined up to win his heart on the show!

"His family won't tell anyone where he is," Lainey said, sticking to what she could—in good conscience—reveal. "And the citizens of Laramie are just as protective of him." Had she not stumbled across him, and been hired to organize the Lazy M, she still wouldn't know where he was currently residing.

"Maybe they'll change their minds," Sybil said as the waiter returned with two bowls of tortilla soup.

"I doubt it. Brad is very well loved in his hometown. More than one person told me they didn't know who that was on the reality show, but it sure as heck wasn't the Brad they knew, before or since."

"So they think he was screwed by the producers."

Lainey nodded, savoring the spicy mixture of flavorful broth, tender chicken, crisp tortillas, creamy avocado and cheddar cheese. "At the very least, portrayed in a deliberately unflattering light."

"Except that doesn't make sense, since the producers very much want their bachelors to be extraordinarily heroic."

And Brad had been portrayed as the world's biggest cad.

"Viewers won't watch if they don't like the bachelor," Sybil continued between spoonfuls.

Except they had watched, in record numbers, if only to see the handsome lothario get what was coming to him.

"Look, you knew him as a kid, right?"

Lainey made a seesawing motion with her hand. "Sort of. He and his family moved to Laramie when Brad was sixteen, a few years after their mother died."

Sybil leaned forward impatiently. "My point is, you have an insight into this guy—a personal connection—that none of my other reporters have. If you can find him, you have the ability to get close to him."

At least in theory, Lainey thought. Right now Brad was so prickly she couldn't see anyone getting close to him, man or woman. Even his beloved younger brother Lewis was giving him wide berth.

"This could be your big break, Lainey. A cover story that could catapult you into the big time and erase all those years when you didn't work as a writer. Getting this story for me would make your lack of journalism degree a moot point. And if I'm hired as editor-in-chief, largely because you got the story of the summer, I promise you a job as a staff writer."

The waiter cleared their plates and returned with warm lobster tacos for Sybil and Texas crab cakes for Lainey. "I told you—I don't want to live in New York City. I want Petey to grow up in Texas, the way I did. Maybe even in Laramie."

Sybil rolled her eyes. "Two weeks out in the sticks and I guarantee you will change your mind about that and go running back to Dallas."

Maybe, and maybe not, Lainey thought. She had already been there a few days, and already she felt calmer, more relaxed, more in touch with her true self than she had in years.

Being back—even temporarily—was like having a fresh start in her life.

Sybil sat back in her chair. "How many times have you said to me, on the phone or in e-mail, that you wished you'd had the chance to work for a while before you got married, to see if you had what it takes?"

Lainey sighed. "Hundreds." Whenever Chip or his family had made her feel small and inconsequential, she had wished she had more of a sense of herself, more inner strength. She had wished she had a life apart from her husband and son. Something to call her very own.

"If you don't want to leave Texas, that's fine. You could work for *Personalities Magazine* as our southwest stringer."

Sybil didn't know how tempting that sounded. "That would still mean travel." Lainey forced herself to be practical.

"Day flights. You could hop on a plane in the morning, interview someone and be home in time to cook Petey dinner. I promise."

Which would make the situation workable, Lainey knew. And the job would fulfill Lainey's long-held dreams of being a reporter and challenge her in ways she hadn't been challenged in a long time. Certainly, being a staff reporter for *Personalities Magazine* would be a lot better than trying to make it as a freelance reporter, selling stories here and there.

"The point is, Lainey, you and I both know that the story the producers presented to the viewing public was not the *whole* story. If Brad McCabe is the wonderful guy at heart that his family and the entire citizenry of Laramie, Texas, think he is, then other stuff *must* have happened behind the scenes that maybe only Brad—and the woman he ended up first choosing and then unceremoniously dumping at the end— know about." She took a sip of water. "And you've read the stuff Yvonne Rathbone's been spouting. That he was a Jekyll and Hyde, her heart was shattered all to pieces…and she will never ever get over what happened in a million years."

"I saw her on one of the morning news shows, after it happened," Lainey admitted reluctantly. Yvonne had been crying her eyes out. "She appeared credible."

Sybil looked cynical. "You and I have both known women who are capable of twisting the truth. It's up to you to discover what really occurred and write it up, so everyone knows what happened, instead of the lies and the half-truths Yvonne and the producers are putting out. In the meantime, I've got some standard contracts and releases for you to sign."

She handed them over. Lainey perused them while they waited for their dessert and coffee. The documents were fairly straightforward. Until Lainey got to the amount being offered for the article. She glanced up. "You're willing to pay me five thousand dollars for one three-thousand-word article?"

"If we publish it," Sybil concurred. "And we won't publish it unless you can come up with something new, factual and fairly sensational."

And therein lay the challenge, Lainey thought, as she kept reading the terms of the contract. How could she become friends with the McCabes, while at the same time secretly investigating—for public disclosure—the true character of one of their own? If what she found out flattered—and freed— Brad from this nightmare of bad publicity, she could very well be a hero in their view. But if the worst happened, if Brad actually had been a cad, for absolutely no reason, as his ex alleged, what then? If Lainey were the bearer of news like that, the citizens of Laramie would not be happy with her. And that resentment could prevent Lainey from returning to Laramie— with Petey—to live.

"You'll notice we have the exclusive right to publish whatever you do find out," Sybil pointed out.

"As well as make any editorial changes you see fit," Lainey noted, all of which was standard.

Sybil handed over a pen. "I'll need you to go ahead and sign this agreement—and then we'll get down to the brass tacks of what the magazine expects from you on this assignment."

Lainey complied and Sybil countersigned, then handed a contract to Lainey and slid the other back into her carryall.

"So this is what I am proposing," Sybil said as they sipped their coffee. "I want you to use your knowledge of Brad and anything else you can find out about him and his family that is not currently known. And then I want you to interview Yvonne Rathbone for the magazine and use that intimate knowledge to try to trip her up, see if you can catch her in some obvious lies. And maybe, just maybe, get her to at least give you a clue, if not an outright confession, about what really happened behind the scenes at *Bachelor Bliss*. Maybe if you get her to admit enough, you'll be able to use your desire to clear Brad's name and rep to get his family to tell you where you can find him for a sit-down interview. That way, he'll see how much you want to help him, and he will fill in the rest for you."

Did she want to help him? How could she not? Certainly, she wanted to know the truth of what had happened, and be responsible for getting that truth out for everyone to know! "That's a lot of ifs," Lainey said finally.

Sybil dipped her spoon into the raspberry sauce on top of the crème brûlée. "I remember very well how tenacious you are when you're on a story. I have faith you will be able to get the job done."

Lainey admitted to herself that she wanted all the answers as much as Sybil did—if not more. Thinking about the task ahead, knowing she was up to the challenge, she savored her chocolate cake. It was time to prove she had what it took to be a reporter, time to build a new life for herself and Petey. "What's the time frame?"

"You have the rest of this week to prepare and do your digging. I've set the interview with Yvonne up for Sunday afternoon. She's going to be in town this weekend to appear at a charity gig—and she agreed to meet with you and a photographer from the magazine at the Fairmont Dallas, where she'll be staying. I'll need the article on her and Brad one week from today."

Seven days. "That's not much time."

"It's enough for a pro. You're a pro, Lainey. You know it and I know it. You've just been off the job for a while. Now it's time to get back to the work you were born to do."

"What if I can't get Brad to talk to me and tell me his version of events? I mean, it's been almost three months and he hasn't told anyone what happened thus far."

Sybil shrugged. "You'll still have the article you write about his ex—Yvonne Rathbone—after you interview her. And you can write the article about Brad whether or not he allows you to interview him. That fact alone might induce him to cooperate." She continued. "And even if it doesn't, you still have your Laramie connections. You'd be surprised what little tidbits you can pick up here and there when people feel comfortable enough to open up to you. Once compiled, they could make a hell of a story, or at least lend powerful insight to what happened to make Brad change his mind about proposing to Yvonne. I'm counting on your intimate knowledge of the family and the town where he spent his teenage years to give you an edge and an in that no one else has had to date."

"Because unless there's something new to be told about the breakup, you don't want it."

"Right. No sense in rehashing what has already been said a hundred different ways. That won't sell magazines. Readers want to know how Brad McCabe could seem so head over heels in love with Yvonne Rathbone one minute, and then treat her like dirt the next."

It was a puzzle.

Brad was ornery but he didn't seem cruel. And yet on the show he had abruptly seemed so cold, irrationally angry and bitter. Lainey paused. "Everything you've said thus far makes sense."

"And—?"

"I have to tell you," Lainey sighed, wishing she didn't have such a guilty conscience. It would be so much better for her career. "It doesn't feel right going after the story in such an underhanded manner." It felt like a betrayal. To herself, to the McCabe family, and especially to the target of her story, Brad McCabe. To the point that at least part of her was already regretting signing that publishing contract.

Sybil studied her. "All I am asking you to do is discover the truth and help Brad McCabe regain his reputation as a good and decent guy."

If Lainey did that, maybe the brooding look would disappear from Brad's eyes. Maybe he would regain his innate good cheer and the optimism he'd once had about love and life. Maybe then all the McCabes would rest a little easier. On the other hand, if he didn't, he could easily end up like her late father—embittered, angry and resentful the rest of his life....

"I'm sure all Brad McCabe needs is a journalist to whom he can tell his side of things and he will open up," Sybil continued.

But how could Lainey get Brad to trust her now, when she had gone out to the ranch to hunt him down? If she told Brad the truth, he would kick her off the ranch so fast her head would spin. If she didn't, she would be staying there under false pretenses.

"I think I understand where you're coming from," Sybil said gently.

Lainey didn't see how *that* was possible, given all she hadn't told her old friend.

"You're scared. You haven't had to work in a long time, whereas a lot of women our age have done nothing but gain experience and devote themselves to their careers the past ten years. But you have to start somewhere if you want a career, Lainey. And I have to be honest with you—offers like mine are going to be few and far between."

Lainey toyed with the last of her dessert, feeling torn between her own ambition and her loyalties to those she had grown up with. "I know that."

"Then be sensible and take me up on this wonderful offer. Put your personal feelings aside and act like the tenacious reporter you were when we were in college! Find the facts. Put them in an article. And to help you get started—" Sybil opened her carryall and extracted a trio of DVDs.

"What's this?"

Sybil smiled. "Copies of the episodes that featured Brad McCabe and Yvonne Rathbone. I know you've seen them, along with the rest of the country, but watch them again, slowly and carefully this time. I guarantee you will see things you didn't see the first time, and that—plus your nose for news—will lead you to the truth about Rathbone and Mc-Cabe."

Chapter Four

Sybil had been right, Lainey thought late that evening as she watched the DVD on her laptop computer screen. Being able to watch the show again—thoughtfully—was going to be a huge help to her as she prepared a list of questions that would need to be answered if she were ever to find out what happened behind the scenes at *Bachelor Bliss*.

And the people who had known Brad forever were also correct in their assessment, Lainey noted. The Brad on TV was different from the smart, sassy, challenging man in real life. His actions, as he was introduced to each of the twenty women vying for his heart, were stiff, almost scripted, as were his deadly dull remarks. Except when it came to Yvonne Rathbone. When Yvonne approached him on the terrace, sumptuous curves spilling out of a glittering evening gown, flame-red hair flowing over her shoulders, something definitely clicked.

Lainey backed it up, and watched again as Yvonne sashayed toward Brad. Instead of simply clasping his hand or kissing his cheek in the same nervous, formal way all the other contestants had done, Yvonne went up on tiptoe and, covering her microphone with one hand, whispered something in his ear that the viewers couldn't catch. Brad's eyes lit up and he grinned, as if he hadn't expected Yvonne to say whatever it was she had whispered to him. And just that simply and quickly, a connection of some sort was made.

Question #1, Lainey wrote. *What did Yvonne say when she and Brad first met?*

Question #2. Was Yvonne the only woman in the bunch Brad was physically attracted to?

Because upon closer inspection Lainey realized that he hadn't looked as if he was enjoying himself with the others.

And if he were the selfish Casanova they had painted him as, Lainey thought as someone knocked on the guest house door, he should have been having fun with all the ladies.

"Who is it?" Lainey called, hurriedly stuffing her paper and pen beneath the sofa cushions.

"Brad McCabe."

Lainey swore as she switched off the DVD, hid the covers for the other two disks beneath that day's *Dallas Morning News,* and moved back to the picture of Petey she used as a screen saver. "Just a minute!"

Satisfied she'd left no clues as to her mission, she hurried to the door.

Brad's expression was impatient. He got straight to the point. "I need printer paper. I know it's late—"

"No kidding." She was already in her pink-and-white-striped cotton pajamas.

For once, he didn't look at her breasts. Not that he would have seen much. They were covered in the demure fabric. "But I saw you were still up—and Lewis said he knows he has some good quality stuff. He thinks it might be over here in a box marked 'Pencils and Scissors.' I've already looked through the ranch house from top to bottom, and I have to have this thing I'm working on done by seven-thirty tomorrow morning, or believe me, I would not be bothering you."

He did look stressed. Lainey realized this might be a good time to get started on gathering her background information from him. "Come on in. You can help me look for the 'Pencils and Scissors' box," she said casually, leading the way past the boxes that were stacked four-high along one wall of the living room, behind the conversation area formed by the green Naugahyde sofa and two easy chairs. A round oak table for four sat beneath the window in the square country kitchen. There were boxes there, too, again pushed against the wall. Lainey noticed Brad had showered sometime that evening. He still smelled of soap and cologne, and his gleaming dark brown hair had the soft, rumpled look that comes from running a towel through just-shampooed hair and letting it dry any which way. Clamping down on her awareness of him— it wouldn't do her story any good to get distracted by his irresistible male presence—she asked, "What are you working on?"

"A business plan for the Lazy M. I've got back-to-back meetings with all three of the town's bankers tomorrow morning. I'm hoping one will be sufficiently impressed to want to lend me the money I need to get the cattle operation up and running. What are you doing?" He glanced at her personal computer sitting on the coffee table. Lainey tried not to feel guilty—and failed. She knew some reporters lied routinely about everything under the sun as they went undercover to ferret out stories that could not be dug out any other way. Lainey was not one of them.

She planned to get Brad's cooperation in the *Personalities* story. That would be a lot easier to do if they were friends and he understood from the get-go that she was there to help him clear up any misconceptions and restore his good name, not malign him as so many others had done. "I was catching up on my e-mail, and doing a few other things on my laptop." *That I can't tell you about...just yet,* Lainey added silently. *But I will, I promise, just as soon as I think you trust me enough to understand.* "Before that I was lining the kitchen shelves."

Brad studied the vintage Fiestaware she had bought at a tag sale the previous month. The rainbow-hued stoneware had been too colorful for her late husband's taste—he'd preferred things subdued and understated—but she loved it because it reminded her of her youth and her flamboyant mother.

"Are those our dishes?" he asked her.

Lainey blinked. "I didn't know you and Lewis had any dishes. Other than paper plates and cups."

"Actually, uh, we don't, as far as I know, which is why I was asking. We could use a few plates and glasses and stuff in the kitchen."

Lainey made a mental note to work on that. "Actually, these dishes are mine."

It was his turn to look surprised.

"I'm going to need them when Petey comes out to stay at the end of the week."

He regarded her with an unreadable expression. "You thinking about taking the job here permanently?"

Was she?

Certainly it would be far enough away from Bunny and Bart that she wouldn't have to worry about them pressuring her. Room and board wouldn't be a factor, either, since that was free as long as she was out here. The fifty-thousand-dollar salary Lewis had talked about paying a housekeeper would go a long way toward Lainey's other expenses, while she made a name for herself as a reporter, either at *Personalities Magazine,* under Sybil, or elsewhere, as a freelance journalist.

But all that depended on Brad understanding what she ultimately had to do here. And, of course, Petey liking it out at the ranch.

His eyes narrowed. Misunderstanding the reason for her hesitant look, he continued wryly, "Don't worry if you are. I won't make a pass at you."

Lainey scoffed as she headed back to the bedroom earmarked for Petey. Brad followed.

"I know what you're thinking about."

The kiss...

"But that wasn't a pass." He stepped past the twin bed with a rough-hewn frame and the bureau, to review the boxes stacked against the wall.

"It wasn't," she deadpanned, looking over at him.

"That was just a kiss." Brad was the picture of lazy male assurance. "If and when I ever make a pass at you, you'll know it."

Lainey's heartbeat quickened. "I expect I would. So it's a good thing you're not going to do it because I'm not one of the women who signed up to compete for your attention."

"Thank heaven for that," he muttered beneath his breath, his lips taking on a brooding slant once again.

Lainey edged closer. "Mind answering a question for me?"

He lifted an indolent hand. "Depends."

"How come you were so…sort of gallant but humorless on *Bachelor Bliss,* at least in the beginning? I mean, I've just been around you a few days and you're always full of witty remarks—"

"Or full of something," he said with comically exaggerated seriousness.

"But you weren't funny on the TV show like you are in real life. Tell me the truth. Did they make you rein in your natural—"

"Don't you mean wicked?"

"—sense of humor while you were on camera?"

Respect glimmered in his brown eyes. "You're the first person who's ever asked me that."

Aha! She'd known it! "So it's true," Lainey said, ignoring the tingle of awareness starting up inside her whenever Brad was near. "The show's staff told you to rein in the repartee. What'd they do?" She regarded him with all the directness she could muster. "Write your dialogue on cue cards or something?"

"Not all of it," he allowed reluctantly.

"How much?" Lainey pressed.

He shrugged. "I don't know. Maybe...ninety-eight percent or something."

Lainey found this distressing. She figured the *Personalities Magazine* readers would, too. "But the TV show is supposed to be reality."

Brad grimaced. "There's nothing real about that particular reality TV show. Everything on *Bachelor Bliss* is a setup, whether it's the circumstances you're in, or the person you're with."

Interesting, Lainey thought. She wished she could dig out her notepad and pen. "Was the breakup with Yvonne part of the script?" Because from what Lainey recalled, it hadn't looked that way. Yvonne had appeared really stunned by what Brad had had to say, or not say, to her that evening during the final proposal ceremony.

An unreadable emotion shuttered Brad's eyes. "I don't know how we got on this," he said gruffly.

"Or in other words, you're not going to tell me," Lainey said, disappointed. Not yet, anyway....

"You got that right." He stalked out into the hall and across to the bedroom where she was bunking. A queen-size brass bed dominated the center of the room. Lainey had outfitted it with a ruffled white spread and several satin throw pillows. The clothes she'd been wearing earlier—including her lacy pink bra—were strewn across the bed.

She blushed as Brad's eyes touched on her lingerie. Silence fraught with sexual tension fell between them as they both turned to scan the writing on the sides of the moving boxes.

"That box must be here somewhere," Brad complained.

"You've got a lot riding on these meetings, I take it," Lainey said, still not finding anything marked "Pencils and Scissors."

Brad pulled a box from the middle of the wall that appeared to have no marking on it and turned it every which way.

Finally, the one they wanted!

"Let's put it this way," Brad muttered as he ripped it open. "I used every bit of my savings to repair the existing pasture fences, purchase the equipment I need for sprinkler and heat-detecting systems in the barn, not to mention what it cost to get a new roof put on the barn, repair the termite damage that had started on one end, and repaint the whole darn thing."

He began taking out wads of packing paper, handing them over to her.

"I've been meaning to ask you about that," Lainey said as he dug deeper and deeper.

"Yeah?" Brad emerged, victorious, with a ream of high-quality printer paper.

Lainey dropped the wads of packing paper back into the box. "Was the barn that color when you bought the place?"

Brad led the way out of her bedroom. "No, I painted it." He paused at her front door. "Why? Don't you like it?"

"It's a nice guy color, I guess." Lainey stepped out onto the porch with him.

"But?"

She turned her glance to the buildings located behind the house. "I thought most barns were either red or white or weathered gray."

Brad grinned and shook his head, suddenly appearing in no more hurry to leave her side than she was to see him go. "See. That just shows how much you don't know about ranching."

Lainey looked back at the barns and stables. In the moonlight, they didn't look so bad, but in the daylight they were so deadly dull they practically faded into the landscape. "There's a reason they're all golden tan, right down to the corral fence?"

"Yep."

And here she'd thought Brad and his brother just had no color sense whatsoever. "I'm dying to hear," she prodded dryly.

"It calms the cattle."

"You're joking."

"Nope. Texas A&M has done studies on color and cattle management. That particular color is very soothing to cattle. They don't know why exactly—seems the cattle aren't talking," he quipped, "but whenever cattle are around that color they are very calm and relaxed, which in turn makes them a lot easier to handle."

Lainey studied him. "You must have some theory as to why that's so," she observed softly.

Brad nodded, more sober rancher now than flirting cowboy. "It probably has something to do with the fact that animals don't see colors the way humans do. Their depth perception is different, too. This particular hue of tan eliminates shadows and blends well with the landscape, and hence the cattle are more apt to stay calm, less prone to balk, when you're leading them toward either a barn or a fence painted this color."

"So how come all the ranches out here don't have their barns painted this color?"

Brad shrugged. "Maybe they haven't done their research."

Lainey regarded him with respect. Obviously there was much more to Brad than he usually let on. "The fact you have should help you with your loan."

"I hope so. I really need a bank to back us."

BRAD SEEMED genuinely worried, Lainey realized. More so than he should be given the circumstances. She asked the questions that would tell *Personalities* readers what Brad planned for his future. "Couldn't Lewis just lend you guys the cash? Given the success of his computer-gaming company… he's supposed to be rolling in dough."

Brad frowned. "He's already put up the entire down payment for the ranch."

Determined to keep him off guard, Lainey pushed on.

"You must have known this was going to be the case when you two decided to purchase the ranch together."

Tired of holding the ream of printer paper, evidently not ready to leave, Brad set the package on the rough-hewn cedar table next to the cushioned glider. He took a seat and stretched his long legs out in front of him. "We purchased it before I headed off to do *Bachelor Bliss*."

Lainey sat down on the other end of the glider and turned to face him. "They paid you to end up so miserable?" she said as they moved back and forth.

Looking even more handsome in the soft glow of the guesthouse porch light, Brad replied, "They gave all the contestants five thousand dollars to appear on the show. The real money for me—and the female contestants the public took a shine to—was to come later, in endorsements. The last bachelor, for instance, made over two million in television commercials when the series wrapped up. They had close to three million lined up for me."

Another fact the show's viewers would be interested in learning. "Only now, because of the way the series ended, you're public enemy number one," she guessed.

"Right."

"Hence the sponsors want nothing to do with you."

"Right again." Brad sighed. He brushed the flat of his palm down his jeans. "Not that I had any business doing those commercials anyway."

Lainey's hair was still damp from the shower; she wouldn't style it in the usual sleek bob until tomorrow. She could see Brad noticing—maybe even liking—the natural waves. Self-consciously she tucked a curl behind her ear and tried not to notice him tracking the movement. "Didn't you believe in the products?"

Brad held her gaze. "I would never endorse something I didn't believe in. The problem is," he confided, frowning, "it's not real work."

Lainey caught the snobbery in his tone. "I think the people who vie for and film those commercials would disagree with you."

He made a face. "It's just not the kind of thing I do."

What was it Chip had said to her, whenever she had talked to him about her ambitions? *Reporting? Come on, Lainey! Get real! That isn't the kind of thing we Carringtons do.* She hadn't liked his snobbery then. She didn't like recalling it now. A person was not defined by his or her profession. Her mother had not been low class just because she worked in a bar and wore the provocative outfit the establishment management demanded during her work hours, and equally flamboyant and sexy clothing when she was off. Her mother had been sweet and gentle and hardworking, beloved by all who knew her and bothered to find out the person behind the ensemble.

"I disagree," she said. "Work is work, and there is value in work whatever it is."

Her irritated tone brought a provoking smile to his lips. "You really think so."

"Yes. I do."

He paused to consider that and seemed to be searching for the exception to the rule, if only to get her goat. "Even for something like—say—stripping?" he asked her playfully.

How had the situation gotten back to sex again? What was it about the two of them that sparks flew whenever they were together? "Okay. You got me there," Lainey replied dryly. "I would not take my clothes off in front of a bunch of leering strangers for money. But that's still work, and if someone chooses to do it to earn a living, then that's their business. It's not up to you or me to judge them."

"You only say it's real work because you've never been in a situation where you've been leered at that way."

Close enough, Lainey thought, and before she could stop herself the words came tumbling out. "Oh, yes, I have."

Brad looked as ready to continue their argument as she was. "Ah, yes. That homecoming parade Lewis was talking about."

Lainey flushed. Why had she started down this road? "That was my fault for letting my friends dare me into wearing that dress." She'd been young, foolish. Reckless to a fault in a way she wasn't now that she was a mom.

Brad stretched his long legs out in front of him. "Well, this was my fault for letting the producers talk me into appearing on that TV show."

"You didn't sign up for it?"

"No." He settled more comfortably on the bench seat of the glider and laid one arm along the back of it. "They came to me. Apparently, cowboys are heroes and Texans are sexy and they wanted a bona fide Texas cowboy for their bachelor this time around. So they looked at rodeo standings, saw my picture and thought I was just handsome enough to be the star of the show."

"What'd you say?"

"Hell, no." Brad turned to her, dark eyes sparkling. "I was already thinking about talking to Lewis about buying a ranch. The last thing I wanted to do was fly to Los Angeles and spend a month on an estate in Santa Barbara with fifteen contestants all vying to be the first Mrs. Brad McCabe."

"So why did you?"

He scowled, his frustration with the situation apparent. "The commercial money afterward. Since I'm not a computer genius capable of starting my own company like my dad or Lewis, I knew it was the only way I'd ever get the kind of cash I needed, so quickly. I should have known a plan like that would backfire on me, and stuck to real work, instead of trying to take the easy route."

Lainey saw his point about that. In a lot of ways, her life had taken a wrong turn when she married money and let the demands of that kind of life control her. "I don't think there is anything wrong with doing commercials for products you believe in," she said, repeating her earlier assertion.

"Moot point now," Brad said.

Just then Lainey's cell phone rang. Alarmed—it was unusual for anyone to call her after midnight—she uncurled herself from the swing and went inside to get it, then came back out onto the porch to stand with him.

"Hello?" she said, nodding at Brad.

"Mom?" Petey's thin voice trembled in her ear.

"Hi, honey," Lainey said, her voice dropping to the gentle tone she reserved just for him. She turned her back to Brad. "Is everything okay? Are you having a good time with your cousins, Aunt Bunny and Uncle Bart?"

"Yeah. We saw fireworks in the shape of cartoon characters tonight. It was pretty neat."

"I bet." He sounded homesick.

"I want to ask you somethin'."

"Go right ahead," Lainey encouraged softly.

"Are you proud of me—for being so big and brave?"

Where had that come from? Lainey wondered, momentarily taken aback. "Honey, I am always proud of you."

"Lainey?" Bunny's voice came on the phone, crisp, businesslike as always. "Sorry to call so late, but Petey wanted to tell you about the fireworks."

"Is he okay? Because he sounds awfully homesick…."

"He's doing fine! What?—oh! I've got to go! We'll check in with you tomorrow, okay? Love you!"

Lainey heard a *click* as Bunny cut the connection. The dial tone sounded in her ear. Frowning, she ended the call on her phone, too, but left it plugged in and turned on in case Petey called back again.

"Everything okay?" Brad asked.

Lainey wasn't at all sure how to answer that.

"I'M SORRY, BRAD," Tommy Johnson, branch manager of Laramie Savings and Loan, said. "Your business plan looks excellent. But without some sort of collateral…" He hesitated. "If you wanted to have Lewis co-sign for you or put up part of the ranch, well, that would be a different story."

"No." Brad lifted a hand to cut off the discussion. "I was looking to stock the ranch on my own."

"I understand. But it's not like the old days, where a handshake or a man's word would suffice. We're all owned by big companies now, and we have guidelines we have to have follow."

No one had to tell Brad it was a conglomerate world. Bigger had always meant better in Texas. But bigger did not always mean better in business. The loss of the personal touch also meant the loss of good service and ample opportunity. Still, maybe there was something he could do, some way to fix this. First, he had to know if lack of collateral was the only reason he was being turned down. "Answer me this. If I hadn't been on *Bachelor Bliss,* would my chances be better?"

"Not for obtaining a loan. But it would probably help you be taken more seriously in this new venture of yours. The last thing any businessperson wants to be thought of is fickle and unreliable."

"And because I didn't propose to Yvonne Rathbone, that's the view of me now."

Tommy made a face and rubbed his knuckles on the underside of his chin. "Actually, it goes a little further back than that."

Brad lifted a brow.

"Unfortunately, your work history speaks to the same sort of problems," Tommy explained. "You dropped out of college, hit the rodeo circuit off and on, and worked ranches here and there."

"For good reason! To supplement my income and learn as much as I could from as many top-rate sources as possible."

"The point is, you didn't stay in any one place for long.

Then you signed up to do that reality TV show, and reneged on that at the end."

He'd had a damn good cause for that action, too. Not that he planned to tell anyone what it was. Bad enough he'd been humiliated that way without letting the rest of the world in on it, too.

"And now you're in business with Lewis, a person who knows a lot about computer software but nothing about raising cattle. As much as the people around here love you, it's going to take time and a lot of stability on your part for you to be taken seriously as a rancher."

Which meant, Brad thought later as he drove back to the Lazy M, it was either start very small and let the ranching operation grow slowly over a number of years, or go back to the fallback plan of letting Lewis pay for everything—the land, the cattle and the operating costs, even Brad's room and board. The two were going to split the profits right down the middle, but it would be years before those amounted to much.

Brad was still scowling as he parked his pickup next to the ranch house and walked inside.

He followed the lilt of Lainey's soft, feminine laughter and the eager sound of his brainiest brother to the formal dining room that was being retooled as Lewis's home office. Brad was claiming the former formal living room as his study, since neither of them planned to give any parties that couldn't be held out on the lawn, or, in inclement weather, in the kitchen and family room.

"The chandelier is going to have to come down and be replaced with another light fixture," Lainey was saying. "Otherwise you'll be in danger of bumping your head on it every time you get up from your desk."

Brad stopped in the portal, shocked by what he saw.

Lainey had only been working on this room since this morning, but already it had been transformed from a mess of boxes with a trio of bookcases and large U-shaped desk into an organized work environment. She'd taken down the dusty drapes that had come with the house, and removed the outdated drapery rod from the wall. Lewis's three computers, fax, two printers, copier and speakerphone were all organized in a way that made sense, with the computers set up equidistant from one another in his workspace for easy access, the other equipment placed on the shelves. They had also brought in the beat-up green leather reclining chair that had been with Lewis since his college days and put it in the corner, along with a pole lamp that made a cozy reading nook.

Lainey and Lewis both had their backs to Brad as Lainey pointed out places on the ceiling. "I think you're going to want to add some track lighting around the perimeter," she was saying, "to really brighten up the space. And maybe a nice rug? And those posters you bought during your travels would look nice on the walls, if you had them framed."

"Can you help me with that?"

"Sure," she replied.

"I never know what to buy."

"You've done just fine so far."

Lewis beamed at her compliment.

Brad's scowl deepened as Lainey and Lewis belatedly seemed to realize they were no longer alone and turned to face him.

"So, how'd it go?" Lewis asked cheerfully. "The banks give you everything you need to get the cattle operation up and running?"

Brad shook his head. He only wished it had been that easy. But he wasn't going to hide from the truth—at least not in this regard. "Seems like we're back to the original plan," he stated matter-of-factly.

Lewis looked disappointed but not surprised.

His brother might not know how to dress or dazzle the ladies, but he had business sense—and instincts about what would or would not fly. Which was why Lewis had tried to keep Brad from going to the banks in the first place.

"No problem." Lewis reached into his desk and took out a business checkbook. He tossed it to Brad. His eyes were filled with the respect that, thanks to the lies that had been spread about Brad, was in short supply nearly everywhere else. "I had your name added to the account. So you can write checks for whatever you need."

"Thanks," Brad said, grateful for the trust, even as he felt like he was choking on his pride.

An awkward silence fell. "Listen, if you two want to talk business, I can get busy elsewhere," Lainey murmured.

Brad had nothing further to say on the matter. Lewis knew where they stood as well as he did. Lewis was the family's biggest success story, and Brad was the family's biggest failure.

BRAD SPENT WHAT WAS LEFT of the day toiling over the sprinkler system in the barn. He was still working on it as dusk approached, and Lainey appeared in the doorway. Deliciously tousled from a day of working hard, she was clad in a trim peach skirt and a sheer white short-sleeved shirt, embroidered with peach-and-green flowers, over an opaque white tank top. Her only concession to the hard physical work she was doing was the white socks and sneakers on her feet, instead of the usual sandals. As she moved toward him, a strong breeze wafted through the open barn doors on either side of the twenty-four stall facility, mussing her blond hair. Brad liked the way she looked. Womanly, purposeful, mouth-wateringly feminine, and flushed with the heat of the June day.

When he had ended his stint on *Bachelor Bliss,* Brad hadn't thought he would want anything to do with romance ever again. Lainey made him reconsider. And it wasn't just her looks, or the way she sassed and challenged him. Or even the way she had kissed him back, all the while swearing the lip-to-lip contact meant nothing. It was the way she listened to him. The way she knew what questions to ask, when to push, and when to back off.

She wanted to get to know him, the real him. Not the stud on TV or on the cover of magazines. More surprising still was the fact he wanted to really get to know her, too.

Not that it was going to be easy. She seemed a lot more comfortable asking the questions than answering them.

She tilted her head back to regard the PVC piping that ran the length of the barn's center, then spread out over each of the stalls. Four-foot fans were placed forty feet apart. Sprinkler heads were mounted eight feet over the floor above each stall. "Wow. This looks state-of-the-art," she said as she walked across the scrubbed cement floor.

"Pretty much." Brad continued mounting the thermostat and timer control on the wall just to the left of the door.

Lainey stood, legs braced apart, hands on her hips. "Have you ever done this before?"

He couldn't say why exactly—usually Brad didn't care what people thought of him—but he wanted Lainey to be impressed with his accomplishments. "I helped put in a system on a ranch in Colorado," he told her matter-of-factly.

She turned around slowly to get a full 360-degree view of his handiwork, and gave him one of her in return. Brad's mouth went dry as he noted the perfection of her curves. "Is it all for fire safety?"

"There is an overheat- and fire-detection system in here." Tearing his gaze from her breasts, Brad pointed out the components to her. "And the sprinkler system will be hooked up to that, as well. But what I'm installing right now is a cooling system that will protect animals against heat stress."

Lainey wrinkled her nose. "Is that a problem?"

"It can be," Brad replied soberly, "especially for newly weaned calves, or animals that have just been transported from one ranch to another."

"I guess you've had experience with that, too."

Brad nodded. "I worked a ranch in west Texas a couple years ago where they would have lost half their new calves if they hadn't had a system like this." He came down the ladder, thinking that standing there face-to-face with her would prompt him to knock off the romanticizing. It just made it worse. That close, he could see the softness of her lips, the flush of color in her cheeks, the clear interest in her forest green eyes.

As the moment drew out, with neither one of them saying anything, the awareness between the two of them increased. Finally, Brad cleared his throat, knowing it was either get back to business or kiss her. "Did you need something?"

Lainey blinked, clearly coming back to reality as slowly and reluctantly as he was. "Um, yes. Lewis is going into Laramie to pick up some pizza for us—apparently your supply of frozen dinners has dwindled precariously and I haven't had time to buy any groceries, either—and he wanted to know if you had any requests."

Brad wasn't sure whether to thank Lewis for the interruption sent his way—or damn him. One thing for sure, he'd be thinking about Lainey, and the way she looked right now, for days and nights to come. Pizza. What did he want on his pizza? "No anchovies on mine," Brad said finally.

Lainey grinned. And still didn't leave. "Okay, that covers what you don't want," she teased. "What *do* you want?"

You, Brad thought, almost as shocked by the thought as he was aroused. *Beneath me. Hair spread across my pillow. Arms and legs locked around me. And me so deep inside of you I don't know where I end and you begin.*

Not that he had any right to be thinking that way.

He had no intention of getting intimately involved with any woman again anytime soon. And Lainey Carrington was the kind of woman who would demand emotional involvement.

Lainey Carrington was a forever kind of woman. And he was, as had been pointed out to him more than once today, a short-term kind of guy. At least as far as everyone else was concerned.

But that didn't mean he couldn't want to make love to her. Wanting was not out of the question.

Acting on those desires was.

"Well?" Lainey's impatient prodding brought him out of his reverie. "What do you want on your pizza?"

Brad straightened. "Whatever you and Lewis want is fine with me," Brad said, distracted at the sight of the Lexus pulling into the driveway. Instead of stopping at the house, as most visitors did, the driver appeared headed directly toward the two of them. "Friends of yours?" he said.

"Oh, my!" The paper in Lainey's hand fluttered to the ground as the rear door of the SUV opened and a towheaded kid sprang out and dashed toward her.

"Mommy!" The little boy threw himself into Lainey's arms.

"Petey!" She hugged him to her tightly. He hugged her back just as hard.

Seeing the resemblance—and the affection—between the two made Brad smile. Lainey's son had her intelligent eyes and warm smile. Even the stubborn way they held their chin was the same.

"Who's this?" Petey asked, looking at Brad.

"This is Brad McCabe. He and his brother Lewis live here at the Lazy M Ranch. Brad—my son, Petey."

Brad shook Petey's hand with the same courtesy and respect he'd offer a grown man. "Nice to meet you, Petey."

The little boy looked awestruck in the way city kids who have never been on an actual ranch usually do. He tipped his face up to Brad's. "Are you a real cowboy?"

"Yes."

"Do you ride horses and everything?"

"I will as soon as we get some, later this week. Right now, we're still in the process of fixing up the stables and corrals to get ready for 'em."

Petey gazed at the barn and pastures wistfully. "I always wanted to ride a horse."

Brad recalled the joy he'd felt when he first sat a horse at his uncle's ranch. It was an experience no boy should miss. "Well, maybe if your mom says it's okay, I can teach you how." Brad looked at Lainey for permission.

Obviously embarrassed, she tucked Petey closer to her side and said, "We didn't mean to put you on the spot."

"It'd be my pleasure," Brad replied, meaning it. There were some things he could still do without a bank loan or a gentleman's reputation.

Petey beamed, thrilled.

Brad cast a surreptitious look at the couple who had driven Petey out to the ranch. They were still in the car and appeared to be deep in some sort of serious discussion that his gut told him spelled trouble.

"So are you surprised to see me?" Petey demanded, going back into Lainey's arms for another exuberant hug, as the elegant-looking couple finally emerged from the front seat of the Lexus. The woman had carefully done hair and makeup. She was wearing an expensive white linen dress, and a sweater tied around her shoulders. Her companion had thinning hair and a slight paunch. He was wearing a grass-green golf shirt and plaid slacks that belonged on a country club tee-off area.

"I sure am," Lainey said, ruffling her son's hair.

Lainey paused just long enough to introduce her sister- and brother-in-law, Bart and Bunny Carrington, then asked them, "What happened? I thought you weren't coming back until the end of the week!"

"Petey was a little homesick," Bunny said.

"Actually," Bart added, "the twins wanted to come home, too."

Bunny's smile looked frozen. "Suddenly they feel they're too old for family vacations," she said, unable to completely disguise the hurt in her tone.

Bart shrugged. "I think they just wanted to be with their

friends. They want to spend as much time as possible with each other since they're all going off to different colleges in the fall. And I can't say I blame them—they have big changes ahead."

"For you, too," Lainey returned perceptively. "I'm sure you're really going to miss the girls."

"It's time for them to spread their wings," Bunny claimed with a smile. "And besides, we'll still have Petey."

Except, Brad thought, Petey was not their son. He was Lainey's. Hence, it really wasn't the same, no matter how much they tried to tell themselves it was.

The back door of the ranch house banged open and Lewis came bounding down the steps, car keys in hand. In his '80s slacks and tie-dyed McCabe Game Company T-shirt, he looked more like the proverbial slacker than the wealthy CEO of his own company. A fact Brad knew Lewis used to sort out the people who would treat him well no matter who he was, from the hangers-on, who were only interested in him for his newfound wealth.

Lewis smiled as he reached the group, and went straight for Lainey's son. "You must be Petey."

Petey cocked his head. He looked at Brad, then back at Lewis. "How'd you know that?" Petey asked Lewis, perplexed.

Lewis ran his hand through his spiked hair. "'Cause your mom talks about you constantly."

"Oh, yeah? What does she say?"

"The usual. That you're the smartest, cutest, nicest kid who ever lived."

Petey looked at Brad for confirmation. Brad nodded. "It's true," he said. It had been obvious from the first that Petey meant the world to Lainey. A fact that pleased her son no end.

"And guess what else?" Lewis continued affably, while Bart and Bunny watched, their expressions wary, almost jealous. "I heard you like playing computer games." Oblivious to the looks he was getting from Petey's aunt and uncle, Lewis bumped fists and slapped palms with Petey in the multistep greeting currently popular with kids. "And as it happens, I'm designing some for eight- to ten-year-olds that I want you to help me test."

"Really?" Petey looked as if he couldn't believe his good luck. First, horses, and now this.

"Meantime," Lewis said, as soon as he, too, had been formally introduced to Bart and Bunny Carrington, "I'm starving. So what do you all want on your pizza?"

Chapter Five

Bunny blinked. "You're making *pizza?*" Obviously pizza wasn't a staple of her high-class life.

"Heck, no," Lewis retorted cheerfully, before Lainey could stop him. "We don't have the makings for that in the house. We hardly have any groceries."

Thanks, Lewis, for thoroughly alarming my sister-in-law. Lainey smiled at Bunny and Bart reassuringly. "I'm going to remedy that first thing tomorrow," she said.

"Meanwhile," Lewis continued affably, "we've got to eat, so I'm driving in to Laramie to pick up a few pies at Mac Callahan's Pizza & Subs. And, of course, you're welcome to stay for dinner."

"Pizza is hardly a proper meal," Bunny countered, her expression stiff with disapproval.

Brad shrugged, siding with Lewis. "I don't know why you'd say that," Brad said lazily. "It's got all the food groups."

"Yeah, and I like it a lot!" Petey piped up, eager to be one of the guys.

Bunny looked at Lainey. "Perhaps Petey should return to Dallas with us, now that he's seen you," she said sweetly.

"No!" Petey grabbed on to Lainey's waist and held tight. "I'm staying with my mommy!"

Bart—who looked like he didn't want any trouble—headed back to the Lexus. "I'll get his suitcase."

Bunny turned her withering glare on Bart.

"Does this mean you're not staying for dinner?" Lewis asked, still looking eager to get on the road to town.

Bunny narrowed her eyes at him. "Obviously not," she replied coolly.

Lainey wrapped her arms around her son's shoulders and tried desperately to end this encounter on a pleasant note. "Petey, did you thank your aunt and uncle for the lovely trip to Florida?"

"Thank you. I had fun even if I did get homesick and miss my mom," Petey said sincerely.

Bunny's expression gentled. She leaned down so she and Petey were face-to-face. "We had fun, too," she told Petey warmly, giving him a hug.

Bart returned with Petey's suitcase. "Here you are, sport."

"Thanks, Uncle Bart." Petey hugged him, too.

"Thank you, both," Lainey said. "I appreciate everything you've done for us."

"Yes, well, we're going to have to sit down and talk soon," Bunny said.

Lainey felt a shiver of unease. Bunny's tone could only mean trouble.

Fortunately, not tonight.

Bart took his wife's hand and drew her away. He appeared as determined to end this conversation as his wife was to prolong it. "We'll see you all later," he said.

"PIZZA FOR BREAKFAST, TOO!" Petey said early the next morning. "This is so great!"

"Don't get used to it," Lainey warned. "Starting tomorrow, we're back to the usual eggs, cereal, fruit and pancakes."

"Is that what cowboys eat?" Petey asked as Brad entered the ranch house kitchen. Lainey was already hard at work lining shelves, while her son sat on a stool at the counter, eating off a paper plate.

Brad flashed one of the smiles that was all too rare these days. "Cowboys usually eat whatever is around." Brad peered into the fridge, sighed, and brought out the pizza box. "Which in this case is not much."

"I know. That's how come I'm having soda with my pizza this morning instead of milk or juice. Mommy says we're all out and we have to go to the store."

"I know." Lewis came in, coffee cup in hand. "Sorry about that." He helped himself to a slice of pizza and ate it cold. "Guess I should have picked up some last night when I got the pizza and wings."

Lainey waved off his apology. "It's fine. I need to run into town and get groceries today, anyway."

"What would you think about cooking for all of us?" Brad asked.

Surprised, Lainey turned to him.

"I know it's not in your job description," Brad said. "But while you're here, it sure would help out."

"No problem," Lainey said. "I love to cook."

"Yeah, my mommy is real good at that," Petey said between mouthfuls. He swung his legs back and forth. "You just got to tell her what you want and she'll make it for you."

Lewis and Brad grinned, seeming both amused and touched by Petey's enthusiasm. Lewis looked at Lainey. "As long as you're going into Laramie, you want to bring Petey by the McCabe Game Company testing facility for a session?"

"Can I, Mom?" Petey practically bounded off his stool he was so excited by the prospect.

Lainey looked at Lewis. "You're sure it's okay?"

"He can stay all day and come home with me tonight, if you like," Lewis said. "We have a group of eight- and nine-year-olds coming in today to play some of the prototypes, and to talk to the focus-group leaders about what they think. Annie and Travis's sons, Kurt and Kyle, are going to be there. If Petey would like to participate, it would be great."

"Thank you." Lainey smiled. She looked at her son. "Sounds like you've got quite a big day ahead of you, then."

Lewis said to Brad, "You okay with helping Lainey with the groceries?"

Brad practically spit out his coffee he was so surprised. It was all Lainey could do to keep her face expressionless. She couldn't imagine a more unlikely partner.

"We need a lot of stuff," Lewis continued. "We can't expect Lainey to carry it all herself."

If Lainey hadn't known better, she would have felt Lewis was matchmaking. As Brad and Lewis stared at each other, a challenge seemed to pass between them. Over what exactly, Lainey wasn't certain.

"Sure," Brad said finally. "Why not?"

"YOU DON'T HAVE TO DO THIS," Lainey told Brad, outside the supermarket. Although, it would help her cause—and his attempts to put the *Bachelor Bliss* fiasco behind him—if the two of them did become friends.

Brad tossed her a look that quickly had her heart racing. He pulled out a cart for them. "You think I'm not capable of a little grocery shopping?" he teased her.

"I didn't say that." Feeling she had no choice but to brazen her way through this sticky situation, Lainey led the way toward the fresh produce aisle once they were inside the store.

"But?" Brad tossed a bag of baby carrots into their cart.

Lainey perused the lettuce, finally deciding on Boston, red-leaf and romaine. Her breath hitched in her chest as she turned her face up to his. Just being near him like this made her blood heat and played havoc with her objectivity. Not good for a reporter on a story. "It's not really most men's idea of a good time." And it certainly didn't fit his reputation.

"I don't know about that." Brad stopped to inspect the tomatoes. "Personally, I like perusing the persimmons."

Lainey grinned at his joke. How did an ordinary summer

morning suddenly end up feeling so much like a date, albeit an arranged one? "Have you ever even eaten a persimmon?" she asked, putting bags of oranges, apples, lemons and limes into the cart.

"I'm not sure." Brad loaded a ten-pound bag of potatoes and a five-pound bag of onions onto the bottom of the cart. "What exactly *is* a persimmon?"

Lainey looked around and didn't see any in the store just then. The Dallas markets would have had them.

"It's sort of like a plum," she said finally, aware how cozy and domestic this felt, how unlike her marriage to Chip. There, the lines had been strictly drawn. He was the one in control, she was the subordinate. Chip had never done anything remotely domestic. Chip had hired people for that. Brad just seemed to do what needed to be done, without giving too much thought to whether he was "too good" for it or not. Lainey liked that about Brad. She wanted to see it revealed in what was written about him. And if she had anything to say on the matter, it would be.

"Oh. Well." He swaggered closer, his steps long and lazy. "Maybe I have tasted a persimmon, then."

"And maybe not?"

He shrugged, looking amused. "I don't always know what it is I'm eating."

Lainey hadn't, either, when she first married Chip and moved to Dallas.

Brad leaned closer. His warm breath whispered past her ear. "What's so funny?" His voice was sexy, self-assured.

She shrugged and stepped back. She had to keep some distance here. And she couldn't do that when they were close enough to feel each other's body heat. "Just thinking about my first taste of escargot." She forced her tone to be casual, unlike her thoughts.

His gaze moved over her in disbelief. "You ate snails?"

"Only because I didn't know what they were."

His brown eyes lit up merrily. "And when you did?"

Lainey rolled her eyes. She struggled not to notice how good he looked, with a cowboy hat pulled low over his brow, how ruggedly at ease. "Let's just say I never acquired a taste for them."

"Or armadillo, either, apparently."

They grinned, recalling her first day on the ranch. Lainey was aware they were flirting. And that Brad suddenly seemed like the old Brad she remembered. Carefree, happy-go-lucky, flirtatious. It was good to see. Their exchange was putting her in a reckless, lighter-of-heart mood, too. "What's put you in such good spirits?"

Brad's smile broadened. He shrugged. "The thought of a home-cooked meal tonight?"

It had to be more than that, Lainey thought. "You haven't tasted my…" Lainey stopped as she saw a man in a tropical-print shirt, Bermuda shorts and straw hat snapping photos of them through the plate-glass window in front of the store.

BRAD SAW THE COLOR DRAIN abruptly from Lainey's face. Instinctively, he moved closer, cupped a protective hand on her slender shoulder. "What is it?"

Lainey's face grew even paler. "That man," she whispered. Standing stiff as a statue, she nodded toward the front of the store.

Brad turned in the direction of her gaze. "I don't see anything."

Lainey swallowed. "I could have sworn that tourist out there was taking pictures of us inside the store."

"Looks like he is with his family," Brad said, as the man directed a woman and two teenage girls—also tourists—to stand in front of the windows, just beneath the sign.

"I'm sorry. For a moment there, I thought we were being stalked," Lainey said.

Brad took their basket and guided it toward the dairy aisle at the rear of the store. "It wouldn't be the first time."

"Since the show ended?"

He nodded grimly. "You wouldn't believe the number of people trying to make a buck off me. The first couple weeks after the last show aired were the craziest. We had tabloid reporters everywhere. Harassing my family, friends, trying to find out where I was."

This wasn't the place or time Lainey had figured on having this conversation. But never one to look a gift horse in the mouth, she said, "It's probably not going to stop, you know."

He looked over at her.

"As long as there are questions, there will be reporters and writers trying to find out the answers to them. The quickest way to end it is to find someone you trust, and just tell them your side of the story."

IF BRAD DIDN'T KNOW BETTER, he'd think she was one of *them*. But that was ridiculous. Lainey was a homemaker, and temporary-professional-organizer-slash-household-manager. Not a bloodthirsty reporter. "They're never going to go away."

"They will once the real story is out there," Lainey persisted, as she added a selection of cheeses, milk and butter to the cart. "Haven't you heard the saying? The only thing worse than no news is old news."

Brad added eggs and fresh corn and flour tortillas, too. "People will forget," he insisted, wishing she would do what everyone else who knew him had finally done and just drop it.

"No, they won't." Lainey continued pestering him. "Not around here. Fifty years from now, everyone who knows you will be still be wondering why you dumped Yvonne Rathbone in front of an audience of seventeen million people."

"So it will be one of the great mysteries of all time. So what?" Brad's expression hardened as he pushed the cart toward the meat case.

"So I would think you'd want to get on with your life," Lainey told him passionately.

"In case you haven't noticed? I am."

Lainey fell silent. She seemed to have realized, Brad noted, that she had overstepped her bounds by a whole hell of a lot.

The rest of the shopping was done in relative silence. Eventually, Brad had to go back and get another cart. They filled that one to overflowing, too, then headed toward the checkout lines.

"I want to split the groceries with you," Lainey said as they reached the conveyer belt.

"Not necessary. Lewis said room and board was included, so he and I will pay for them."

Lainey got out her billfold at the same time as he did. "We'll put it on my card—you and Lewis can reimburse me for half later."

Brad knew he had offended—or maybe just disappointed?—her with his refusal to go public with his side of the story. But she seemed to be taking it awfully personally. Too personally. Which was odd, he mused as their groceries were scanned and sacked. He had never figured her for one of those women who always had to be right….

Finally, the total appeared. Lainey removed the bank card from her wallet and slid it through the machine mounted on the counter. "Debit or credit?" the clerk asked.

"Debit," Lainey said.

The clerk punched in a few numbers. Frowned. Punched them in again. "I'm sorry." She looked at Lainey. "It won't take it—insufficient funds."

Lainey did a double take. Her cheeks grew pink. "Try the credit, then," she said finally. Turning to Brad, she murmured, "There must be some screwup at the bank. I've got plenty of balance in there to cover this transaction."

Brad nodded.

"I'm sorry," the clerk said again, "it won't take the credit card, either."

"Now I know there's some mistake," Lainey said, visibly upset.

Brad pulled out his wallet, handed over his bank card. "Let's try mine."

It went through like a charm.

LAINEY FUMED about the mistake with her card all the way back to the ranch. She was still stewing as they carried the groceries inside and put them away. As soon as they were finished, she pulled out her cell phone, dialed her bank in Dallas and asked to talk to Customer Service. "What do you mean my account was emptied this morning?" she said, aghast. She listened some more, her face growing first a stunned white, and then an angry red. "I see. No. Thank you." She hung up the phone. Her hands were trembling.

"Anything I can help out with?" Brad asked.

She shook her head and picked up her cell again.

Feeling like he would be prying if he stayed, he went to check on his own phone messages. He had several. By the time he returned those calls and made his way back to the kitchen, she was off the phone again. She looked very upset.

He knew it was none of his business. He had tasks that needed accomplishing, too, but he couldn't just leave her like this. For the first time in a long while, it looked like someone close to him was having a worse time than he was. "Anything I can do to help?" he asked gently, his heart going out to her. She had been terribly embarrassed at the grocery store.

Lainey stared straight ahead. "Bunny has cut all my funds," she said, her tone as tense and upset as the look on her face.

"What do you mean?" he asked, moving closer yet.

"She called the bank this morning and had all the money transferred out of my account, and a hold put on my credit card."

Brad pulled up a chair and sat down at the table opposite her. "I don't understand. How can she do that?"

She steepled her hands. "She is the executor of Chip's estate. She controls all the funds he left for Petey and for me."

His glance dropped to the visible softness of her entwined hands. "Has Bunny done this before?"

Her lower lip formed a resolute line. "She's quarreled with me about money and decisions I've made about Petey before, but she's never done anything like this."

He paused. "Why would your sister-in-law be doing it now?"

"Easy." She sighed, discouraged. "She doesn't want us to move to Laramie."

"She said that?"

She bit her lip. "Not in so many words."

Brad edged closer, wishing he had the right to put his arm around her and offer the kind of physical comfort she obviously needed. "What did Bunny say?"

A bleak light came into her eyes. "That she was going to do some financial restructuring where the money being doled out of the trust was concerned, and that she and I should probably sit down to talk it over as soon as possible. She said if I wanted to bring Petey back to Dallas this afternoon, she'd make time to talk with me."

"Whoa."

Her expression was grim as she nodded. "Definitely a shot across the bow."

And a hell of a warning at that, he thought sympathetically. What was Chip thinking, to have left Lainey and Petey in a situation like this? Shouldn't he have foreseen his sister's irrational tendencies? "There's no way you can rearrange things so that you're in charge of the trust?" he asked.

"No. The beneficiaries of a trust are never the executors, too. Someone else always controls the money. And the person who sets up the trust—in this case, Chip—also decides who will control the dispersing of the trust's funds."

Not good. Brad sat back in his chair, drew a deep breath. "What are you going to do?" he asked.

Determination lit Lainey's eyes. "I'll tell you what I'm not going to do." She looked Brad straight in the eye. "I'm not going back to Dallas. And I'm not going to grovel. Not anymore."

"THAT'S SOME MEAL my big brother just missed," Lewis said, as Lainey cleared the plates and returned with a golden peach cobbler, still warm from the oven. She got out the ice cream and several dessert plates.

"My mom makes the best fried chicken," Petey said with a contented sigh.

"Don't forget the mashed potatoes and cream gravy and the green beans," Lewis said.

"And the salad," Petey added.

Lainey grinned, glad her efforts had been appreciated.

"Brad is going to be sorry he wasn't here," Lewis continued warmly. "Where is he, anyway? Did he say where he was going?"

Lainey shook her head. She regretted that Brad had missed the sit-down dinner in the ranch house kitchen, too. And not just because it would have helped set the stage for her eventual request for an interview with him.

"A couple of ranches to look at cattle. I'm not sure where exactly. He borrowed a livestock trailer from Travis, though. He expects to be coming back tomorrow with some of the herd."

"I can't wait to see that," Petey enthused. "I like trucks and animals as much as I like video games." Petey looked at Lewis shyly. "Thanks again for letting me be a tester."

"You're welcome, Petey. You and the other kids had some really fine ideas on how to improve the new prototypes."

Petey grinned and turned to Lainey. "Aunt Bunny said I wasn't going to like being out here, but she was wrong. This place really rocks!"

"I'm glad you like it," Lainey said quietly, doing her best to keep her temper in check. She was still angry at her sister-in-law for the stunt she'd pulled with Lainey's sole bank card. Lainey also knew she had only herself to blame for allowing herself to be in such a predicament. She could have gotten a job and her own money a long time ago. She hadn't.

She would now.

"I'm glad you enjoyed yourself, too," Lewis said, oblivious to the dark nature of Lainey's thoughts. "It's fun having a kid around here. Reminds me of when I was growing up."

"Were there a lot of kids in your family?" Petey asked.

"Five, besides me," Lewis said. He launched into tales of growing up one of five boys, with only one baby sister, Laurel. Petey was spellbound all through dessert, and dishes.

Lainey hung up the dish towel and checked her watch. Eight o'clock.

"You've done enough for today," Lewis said, reading her mind. "Why don't you knock off?"

Lainey looked at the rows of moving boxes stacked in the utility room and back hall. "I didn't get as much done as I had hoped to."

"So you'll stay a few days or weeks longer." Lewis winked at Petey. "You won't mind, will you, sport?"

In answer, Petey beamed.

Exhausted from the excitement, Petey was showered and tucked in bed by nine, and asleep by ten. When she was certain it was quiet, Lainey curled up with her computer again, and the DVDs of *Bachelor Bliss*. Lainey watched two more episodes. The closer she looked, the easier it was to see that Brad was not enjoying himself. The smile he wore was plastered on his face. He was genial, easygoing, gallant. But only around Yvonne Rathbone did he seem at all genuine. Yvonne appeared as if she was enjoying Brad's company just as much during the half-dozen or so outings that the two had.

Their last evening alone together was particularly romantic. Brad appeared totally smitten.

So what had happened to change that? Lainey wondered.

Why had he gone in the next day, clad not in the tux he was supposed to be wearing, but a pair of jeans and a Western shirt, stuck his hands in his pockets and told her, "You know what? This isn't working out. So what do you say you and I just do ourselves a favor and call it quits here and now?"

Yvonne—wearing a beautiful evening gown—gasped and broke into tears.

Brad turned and walked out.

The camera cut back to Yvonne, and her gasping, wrenching sobs.

Frowning because once again it seemed like Brad was a real cad, and not the quick-witted, warmhearted man she was getting to know, Lainey went back to the menu and clicked on the last episode of the series of shows featuring Brad. Brad and Yvonne were seated with the show host, discussing what had not happened during the final "ceremony."

Yvonne was tearful and obviously hurt by the fact Brad hadn't asked her to marry him. Brad didn't care. He was alternately ignoring or glaring at Yvonne as they "discussed"— or, to put it more aptly, *didn't* discuss—the situation. His anger was subtle, but there nevertheless.

Obviously, Lainey concluded as she watched it over and over again, Yvonne had done or said something to really anger Brad. Maybe not in front of the cameras, but away from them. The question was, *what?*

Chapter Six

"Mommy, look!" Petey ran into the upstairs hall, where Lainey was organizing the linen closet early the next morning. Bypassing the snap-together building block set he had been playing with, he took her by the hand and dragged her to the window. Out in the yard, Brad was backing his pickup, and the livestock trailer behind it, toward the pasture gate.

"You think he's got another horse in there?" Petey asked.

Lainey hadn't seen such pure excitement on her son's face in a long time. She put her arm around his shoulders. "I don't know, honey."

"Can we go see? Please, Mommy!"

"All right." Lainey smiled. "But on one condition. We have to make sure we don't get in the way, so I want you to stay right by my side."

Petey nodded eagerly, already latching on to her hand. "I will, I promise."

By the time they reached the yard, Brad was out of the pickup and opening the rear doors of the trailer, which were situated inside the fence. "Whoa, there!" Brad said. "No. This way. Come on, fella. That's it. Right this way…."

Seconds later, a large rust-colored bull with horns at least four feet wide came lumbering down the ramp and onto the pasture grass. Brad followed, apparently unafraid, as the bull hit the ground and kept right on going, out onto the pasture. When he reached the watering hole in the center of it, he bent his head and began to drink.

Brad closed up the rear of the trailer, got back in the truck and moved it forward enough that he could go back and close and latch the gate.

As soon as that was done, Petey broke away from Lainey and ran toward Brad. "Wow!" Petey said. "Is that a real cow?"

Brad grinned. "It's a bull, Petey. And his name is Tabasco Red."

It also weighed a good thousand pounds. Lainey had only to look at her inquisitive little boy's face to know what he was thinking. "You aren't to go near him, Petey."

Petey frowned, disappointed and upset. "But Brad went near him," he complained.

"Brad is a grown-up. When you're a man, you can go near bulls, too. Not until then," Lainey said firmly.

Brad looked at Lainey. He appeared ready to differ with her. She sent him a look, letting him know that would not be wise. He remained blessedly silent.

"Are you going to get more bulls?" Petey asked.

"We've got twenty virgin heifers being delivered tomorrow," Brad told her son matter-of-factly.

"What's a virgin hecker?" Petey asked.

It was all Lainey could do not to cringe and cover her face.

"Heifer," Brad repeated, seeing Lainey's embarrassment and leaving out the "virgin" part this time. "And it's a young female cow who has never had a baby cow—or calf," Brad explained seriously.

"Oh." Petey mulled that over. "Are they going to be out in the same place?" He pointed to the pasture closest to the house, where Tabasco Red stood chewing on grass.

"Not right away, no."

"Okay. That's enough questions, Petey." Lainey smiled, doing her best to pretend she wasn't the least bit discomfited by the conversation. She made a show of looking at her watch. "It's almost nine o'clock."

Petey perked up. "Time to go to my play date?"

"Yes," Lainey said.

Brad shot her an inquiring look.

"I got invited to go to another ranch," Petey informed Brad excitedly, "where there are two boys almost my age. Kyle and Kurt McCabe. They're supposed to be your cousins—I met 'em at the game company yesterday. They were testing stuff, too."

"That sounds like fun," Brad said, suitably impressed.

"It's going to be," Petey told Brad. "They have a swimming pool and a basketball hoop."

"If you want, I can drop Petey off," Brad said. "I'm on my way into town to buy feed, anyway. I'll go right by there."

Lainey looked at Petey. "That okay with you?"

Petey nodded. "Do we get to ride in the pickup?"

Brad slapped his hand on Petey's shoulder. "You bet!" The two swaggered off, side by side, with Petey doing his best to imitate his new hero.

LAINEY HAD MOVED ON to Lewis's bedroom when her cell phone rang, shortly after noon. She continued hanging up clothes with one hand even as she answered.

"So, how's the search coming?" Sybil asked, shifting into editor mode the moment hellos had been said. "Have you been able to talk to Brad McCabe yet?"

"I'm working on it," Lainey said, frowning as she looked at a suit of Lewis's that would have been better suited to the Beatles, circa 1965. "I have to tell you, though, Brad McCabe is still in no mood to be interviewed."

"I assume you're working on getting him to change his mind."

Not as hard as I should be, Lainey thought guiltily, aware if truth be told that she was more interested in getting to know the man he was now, than what had happened on *Bachelor Bliss*.

"You've got a great opportunity here," Sybil stressed.

"I won't blow it," Lainey promised.

"That's what I wanted to hear," Sybil countered cheerfully. "In the meantime, I've been using my contacts in the business to see what I could uncover, too."

"Got anything?" Lainey switched into reporter mode.

"I just got off the phone with Yvonne Rathbone's manager. Apparently, she's been hired to do guest spots on two of the network's dramas. The episodes are going to air early in the fall." There was a rustle of paper on the other end. "I managed to get you a telephone interview with the producer who hired her. Call this number—" Sybil paused to read off a ten-digit number and extension, while Lainey wrote it down "—at precisely two o'clock Pacific time, and Rocco Talmadge will speak with you. Have your questions ready. Five minutes is all you've got."

Lainey was alone in the ranch house, working on Brad's bedroom, when the time came to make the call. She perched on the edge of the bed, notepad of questions in hand. As promised, she was put right through to Rocco Talmadge, the producer who had hired Brad's ex.

"Were Yvonne Rathbone's appearances on two network dramas part of the deal when she signed on to do *Bachelor Bliss*?" Lainey asked.

"No. This was arranged after that stud broke her heart and the whole country fell in love with her."

"So, it's just a publicity stunt, then, to attract viewers?"

Rocco sighed. "Could have been. That's what I figured it would be—if we hired her. But that was before she came in to do a screen test for us last week. Yvonne was just flat-out amazing. She nailed her dialogue and conjured up all the right emotions at just the right time. She even had the camera work down, although I guess that's not surprising given the fact she just spent six weeks filming *Bachelor Bliss*."

Lainey recalled Yvonne had been a copier sales rep before she quit to do reality TV. "Has Yvonne acted before?"

"No. She's just a natural, I guess."

Interesting, Lainey thought. Had Yvonne's stellar "acting" ability somehow played into the breakup with Brad, his reasons for wanting to dump her, regardless of what was expected of him? "Do you think Yvonne will have other acting opportunities after this?"

"If she manages the actual taping as well as the auditions? Absolutely! Listen, I've got to go. Thank the people at *Personalities Magazine* for mentioning this. It's bound to boost our ratings."

Lainey knew a little free publicity never hurt. "No problem."

Still musing over what she had learned, Lainey cut the connection and put her phone back on her belt, just as a door slammed downstairs. Quickly, she put her notepad and phone into the deep slash pocket of her skirt and went back to hanging up jeans.

Seconds later, Brad strode into the room. His hat was off and his shirt was unbuttoned to the waist. He seemed surprised to see her standing there.

"What?" he said abruptly, looking her up and down. He took off his shirt and tossed it into the hamper Lainey had put in the adjoining bathroom.

She blinked, unable to take her eyes off his broad shoulders and nicely muscled chest. The satiny smooth skin had been shaved when he was filming *Bachelor Bliss*. No more. The suntanned flesh was covered with sable-brown hair that spread across his pecs, and arrowed down past his navel to disappear beneath the waistband of his jeans.

"What do you mean—*what?*" she mocked.

He strode closer, smelling like sweat and man. "Why do you have that look on your face?"

The one that indicated her heart was racing, her knees

were weak, and there was a fluttery, melting sensation in the middle of her tummy? Knowing it would irritate him, Lainey played dumb. "What look?"

Brad's brown eyes narrowed as he studied her intently. "I don't know. Guilty, maybe?"

Of course—since she was here under at least partly false pretenses. But unable to tell Brad any of that yet, Lainey shrugged. "I'm uncomfortable, definitely."

His brow furrowed. "Because?"

"I was in here, in your bedroom, working, when you came striding in, tossing off clothes right and left."

"I wouldn't call one shirt 'clothes.'"

Lainey ignored his joke. "I would. And I think I should be leaving now…." She started to step past, heart racing all the more.

"Don't you want to know why I'm undressing?" Brad called after her in the low, sexy voice that had broken so many bachelorettes' hearts.

She turned, discovering Brad had his boots, belt and socks off, too.

"We've all been invited to Annie and Travis McCabe's for dinner." He disappeared into the bath, returned with a can of shaving cream in hand.

What was it about a man in nothing but a pair of jeans, and whatever he had under them…? "Thanks for letting me know." She folded her arms in front of her and watched as he spread lather over his face. "But I'm not sure I can go. I have an awful lot of work to do here." And an awful lot of research and interviewing to do, too….

Brad plucked his razor off the sink and began running that through the cream, disappearing from view from time to time to watch what he was doing in the mirror. "Petey will be awful disappointed if you don't show up. He's having a great time over there. I think he wanted to share the ranch with you."

Put like that…how could she say no? "Well, maybe for a

little while." She wanted her son to be happy as much as she wanted the truth about Brad and Yvonne and their *Bachelor Bliss* experience to be known.

Brad rinsed his face and blotted it with a towel. "Be ready to go in an hour?"

"No problem." She edged toward the door, reluctant to leave, knowing she had no apparent reason to stay.

"Something on your mind?" he asked curiously, moving with her.

Damn him for being so intuitive. "I was just thinking," she said finally.

"About?"

How someone so obviously sensitive to others could be so cruel to a woman he had—at least on TV—fancied himself in love with. But aware this wasn't the moment to bring that up—that it would take a lot more subtlety to work the question into the conversation—Lainey said, instead, the first inane thing that came to mind. "I was just wondering about those cows you are having delivered tomorrow," she fibbed. "They're not going to be in the same pasture as that bull, are they?"

Brad gave her a bemused look as he went to his closet and flipped through the Western shirts Lainey had just ironed, organized and hung up. "That's kind of the point of buying twenty virgin heifers," he told her drolly.

She cringed. It was all she could do not to cover her ears. "Please don't call them that." It conjured up thoughts of sex. And sex was the last thing she needed between her and Brad.

"What would you *like* me to call them?" he asked, mischief turning up the corners of his lips. He leaned against the bathroom door frame, brawny arms folded in front of him.

Lainey knew her eyes were suddenly sparkling, too. "Cows?" she guessed timidly, knowing her lack of knowledge about ranching matters was endless.

"How about longhorns?" he said dryly.

"Fine." She took a deep steadying breath and tore her eyes from the sleek masculine contours of his chest. She was *not* going to wonder what it was like to touch him. There. Or there… "Back to the, uh…um…" Oh, dear heavens. Couldn't she keep her mind on the conversation they were having for one second?

"Inseminating?" Brad asked helpfully, even more mischief in his eyes.

"Yes." She steeled herself not to be so attracted to him. She had a job to do here, she reminded herself sternly. Two jobs! "Can you please not have the longhorns mating in front of Petey."

His chuckle filled the air. "Where would you like me to take them? A bedroom?"

Lainey failed to contain the blush rising upward from her neck. "How about the barn? Couldn't they, um, do it there?" She couldn't believe she had just said that. And judging from the look on Brad's face, neither could be.

"These are longhorns," he told her matter-of-factly. "They need room to maneuver and the freedom to—how should we say it…engage?—when they feel like it."

Lainey sputtered, "But Petey—"

"Probably knows a lot more than you think," Brad interjected.

Lainey scoffed and folded her arms over her chest. "He doesn't know about this," she stated firmly.

Brad straightened and sauntered toward Lainey. "Then maybe it's time he did."

Lainey watched as Brad carried the jeans and shirt he had selected into the bathroom and hung them on the hook inside the door, then returned to his bureau to search for the black knit Jockey shorts she had also put away. "I'm not prepared to talk to him about the birds and the bees just yet."

He took his socks and underwear into the bathroom and plunked them down on the nicely organized black ceramic tiled counter. "Then just talk to him about bulls and heifers," he said.

Lainey paced back and forth, her slides echoing against the wooden floor. "That might lead to other questions," she said.

He looked down at the hot pink polish she had put on her toenails the evening before. "Yes, it certainly might," he drawled.

She struggled not to react to the way his glance was slowly moving up her bare legs. "You're not being at all helpful!" she scolded.

For lack of a better place to sit, Brad went back to lounging on his bed, legs spread, arms resting on the mattress on either side of him. He looked at her and slowly shook his head. "You're not being at all realistic if you think a kid can be around animals and not eventually get some idea of how Mother Nature works."

Lainey didn't know whether to slug him or kiss him. Truth was, she wanted to do both. "So you won't help me out with this?" she asked, piqued.

Brad rubbed the underside of his jaw, testing the just-shaved smoothness of his skin. "I'll talk to Petey, and explain to him what's going on and why, if you want," he offered, all cocky male.

"That wasn't what I meant!" Lainey threw up her hands in exasperation and stomped closer.

He offered an engaging half grin. "I know what you meant."

Lainey moved even closer. "You can be very aggravating," she told him, even as she was aware a chance like this might not ever come again.

"So I've been told," he admitted rakishly.

"Is that why you broke up with Yvonne Rathbone the way you did, just to be aggravating?" Lainey asked.

THE QUESTION CAME out of nowhere, and spoiled the playful mood that had sprung up between them. "Why do you care?"

Brad asked her, aware she was one of the most natural beauties he had ever seen in his life. Everything about her was extraordinarily fine. From the top of her honey-blond hair to the tips of her toes, she was one memorable woman. Which of course made her unprecedented nosy question all the harder to take.

Lainey shrugged. A self-conscious flush darkened her cheeks but she didn't back down. "I'm curious."

"Curiosity killed the cat."

She kept her eyes on his. "I'm no feline."

Brad sighed, not about to argue that point. "You're all woman, all right." Palpable tension arose between them as Lainey edged closer.

"So what happened?" Lainey pushed him deliberately. "Did the two of you sleep together? Did Yvonne disappoint you in bed? Is that what happened to make you walk away?"

Brad's gut told him two things. One, Lainey didn't look as if she wanted him to have that kind of past with Yvonne. Two, he had the feeling Lainey had said that just to get a reaction. He and his brothers used to do that to each other, when they were growing up, whenever they wanted to dig out the truth. They'd say something so outrageous that the target of the innuendo would have to say something to defend himself. Before they knew it, the real story was out there.

But the two of them weren't kids.

They were adults. Who were ready to cross a boundary from which Brad sensed there would be no turning back.

"You're aware you're really out of line, here," he informed her.

Lainey tilted her head. "At least I'm not afraid."

She headed for the door. Brad was on his feet before she could take two steps. He clamped a hand on her shoulder and swung her around to face him. "What does that mean?"

Her slender shoulders lifted in a shrug. "I just don't understand why you refuse to talk about what happened with Yvonne."

Back to that again. "Maybe I like my privacy."

"And maybe you're embarrassed."

"What do I have to be embarrassed about?" he demanded gruffly. Aware her skin was heating where his fingers rested, he dropped his hand.

"Your behavior?" she countered sweetly. "I mean, it's not every day that a guy dumps a perfectly nice woman without provocation on national TV."

Anger roiled inside him once again. "My actions weren't without provocation," he defended himself hotly.

Her teeth worried the softness of her lower lip. She searched his face and asked the question Brad had already heard a thousand times, from family and friends. "What did Yvonne do that was so bad?"

He hadn't answered anyone else. Maybe it was time that changed. He knew if he didn't tell someone at least part of what happened soon, he was going to explode. "Yvonne led me to believe some things that were not true. And then she made damn sure I'd find out what kind of person she really was fifteen minutes before the taping of the final ceremony was to start."

Brad had hoped Lainey would leave it at that. Of course, she didn't.

"I don't understand," she said slowly. "Why would Yvonne do something like that when you were about to propose to her and she was in love with you, and you both could have walked away with lucrative endorsement contracts if only you had stayed together?"

He sighed. "Yvonne wasn't in love with me."

Lainey lifted her brows. "She sure looked like she was on TV."

"Well, she wasn't," he said harshly.

"That still doesn't answer the question as to why she

would do something guaranteed to make you break up with her, at the very time she was set to win everything," Lainey persisted.

"Maybe," Brad said harshly, "because Yvonne got a lot more attention playing the victim after she was dumped than she would have had if she rode off into the sunset to live happily ever after with me."

Well, that much was true, Lainey had to admit. The story of Brad and Yvonne's live on-air breakup had captivated the media for weeks. Still, the smitten way Yvonne had looked at Brad as "their love" unfolded had certainly seemed genuine enough. Which meant Lainey had to ask the hard questions, even if Brad didn't want to hear them. Shifting into full reporter mode, she continued her probing. "So you're saying what—that Yvonne was just pretending all along?"

"Who knows." He shrugged.

Once again, Lainey had the sensation he was withholding tons more than he was telling.

"All I can tell you is that she sure had me fooled."

Not to mention the rest of the country, Lainey thought. She sat down on the edge of the bed. "I guess that explains why you acted so cold and hostile and uncaring toward Yvonne during the last show." If Brad had felt personally betrayed—duped—by Yvonne, his actions made sense.

He exhaled. "It was all I could do to get through that Heart Ceremony."

"Then why did you?" Why stride in there, hell for leather, and treat someone badly on camera when you knew millions of viewers were watching? she wondered.

He shoved his hands through his hair. "I went because I'd signed a contract. And the show's producers told me they'd sue me for five million in damages if I walked. So I met my obligation."

Now that was a scoop. "The producers must have been unhappy."

"Are you kidding? That was exactly what they wanted. Ratings had been going down on all the *Bachelor Bliss* shows. The novelty of TV romance was wearing pretty thin. The show's creator, Gil Hewitt, knew the only way to keep the show on the air was to create some real-life drama."

"But you weren't in on the game," Lainey said carefully.

"I wouldn't have cooperated had I known what kind of behind-the-scenes minidrama Gil Hewitt had planned."

A drama Brad still hadn't fully explained—and he didn't look likely to, either. "Were *all* the women in on this?" Lainey treaded carefully, wary of scaring him off with questions that were too pointed and probing.

"I don't know for sure, but I don't think anyone witnessed what happened except me, Yvonne, and the person on the show who made darn sure the grand finale all happened according to plan."

And that was the way Brad obviously wanted it to stay, Lainey realized in mounting frustration. "So the big reveal wasn't on camera?" she guessed, wondering why the *Bachelor Bliss* producers had stopped short of showing that, too. Unless doing so would have tipped the hand as to what would happen next.

"No. Thank God. Although—" Brad stopped, shook his head and didn't go on.

Frustrated but not defeated, Lainey persevered. "And you never suspected…during the show's filming…that anything was amiss?"

He shrugged and took on a brooding expression. "Looking back, I see the way the show's staff kept pushing me toward Yvonne as a mate," he allowed finally.

"And you were okay with that." Lainey knew it had sure looked that way on the TV screen.

"It sounds crazy now, knowing what I do about the conniving…sneak, but at the time, I thought Yvonne might very well be the perfect woman for me. She appeared to be everything I had ever wanted."

Lainey pushed aside a flare of jealousy. With effort, she stayed professional and zeroed in on his suspicions. "You don't think that happened by chance, do you?"

Brad shook his head. "No. I think someone gave Yvonne advance access to the questionnaires that we filled out when we were accepted as contestants. There were pages and pages of them, plus interviews with psychologists to make sure we were emotionally fit to be in this type of program."

"And Yvonne used the information she gleaned to—?"

"Simultaneously undercut other contestants and make herself into a persona that fulfilled my every fantasy."

For reasons Lainey preferred not to examine too closely, she didn't ask what precise "fantasies" were fulfilled. "That's a pretty hefty accusation," she stated calmly, wishing she weren't thinking about taking Brad in her arms again and claiming him as hers and hers alone.

"But true, nonetheless."

They sat there in silence. "Now do you see why I want nothing to do with the show or anyone on it ever again?" Brad said finally, meeting her eyes.

Lainey nodded sympathetically, understanding that he had been humiliated and betrayed, and was—as most men would be—still very reluctant to talk about an incident that had so damaged his pride. But he needed to talk about it, and get it all out, as much as she needed for him to do so.

Unfortunately for her, Brad hadn't yet divulged the details that if disclosed would make Lainey's story a sensation. Which meant she had to try harder to help him, and herself, and her friend, Sybil. Most of all, she wanted to set the record straight. Get the truth out there once and for all. End the innuendo, the lies, and most of all, the damage to Brad's reputation.

"The thing is, Brad," she said, looking deep into his eyes, "ignoring what happened is not going to make it all go away."

Chapter Seven

Brad knew he shouldn't have started down this road. He wasn't even sure why he had. Except, there was something about Lainey, the way she asked questions, the way she wanted to understand everything about him, that held him spellbound. She fascinated him in a way no other woman had.

"You should tell your side of the story, and I mean every bit of it, Brad, and clear your name," Lainey said.

So everyone said. Trying not to notice how pretty she looked in the late-afternoon sunlight streaming in through the windows, Brad turned his gaze away from her and removed his boots. "I'm tired of explaining myself," he stated gruffly.

"Then let someone else do it for you," Lainey persisted. "Someone you trust."

Annoyed, Brad leaned forward, elbows resting on his thighs. "And who would that be?" he demanded, giving her an arch look.

For a second, Lainey looked as if she had a very specific idea who that might be but was afraid to suggest it. The moment passed, and she shrugged. "There are a lot of different venues," she said carefully, coming closer, so they might continue talking in the low intimate tones that fit the situation. "Magazines, TV shows, even newspapers. But the avenue that would benefit you most financially would be a book deal."

"A book," Brad repeated.

"Yes. A tell-all." Lainey remained directly in front of him, her body braced in challenge. Knowing she wasn't going to back down kicked his heartbeat up another notch.

"Forget it." He stood, restless as ever. Then made the mistake of looking at her again. For the life of him, he couldn't figure out why she persisted in dressing so nicely for such rigorous work. Most people wore old clothes—shorts and T-shirts—when they unpacked moving boxes. Lainey was clad in a sunny yellow cotton skirt and matching white-and-yellow diagonal-striped top. Her legs, arms and shoulders were bare, the exposed skin soft and silky looking. Facts that only added to her appeal. And his bad judgment for noticing. Hadn't he determined after the *Bachelor Bliss* debacle that he wasn't going to get involved with a woman again for a good long while? And a woman like Lainey would, by definition, require emotional involvement.

"You're such a hot commodity right now that with the proper agent you could probably get a deal well into the six figures. Now, that may not be what you would have earned doing commercials after the show, but it's still a lot of money, and it would go a long way toward helping you buy into this ranch as a full partner the way you had planned."

That did sound good. Baring—no, *selling*—his soul did not. Deliberately, he kept his eyes on her face. "For starters, I can't write."

She offered a tantalizing half smile. "I'm sure the publisher could pair you with an excellent ghostwriter."

The thought of furthering his public pillorying was unacceptable. "No. My private life remains private." He started toward the bathroom.

Lainey followed, looking just as determined as he felt. She leaned a slender shoulder against the door frame as he bent to splash cold water on his face. "You're fooling yourself if you think what happened will remain secret forever.

Someone is going to find out about it, and then they'll benefit, and you won't. Again!"

She was calling him a chump. And maybe he *was* one for letting the conversation go on this long. Brad dropped the towel onto the sink. "You want me to benefit from all this?" he said, his mood shifting as he moved toward her.

Pique flashed in her eyes. "That's what I've been saying, isn't it?"

"Then how about you help me out?" Brad retorted as he stopped in front of her.

Giving her no chance to respond, he wrapped his arms around her and pulled her close. He heard her soft gasp of surprise as his head dropped, and then his lips were on hers, their mouths fusing as one, their bodies pressing close together. Heat flooded through him. Lower still, blood pooled into an insistent ache.

Brad hadn't meant to do anything but shut Lainey up in the most shocking way possible. He hadn't expected her to melt against him, or to open her mouth to the plundering pressure of his, or to kiss him back. He'd figured he deserved a slap across the face. Not this sweet, gentle, loving invitation to dally.

Lainey knew it was a mistake pushing Brad, just as it was a mistake to allow him to take her in his arms. She should be fighting for what she wanted here, instead of devoting herself to helping him. But she couldn't help it. Something about his stubborn male pride, the hidden vulnerability in his heart, combined to draw her like a moth to the flame.

And full of fire, he was.

She'd never been kissed like this. With such fierce possessiveness and total mastery. Nor had she ever allowed herself to melt into anyone so completely. Always before, there had been that careful wall of restraint. The veneer of cool sophistication she had worked so hard to achieve.

There was nothing reserved about the way he was dancing her backward toward the bedroom wall. Nothing subtle about the way he held her there, arms flattened on either side of her head, body pressed warmly against hers. Brad was kissing her as if she were already his woman, and damn if she didn't feel like that just might be the case.

But deep down she knew that if she allowed him to make love with her, then and there, it would mean no turning back. Brad McCabe would have not just her body, but her heart. That truth brought Lainey crashing down to earth. Realizing she had no other choice, she removed her arms from about his neck, tore her mouth from his and pushed him away with all her strength.

BRAD WATCHED HER MOVE a short distance away. Sauntering closer, he girded his thighs and crossed his arms as if for battle. "What? No slap?"

"Not that you don't deserve it." Feeling heat in her cheeks, Lainey spoke as if underlining every word.

"But?"

Not about to let him get the better of her, now or at any other time, Lainey held her ground, despite the fact they were now uncomfortably close. Close enough to start kissing again. Close enough for her to inhale the musky scent of man and sweat clinging to his skin. Close enough to see the speculation gleaming in his brown eyes. "If I'm going over to Annie and Travis's for dinner with Petey, I need to get cleaned up."

A devilish smile tugged at the corners of his lips. "I like you the way you are," Brad said. Bracing his legs a little farther apart, he skimmed her provocatively with his gaze. "All mussed up."

When he looked at her like that, Lainey felt sexy and powerful, in a very decadent and satisfying way. Unwilling to consider what it would be like if someone as used to having his own way as Brad McCabe became part of her life, Lainey drew an unsteady breath. "I'm not one of your women," she said. Although, she noted in dismay, she had been acting as if she were—advising Brad to seek a book contract instead of an exclusive interview with her.

Times like this she had to wonder if she possessed the necessary single-mindedness required for her profession. An ace reporter destined for fame and fortune would have been focused on the story they were trying to research, not looking out for the best interests of others to her own detriment.

"Women?" he repeated with a look of utter male supremacy, drawing her back to their conversation.

Finding his low, seductive voice a little bit too disarming, Lainey turned away. "You know what I mean."

"I know what you think you mean." Ignoring her resistance, he pulled her back into his arms. "And just so you know—" he leaned forward and whispered in her ear "—I never thought you were one of my women."

Heart pounding, she studied him. He wasn't hitting on her, wasn't attempting to kiss her again. He was just playing mind games with her. Giving her reason to stay away from him and not bring up the subject of his experience on *Bachelor Bliss* again.

Still, the embrace, and her reaction to it, stayed with her all through dinner at the neighboring Rocking Diamond Ranch. She was still distracted by the searing memories as she, Annie and the other adults—Lewis, Travis and Brad—took their coffee out onto the wraparound porch. The three boys were out in the side yard, playing fetch with Duke, the family's big black Lab.

"So, how's Tabasco Red doing? Has he settled in okay?" Travis asked Brad.

Brad nodded. "So far, he's doing fine."

"I've got a heifer in the barn you might want to take a look at," Travis said. "A little on the scrawny side," he continued as the three men set their coffee cups aside and ambled down the porch, "but good bloodlines and I'd be willing to let her go cheap, if you're interested…."

As soon as the men were out of earshot, Annie kicked back in her rocking chair. "So, how is the organizing going?"

Relieved to think about something other than the man who had her totally fascinated…and confused, Lainey smiled. "I've got the kitchen and two offices downstairs done. Today, I've been working on the bedrooms."

"Lewis said you've been amazing."

She flashed Annie a look of gratitude. "Thanks to your help getting the furniture in the right place, and some of the extraneous junk cleared out, I got off to a mighty fast start." Almost too fast, as she was going to be finished in no time. And once she was, she would have no more excuse to stay on. She didn't want to think about how depressing that was. She was enjoying being back in Laramie, living on a ranch for the first time in her life. Petey liked it, too. "Besides, all I really had to do was unpack boxes and put things away. It hasn't been all that hard."

Annie poured more coffee, then set the carafe back on the white wicker table between them. "You wouldn't know it to hear Lewis talk. He thinks you're a miracle worker. And speaking of men in need of miracles…" Her smile widened. "My nephew—Lewis and Brad's brother, Riley—is moving back to Laramie in August. He just finished his residency and has taken a position at Laramie Community Hospital. Anyway, he's going to need some similar work, and he'd like to hire you to help him get organized, if possible."

"No problem." Lainey planned to take on as much work as she could handle.

"You ought to start your own business as a professional organizer," Annie continued.

Was that what she wanted? Or did she want to continue to pursue her long-held dream of being a journalist? All Lainey knew for sure was that she had some serious choices ahead of her. Like how far she was willing to go to uncover Brad McCabe's secret.

Annie studied Lainey. "Is that frown related to our discussion—or to the man who has you tied in knots?"

Lainey wasn't used to talking about her personal life, but heaven knows she needed to confide in someone. "It's that obvious?" she asked wearily.

"Let's just say I recognize the particular type of tension flowing between you and Brad because it used to flow like the Rio Grande between Travis and me before we hooked up."

Lainey recalled Annie and Travis had enjoyed the kind of high-profile romance that'd had the whole community buzzing, yet they had come out of it with a relationship that only seemed to get stronger and more loving every year. Lainey gazed at the rosebushes Annie had planted next to the porch.

"Is Brad the kind of womanizer everyone says he is?"

"There's no shortage of women pursuing him. He's so handsome and charming. I just don't think he's allowed himself to get caught very often, if at all."

"A good-time guy," Lainey paraphrased, her mood as careful and wary as it should have been earlier.

Annie sighed, worry coming into her pretty eyes. "Let's just say, before Brad did *Bachelor Bliss*, he never minded entering a party with a pretty woman on his arm. Now, he's lucky if he gives any female the time of day."

That was certainly how Brad had behaved when Lainey had first showed up at the Lazy M to talk to Lewis. But lately, Brad had been giving her a lot more than the time of day. But then, she had kind of gotten in his face, in her efforts to get the real story out of him. If Lainey were half the reporter Sybil seemed to think she was, she would have told Brad right away who she was working for and pressed a lot harder to get him to 'fess up. Instead, she was letting Brad's comfort level—instead of her own pressing timetable—dictate her reporting. She was easing off on the scoop of the summer, wishing instead that she could spend more time with Brad, just for the sake of their getting to know each other. How crazy was that?

Annie shook her head at Lainey. "He's really gotten to you, hasn't he?"

Whoo, boy, had he. Lainey had never been this distracted—and fascinated—by a man before. She pushed out of her rocking chair, and moved to the edge of the porch. Abruptly, she realized the ranch had gotten awfully quiet. Never a good sign where kids were concerned. She peered around to the side yard. No boys. No dog. Uh-oh. "Do you know where the kids went?" she asked.

Annie's brow furrowed. "They're supposed to be right there."

Worry slid to panic. "They're not."

Annie leaped out of her chair. She was halfway down the front porch, with Lainey right after her. At the same time, Travis, Brad and Lewis emerged from the barn closest to the ranch house. Annie cupped her hands around her mouth and yelled at Travis, "Are the boys with you?"

Travis shook his head.

In the distance, there was a bark.

Then another.

And another.

They all turned in the direction of the sound.

In the distance, Duke could be seen leaping and bounding through a pasture of four-foot-high grass, bordering a thicket of cedar trees and juniper bushes.

"Oh, no!" Annie said, frowning.

Travis frowned, too. "I'll get 'em," he said.

"YOU BOYS KNOW BETTER than to go out there in shorts and tennis shoes," Annie scolded, as the boys and their dog returned to the yard where they were supposed to be hanging out.

"We were just playing ranchers and rustlers," nine-year-old Kurt explained to the five grown-ups who had been worried about them.

"Yeah." Eight-year-old Kyle chimed in, more interested in the game they had been playing than the safety issues in question. "Kurt stole Rocco—he was pretending to be our prize bull—and me and Petey had to go and get 'em."

"That's all fine and good," Travis said sternly. "But you need to play that game in the yard where we can see you."

Brad nodded in agreement, looking sober indeed. "Those woods are deceptively deep. You guys could get lost out there."

"Or at the very least come down with a good case of poison oak or ivy!" Lainey said, belatedly aware she hadn't once thought to caution Petey about that. But she hadn't expected him to run off, either. "You don't have jeans and long-sleeved shirts on," she explained, more to her son than to the other two boys who lived on the ranch and knew the precautions necessary. "You're in shorts and T-shirts."

Abruptly, Petey's temper flared. "I don't even have any jeans here, Mom!" he fumed.

Lainey stared at her son in shock, embarrassed by his sassy tone. "Since when do you talk back to me?"

Petey folded his arms and glared at Lainey petulantly. "Since you treat me like a baby instead of a grown-up guy."

Well, maybe that's because you're not a grown-up guy, Lainey thought, aware this was not a discussion she wanted to have here. "I think we need to go home," she said, plastering a cordial smile on her face. She knew she was being abrupt, but it had been a very long day and she could see Petey was close to a meltdown. "Thank you so much for a lovely dinner and play date."

"I don't want to go home!" Petey shouted in a manner that was completely unlike him.

His two playmates, who might be prone to mischief but knew better than to talk back, fell silent, looking shocked, too. Duke lay on the ground at their feet, panting hard after his exertion in the heat of the summer evening.

"We're going," Lainey said firmly. She put her hand on Petey's shoulder.

Petey jerked free. He was already scratching furiously at his neck, legs and arms.

Brad's expression went from sympathy to concern. "Better get him in the shower as soon as possible. Lots of soap and water everywhere he might have come into contact with poison oak, ivy or sumac."

"You guys, too." Annie herded her two youngest sons toward the house.

Travis nodded before turning to follow his wife and boys. "And be careful handling his clothes," he told Lainey. "They could have the oily residue from the poison weeds on them, too."

"Thanks," Lainey said. She knew all this, but it had been so long since she'd been out in the Texas countryside and had had to deal with it that she had almost forgotten.

"You can't make me do anything I don't want to do!" Petey continued to shout ferociously.

Tired of fooling around, Lainey took Petey by the arm, her manner no-nonsense. "We'll just see about that, young man," she said, already guiding him in the direction of their SUV. "Now march!"

LAINEY PHONED THE RANCH HOUSE as soon as Petey was out of the shower. "Do you guys have anything for chigger bites on hand?" If they didn't, she was going to have to pack Petey in the car, pajamas and all, and drive to town.

"Be right over," Brad said.

He was at the guest house door two minutes later, bottle of Listerine mouthwash in hand, looking ready, able and eager to help.

"The insect bites are on his arms, legs, neck and face, not in his mouth," Lainey said dryly, feeling ridiculously glad to have him there as backup. She ushered him inside.

"Oh, ye of little faith," Brad said dryly. Petey emerged from the bathroom, clad in a pair of cotton sleep shorts and a Texas Rangers T-shirt.

Brad knelt in front of Petey. "Pretty miserable, huh?"

Petey glared at Lainey, like she was the worst mother on the entire planet, then looked back at Brad with a sad little nod. "I itch so bad," Petey whispered, as if Brad were his only friend left in the world.

Brad gave Petey a reassuring pat on his shoulder, letting Petey know with a look that things were going to be all right very soon, then asked Lainey quietly, "Do you have a small bowl or something I could pour this into?"

Lainey went to get it. Brad followed, her son in hand, and hefted Petey onto the kitchen counter as if he weighed five—not sixty-five—pounds. "This seem strange to you?" Brad asked Petey as he dipped a cotton ball into the minty-smelling mouthwash and began daubing it on the red welts on Petey's legs.

Petey nodded.

"Well, give it a minute," Brad advised.

"That feels kind of good," Petey said, after a moment. He looked at Brad gratefully. "It doesn't itch no more."

"Anymore," Lainey corrected.

Petey glared at her again.

"Forgive me for being a mother," she muttered under her breath.

Brad grinned. He gave Petey a commiserating look as he dipped the cotton ball in mouthwash and began attending to the angry red bites on Petey's arms. "Women." Brad shook his head. "What are you going to do?"

Petey mimicked Brad's droll gesture and heaved a great big sigh. "I don't know," he said.

Grateful to Brad not only for making her son more comfortable, but for defusing the potentially explosive situation, Lainey leaned against the counter, watching. Chip had loved

Petey dearly, but he had been a hands-off father when it came to anything practical. Chip had never changed a diaper, or gotten up with Petey in the middle of the night, or helped him learn his spelling words. She sensed Brad would do all that for any child of his, and more.

"Where did you get the idea to do this?" she asked.

"My brother, Riley."

"The physician who is coming to town soon?"

"Right. He learned it in medical school. I guess they did some studies and found that the herbal ingredients in Listerine have both antifungal and anti-itch properties. It kills the chigger, soothes the site of the bite, and voilà…you're better before you know it." Brad daubed Listerine on the spots on Petey's neck, then stood back. "Okay, cowboy, do you feel like I missed any? Are you still itching anywhere?"

Petey shook his head. "Thanks, Brad."

"You're welcome." Brad held out his hand. "Put her there, pardner."

Petey shook his hand.

Lainey hated to break it up, but she knew Petey was tired to the point of exhaustion. "Okay, sport, thank Brad and then head to bed."

Petey turned to Lainey, the anger gone. In its place was the need to make up with her, at least most of the way, before he went to sleep. "Can I read for a little bit?"

Lainey doubted he'd get past two pages, but she never discouraged reading. She knew it was the key to his future success. "Yes."

Petey turned back to Brad. "Thank you for helping me out. My mommy wouldn't have known what to do to make me stop itching so fast."

Lainey's jaw dropped. That wasn't quite true. And the glint in Brad's eyes as he glanced at her told her he knew it, too.

"Anytime you need anything you let me know." Brad ruffled Petey's head. The boy grinned and started back to his bedroom. Lainey was about to say something when her son turned back, gave her a brief, sorrow-laced hug, and then departed once again. Brad returned to the kitchen. He capped the bottle of Listerine. "You want to keep this? I've got an extra bottle at the house."

"If you don't mind, I think I will. And thanks—for helping and coming over." Lainey walked him out to the front porch. Darkness was descending. It was going to be a clear, pretty night, with lots of stars in the velvety Texas sky overhead.

"I'm sorry he was upset earlier."

"He was just overtired," she said.

"Sure that's all it is?"

Leave it to Brad to hit the nail on the head. Lainey bit her lip. Who would have thought he could be this easy to talk to? "He's having a hard time lately."

Brad's expression gentled. "Because he lost his dad?"

Lainey hesitated, more unsure of herself than ever. Something else that was unusual. Her ability to mother was the one thing she had always been confident about. "I don't know. It's been two years."

"Yet—?" He studied her, guessing there was more.

Lainey perched on the porch railing, her back to the yard, and ran a hand down the sturdy wooden post that supported the roof. "He was doing so well. I mean, initially, when Chip died, he had trouble concentrating at school, cried a lot and missed his father terribly during holidays. But as time wore on and almost two years passed, he seemed to be coping great. Then, suddenly, this last spring, he wasn't coping so well anymore. The things that used to make him so happy— spending time with his cousins, going on family outings, even going to the playground at the park—have left him tense and irritable."

Compassion crossed Brad's face beneath the warm glow of the porch lights. "Because he misses his dad?"

"And because he's growing up without one and thinks I treat him too much like a baby."

Edging nearer, Brad stood with his legs braced apart, hands in the back pockets of his jeans. "You don't. I've seen you with him. You are remarkably gentle and respectful, even when Petey's in the midst of having a meltdown."

"Thank you." She ducked her head. "But I don't feel so competent." She lifted her head again and looked into his eyes. "That's why I wanted to spend some time in Laramie this summer and let him participate in the game-testing program at Lewis's company. And be out here at the ranch, too. I thought a change of pace might lift his spirits. Take the quarrelsome edge, that occasionally seems to appear with no warning or reason, off his demeanor. I thought it was working, that he was really happy again. Now, I'm not so sure."

Brad moved to perch beside her on the railing. He reached over and took her hand in his. "He's just a little kid, Lainey. He's going to have his good days and his bad, regardless of how you mother him."

She tried not to think about how good it felt to have her hand clasped in that warm, strong palm. "And how would you know that?" she probed.

Brad grimaced, the brooding look back in his eyes. "Because I lost a parent, too."

Chapter Eight

Compassion filled Lainey's heart. "How old were you when your mom died?"

"Fourteen. But she was ill for months before that."

"Breast cancer, right?" Lainey asked, aware this was the first time Brad had allowed himself to be really vulnerable to her.

He nodded. "I was a lot older than Petey. Old enough to understand that life isn't always fair, and sometimes people get sick and they die. But it was still hard for me and my siblings and especially my dad, because he loved my mom so much. We all did."

Lainey had been married with a family of her own when she lost her parents. That had been difficult enough. She tightened her grip on Brad's hand. "As a kid…as a family…how did you cope?" Did the McCabes have some lessons they could impart to her?

"At first we were just so numb," Brad allowed reluctantly. His eyes took on a distant look. "I think to outsiders it looked like we were doing better than we were because everyone was still going through the motions, just the way we had when Mom was alive. But then as time went on the charade got harder and harder to maintain and everything began to fall apart. We went through nanny after nanny. Finally, in desperation, Dad moved us here, and that's when Kate Marten—my stepmother—came into our lives and made us deal with our loss."

"That's just it, though, Brad," Lainey said softly. "I'm almost certain Petey has already worked through his loss."

"Then what could be causing this difference in his behavior?"

She shrugged, averting her gaze from the tempting proximity of his chiseled lips. "My sister-in-law, Bunny, thinks it's growing pains combined with the lack of male influence in his life."

He cupped her hand in both of his. "But you don't agree."

She studied their clasped hands, aware of how natural this felt. "I know he misses being around Chip. All you have to do is look at how he perks up whenever you, Lewis, Travis and all the other guys around here pay him attention."

"He's a great kid. We enjoy being around him."

"And he, you."

An awkward silence fell between them. She knew she should either end the evening now…or risk kissing again. Deciding she needed her wits about her to complete the story she'd been assigned, she stood.

Before she got more than two steps away, Brad caught her wrist and tugged her back.

She pivoted to face him.

"I feel like I shouldn't have to say this," he stated seriously, "but what I told you earlier about Yvonne pretending to be one kind of person when she was really another…that stays between the two of us. I don't want anyone else—even my family—suspecting how I was duped."

Guilt flooded her. Much more than just Brad's pride was at stake here. "Until you tell me otherwise, absolutely," she promised, meaning it.

"I'm not changing my mind about this, Lainey," he warned gruffly, closing the distance between them. "My private life, the way I was deliberately set up, is not for public consumption."

Well, there went her article for *Personalities* and the

chance to jump-start her journalism career at the national level, Lainey thought, depressed. Unless she could convince him to change his mind, of course.

Did she want to?

Brad picked up on her confusion. And misjudged the reason for it.

"About earlier," he said after a moment.

She had only to look into his eyes to know he was talking about the passionate clinch that still had her insides humming with unslaked desire. Embarrassed at the lack of restraint she had shown when he pulled her into his arms, she moved to the edge of the porch and glanced away. "We don't have to talk about that."

He followed her, standing so close she could feel the warmth of his body and hear the slow, steady meter of his breath. "Suppose I want to?" he said quietly.

If she let her guard down, she knew what would happen. She couldn't risk falling head over heels in love with a man she was trying her best to remain objective about. She knew full well that business and pleasure did not mix. So she pretended this was about something other than what it was, too. "Look, I know you're more experienced in that particular arena than I am," she said, focusing strictly on the highly sexual nature of the encounter.

"Don't bet on it. I haven't been married or had a child with someone—both things that I am guessing lead to greater intimacy and satisfaction."

Lainey didn't want to admit how lacking her previous marriage had been in that regard. She paused, worrying her lower lip with her teeth and looked deep into his eyes, finding all the understanding—and respect—she ever could have wished for. "But I don't mess around for sport," she noted softly. "When I kiss someone it means something."

Too late, she realized how insulting that sounded.

To her surprise, Brad didn't seem to mind. Or even disagree.

He leaned toward her intimately, looking sexy as hell. Every bit the intimidating bachelor he had been on TV. "Maybe that's the problem," he said, grasping her by the shoulders. "Whenever I've kissed someone, prior to you, anyway, it's never once meant anything close to what it should."

The gentle warmth of his fingers penetrated her skin. "What are you trying to say?" she murmured, wishing she didn't recall quite so vividly how passionately he'd kissed, or how tenderly he'd held her in his arms.

His gaze drifted over her as he favored her with a rakish smile. "It's high time my kisses did mean something." He took her all the way into his arms and tilted his head over hers. "It's high time," he told her, mouth lowering, "I felt something more than simple desire."

He gave her an instant to pull away if that was what she wanted. When she went toward him instead, he murmured a soft sound of approval and took her mouth deliberately, kissing her deeply. She clung to him, kissing him back, savoring the scent and feel and taste of him. Sensations swirled through her. His hands moved down her spine, working their magic.

"It's time I let myself feel what you and I were both meant to feel about each other," he whispered, probing her mouth with evocative thrusts of his tongue.

The kiss turned sweeter, more tender. "Brad, I—we—really shouldn't do…" Her will faltered.

"Do what?" he prompted lazily, kissing her again and again and again.

"This," she said, kissing him back.

When he finally let her go, she was so dizzy she could barely stand. Her insides were humming.

Brad smiled as he stroked his hands through her hair, caressed her face. "I know we have to say good night," he told her reluctantly. "I know Petey is sleeping inside and we have to set an example, but something is happening here, Lainey. Something good."

As much as she wanted to, Lainey could not deny it.

"I NEED TO KNOW you're making progress," Sybil said, early the next morning.

Lainey was certainly trying. She wanted nothing more than to get this assignment behind her. She had been up half the night, researching Yvonne Rathbone and Brad McCabe and everything she could find that had been written about the *Bachelor Bliss* episodes starring them. The Internet was full of previously published articles about the couple. But no one knew even a smidgen of the truth about what had happened to break them up—except Lainey. And unfortunately, Brad had not yet consented to tell Lainey everything or let anyone else, even his family, in on the secret.

Lainey still hoped that would change.

The secrets were eating him alive.

In the meantime, she was between a rock and a hard place, trapped between a man who was quickly becoming very important to her, and the job she had been contracted to do.

Aware her boss was waiting, Lainey briefed Sybil on the telephone interview with the Hollywood producer who had hired Yvonne to guest-star in two prime-time dramas.

"She certainly hasn't lost out on anything since Brad McCabe broke up with her on national TV."

Sybil was right, Lainey thought. Brad had been the one who had done all the losing, who'd had his reputation trashed. The unfairness of it all bothered her immensely. "I tracked down the phone numbers of the other female contestants on the show. I've been talking to them one by one."

"And?"

"Let's just say Yvonne was not well liked by the others," Lainey said.

"That could be shrugged off as jealousy, since Yvonne won more time alone with Brad and the chance to win his heart."

Which Yvonne hadn't. "Somehow, I think it's more than that."

"But no one's told you why Brad McCabe pulled the Jekyll and Hyde act," Sybil said.

"No, so far everyone has been very diplomatic," Lainey admitted reluctantly. "But I watched the DVDs of the show on my laptop again last night." After Brad had left and she was sure Petey was sound asleep. "And I zeroed in on the three most emotional women of the group. I'm hoping one of them will tell me something everyone else has been too discreet to say."

"You know you've got less than a week left to pull this off."

Lainey did not need reminding.

"I'm counting on you, Lainey," she persisted, sounding every bit as determined to succeed as she had been in college. "My winning the top slot at *Personalities* depends on my being able to pull this off. A lot is riding on my all-Texas issue," Sybil finished emphatically.

Including, Lainey thought, her own future.

"CAN I, MOM? PLEASE?" Petey asked over breakfast that morning. "It's my big chance to be a real cowboy, just like Brad."

Lainey grinned at the exuberance in her son's voice. How long since he had shown such enthusiasm for anything? Months, she knew.

Lainey looked at Brad. "You're sure you want to take Petey with you to pick up the heifers this morning?"

He nodded. "The Triple T isn't that far. Only about an hour from here."

"You're sure he won't be in the way when you're loading the animals?"

"The cowboys at the Triple T will be putting them on the truck. All Petey and I will be doing is making sure that the animals they are loading are the ones I bought last week."

"How are you going to do that?" Lainey put platters of scrambled eggs, crisp apple-wood-smoked bacon and piping hot blueberry muffins on the table. "Don't they all sort of look alike?" They did to her, anyway.

"The animals are tagged with numbers on their ears," Petey explained. "Brad says it's sort of like cattle earrings."

"Good thing they're female, then," Lewis teased.

"Steers have 'em, too," Petey explained importantly. "That way the cowboys can tell 'em apart when they get to the rodeo."

Lainey looked at Brad in surprise. She knew she should be accustomed by now, but she couldn't get over how ruggedly handsome Brad looked in the morning, even with rumpled hair and in need of a shave, as he was right now. She'd been around long enough to know that he showered twice a day but used his razor only once, in the evening after work. He wore nicer clothes in the evening. The jeans and shirts he wore during his ranching hours were worn and clung to the muscled contours of his tall body.

When he had come into the kitchen, she'd caught a whiff of soap and man and cool mint mouthwash. Just that easily, her motor began to race. Doing her best to ignore her awareness of Brad, Lainey asked, "These animals are slated for the rodeo?"

He nodded, digging into his breakfast with enthusiasm while Petey watched and followed suit. "The steers we get from the breeding operation will be sold to the rodeo when they're fully grown. I'm keeping the female cattle for breeding more rodeo stock."

"And that means nearly every year the size of Brad's herd will practically double," Petey explained. He looked at his mother seriously. "You hafta know your math, if you want to be a rancher."

Lainey smiled, glad Brad was having such a positive influence on her son. "When will you be back?" she asked.

Brad shrugged. "Noon, probably." He paused. "Sure you don't want to go? We've got room in the truck."

Lainey was tempted. "I've got work to do here." Reporting work. And because she was uncomfortable doing it, she'd just as soon get it over with. The sooner she got this writing assignment over, the better, as far as she was concerned. Never again was she going to sign a contract to clandestinely investigate anyone she knew, or had personal ties with on any level. It was just too darn hard. But she had sworn she would do this one article, so she had to follow through. Because she owed it to herself—her friend Sybil, too.

"Next time," Lainey promised. *If you still want me to go.* There was no guarantee that would be the case after the *Personalities* story came out.

As soon as the men cleared out, Lainey got right down to work doing the sleuthing that would allow her to expose the truth of what had really happened between Brad and Yvonne to the public without ever involving Brad.

First up was Susie, a bubbly brunette from Kansas City. The charming elementary-school teacher had been fourth from the last in the elimination, and had struck Lainey as being a very pragmatic, as well as beautiful, woman. "Are you asking me to be honest?" Susie asked.

"Nothing but," Lainey replied, holding the phone closer to her ear.

"I think the outcome was rigged from the first."

Lainey scribbled down Susie's exact words. "What makes you think that?"

"The rest of us had to make do with the outfits we brought with us, or what was on the wardrobe racks. Yvonne Rathbone came in with a whole suitcase full of designer clothing. And you can't tell me she could afford Prada and Marc Jacobs on a copier sales rep's salary."

Interesting, Lainey thought. "Did anyone ever ask Yvonne where she got her clothes?"

"Oh, yes. She just smiled and said it was all in who you knew."

Lainey paused, her pen resting just above the paper. "Are you saying that the *Bachelor Bliss* producers gave her this clothing, and didn't make similar accommodations for the rest of you?"

"All I know is that when Yvonne didn't like the way she looked in something, another designer garment magically appeared for her to wear," Susie concluded. "It was always found on the wardrobe rack. Yvonne always waltzed in just in time to claim it as her own, before anyone else ever even knew it was there."

Up next was Abigail, a ski instructor from Idaho. Abigail also felt Yvonne Rathbone had received special treatment from the beginning. "Several times during the filming of the show, there was a shortage of rooms where all the contestants were quartered and she got bumped to another hotel."

Lainey wrote furiously. "Were the accommodations the same quality?"

"Are you kidding? The room she was moved to was much nicer!"

Lainey followed the lead. "Was anyone else from the show staying there?"

"Yes, the producers, and the show's creator, Gil Hewitt."

"But no other contestants."

"No. Just Yvonne."

Last on Lainey's list to telephone was Shelley. The gregarious travel agent was even more direct when asked if she thought Yvonne Rathbone had ever been given special advantage over the other contestants. "I just found it odd how Yvonne always seemed to know stuff about Brad—like which type of rodeo contests he did—before Brad even told us. Yvonne said it was because she followed the sport. She even claimed to have seen one of his events in Wyoming a few years ago."

Lainey zeroed in on the skepticism in Shelley's voice as she continued taking notes. "But you didn't buy it."

"No."

"Any reason why?"

"Yes!" Shelly replied emphatically. "Yvonne had a real aversion to stable smells. She almost threw up the day Brad took us all riding, on that first group date. I just couldn't see her willingly sitting in the stands in the heat and the dust, the smell of manure wafting up around her."

Lainey smiled as the pieces began to come together. From what she had seen on TV, she couldn't see Yvonne doing that of her own volition, either. "Mind if I quote you on that?" she asked Shelley.

"Sure. Why not? It's not as if the outcome of the contest for Brad's heart is still in question."

But it had been then. And it was becoming more and more clear that Yvonne had cheated to win. The question was, who had helped her get the edge? And what had *that* person stood to gain?

"Did you see me on the horse, Mom? I was up in the saddle and everything!"

"I did see." Lainey smiled down at her son. Petey's day "helping" Brad had obviously thrilled him to no end. "You looked great!" She gave Petey a big hug, then looked over at Brad. "Thanks for giving Petey his first riding lesson," she said sincerely.

Brad radiated contentment, too. "Glad to do it."

Lainey led her son over to the kitchen sink. She handed him the soap and watched as he washed his hands. Petey babbled on in excitement. "Brad is teaching me how to be a cowboy. Cowboys are the strongest, smartest kind of grown-up guys, right, Mom? I mean, cowboys always know what to do in every situation. That's what Tyler, Trevor and Teddy McCabe said."

"Not surprising since they're all cowboys," Brad said with a patient smile. When Petey had finished, Brad went to the sink.

Lainey worried what would happen if Petey got too attached to Brad and then things did not work out between

Brad and her. Momentarily distracted, she watched as Brad rolled up his sleeves. His forearms were muscular, feathered with sable-brown hair. She knew…from some of the swimming and beach shots done on *Bachelor Bliss*…that the rest of him was just as beautiful.

She really had to stop watching those DVDs….

Petey wrinkled his nose as Lainey handed him a towel. "Huh?"

"There are other jobs, too, like Lewis's," Lainey explained. "You think Lewis's job is a good one, don't you? And the one your father had?"

"Daddy mostly got on airplanes."

"He traveled a lot for business," Lainey explained to Brad.

"I don't think Daddy's job was a lot of fun, at least he didn't act like it. What I want to be when I grow up is a cowboy who makes up computer games."

"Could happen," Brad allowed with an admiring smile, as his brother Lewis strolled into the house via the back door, the canvas carryall containing his laptop computer slung over one shoulder.

"Something smells good in here," Lewis said.

"Dinner will be ready in about thirty minutes."

"I have a new prototype of the game you tested the other day," Lewis said to Petey. "Want to take a look at it and tell me if you think it is any better?"

Petey looked at Lainey. "Can I, Mom?"

"Sure."

They ambled off, chattering all the while.

Brad remained. Feeling far too aware of him for comfort, Lainey went back to cooking dinner. "Thanks for letting Petey hang out with you today."

Brad came up behind her. Placing one hand on her shoulder, he took the lid off a saucepan. "I enjoyed it. He's a great kid."

Warmth swept through Lainey in undulating waves. She knew he was not thinking about the food she was preparing.

He was thinking about the way he had been kissing her the evening before. An embrace she was still reeling from. *Something is happening here, Lainey. Something good.*

Lainey gave the spicy shredded chicken a stir. "I also noticed you put the heifers in the barn instead of in the pasture with the bull. Is that so Petey wouldn't see, um, you know…"

Brad leaned in closer, the front of his thighs pressing the backs of hers as he lifted yet another lid. "Any mating going on?"

Lainey swung around quickly, as the steamy aroma of Mexican rice filled the air. She pressed her index finger to his lips. "Shhh. I don't want him to hear."

Brad grinned down at her, eyes twinkling. "He's going to figure it out sooner or later."

Feeling warmth everywhere their bodies touched, as well as where they didn't, Lainey flushed. "Do you really have to let them do it before we leave?" she whispered, embarrassed. "We're only going to be here another week." She slipped by him and went to the cutting board next to the sink. She lifted the serving dishes of chopped tomatoes and shredded lettuce and put them on the table.

Brad trailed after her. "Relax," he told her. "The heifers are getting hormones to synchronize when they will stand in heat."

Oh. "Is that why you put them in the barn?" Lainey asked curiously.

"Traveling is hard on them. It'll be easier to keep them cool in there and let them recover from being jostled around, before we put them out to pasture and let Tabasco Red do his stuff."

Lainey blinked as she picked up blocks of cheddar and Monterey Jack cheese. "One bull is going to service all those heifers?"

Brad took both cheeses from her and lent a hand with the

NO POSTAGE
NECESSARY
IF MAILED
IN THE
UNITED STATES

BUSINESS REPLY MAIL
FIRST-CLASS MAIL   PERMIT NO. 717-003   BUFFALO, NY

POSTAGE WILL BE PAID BY ADDRESSEE

HARLEQUIN READER SERVICE
3010 WALDEN AVE
PO BOX 1867
BUFFALO NY 14240-9952

Get FREE BOOKS and a FREE GIFT when you play the...

LAS VEGAS GAME

*Just scratch off
the gold box with a coin.
Then check below to see
the gifts you get!* →

YES! I have scratched off the gold box. Please send me my **2 FREE BOOKS** and **gift for which I qualify**. I understand that I am under no obligation to purchase any books as explained on the back of this card.

354 HDL D7ZU   154 HDL D7YL

FIRST NAME	LAST NAME

ADDRESS

APT.#	CITY

STATE/PROV.	ZIP/POSTAL CODE

(H-AR-08/05)

7	**7**	**7**	Worth TWO FREE BOOKS plus a BONUS Mystery Gift!
🍒	🍒	🍒	Worth TWO FREE BOOKS!
🔔	🔔	♣	TRY AGAIN!

www.eHarlequin.com

grater. "One male to every twenty-four to thirty cows is considered normal."

"Or in other words," Lainey said dryly, as she added flour tortillas to a skillet, "every male's dream."

Brad made a dissenting face. "More like nightmare if you're talking about humans, and I'd guess—from your tone—you are."

Time to proceed with her reporting again. "You're telling me you didn't enjoy yourself on *Bachelor Bliss.*"

"All those women vying for my attention at once?"

He hadn't earned his Casanova rep sitting home alone every Saturday night. "It was what you seemed to want back in high school," she pointed out.

Brad finished his task and lounged against the counter. "That was only because I didn't want to hurt anyone's feelings. I was the new kid in town—at least in the junior class at Laramie High—and it seemed like every female my age wanted to date me. I'd never had that before and I didn't know how to say no. So—" he shrugged affably, taking a bite of the cheese he had just shredded "—I started stacking dates one on top of the other."

"I remember." Lainey gave the salsa a taste and added another sprinkling of cilantro and a tad more red onion.

"It was hell when the girls figured it out."

Cocking her head, she offered a spoonful to Brad. He tasted it, nodding his approval. "They tarred and feathered you," she remembered.

"With lipstick and perfume." Brad shuddered in disgust and made her laugh. "I can still remember that awful smell, all those fragrances mixed together. Anyway, I learned my lesson and I never dated more than one woman at a time after that."

Lainey plucked the hot, soft tortillas from the skillet, put them into the warmer and closed the lid. She turned off that burner and leaned against the counter, mirroring his stance and half smile. "How many of those were a one-night-only type of thing?"

Brad looked her up and down, too. "I have no idea."

Aware the meat filling had another ten minutes to simmer, and that the rest of dinner was ready, she bided her time. "How many serious relationships have you had?"

He lifted a brow. "Define 'serious'."

Aware he didn't want to go down this path, but determined nevertheless, Lainey specified, "Where you dated someone more than a couple of times."

Regret crossed his face. "I, uh, haven't."

Just as she had feared. "Which then raises the question, why in the world did you ever go on *Bachelor Bliss*?"

GOOD QUESTION, BRAD THOUGHT.

"You knew the show was designed to get you engaged and married in six weeks. If you weren't the settling-down type…" Lainey continued.

If he didn't know better, he'd say he was being interviewed. But that was ridiculous. Lainey wasn't a reporter. She was, however, interested in him—her kisses and the way she responded to him demonstrated that. And, as such, maybe there were things she needed to know if this whatever-it-was they were starting was to go any further.

He could deal with that.

Even respected it.

"I am interested in marriage," he told Lainey honestly.

Her green eyes widened. "You really expect me—or any other woman in this country—to believe that?" she asked in astonishment.

"I don't care what the others do or don't believe." *I care about you.* The thought shocked him, even as he realized it was true. "I'm tired of dating. Tired of not having someone to come home to at night, someone who cares about me—not where we are going or what we might be doing or who we might be seeing that evening." To his surprise, she was listening. Wanting to be near her, he crossed to her side. "I see what other men my age have who are married and have kids of their own. They're happy, Lainey. Content. So, yeah, maybe it was stupid and naive of me, but when I signed up for *Bachelor Bliss* and they told me they would use my answers to the show questionnaire and the information gleaned from the psychologist interview to handpick women who would be just perfect for me, I thought maybe it would work. The old-fashioned way of trying to hook up with a woman by chance certainly hadn't been successful. I figured, statistically, why not give this a try." He paused, aware he had just told her more than he had told any woman. "What about you?" he asked.

Lainey blinked. "What do you mean, me?"

Brad brushed a strand of blond hair from her cheek and tucked it behind her ear. "Are you looking to get married again?" Reluctantly, he dropped his hand.

He wanted to kiss her again. Make his move. Stake his claim. But the thought of Petey or Lewis walking in…

Lainey bit her lip. She looked as vulnerable as she did beautiful, standing there, an embroidered blue denim chef's apron over her clothing, her cheeks flushed from the heat of the stove. "I hadn't thought about it."

Knowing he had to touch her or go crazy, Brad slipped his fingers into the curve of hers and rubbed a thumb over the back of her hand. He studied her until she looked back. "Does that mean you have now?" he asked.

Lainey hesitated. Obviously not sure how much of herself to give away. "Petey wants a father again," she said finally. "That's pretty clear."

Not exactly what he had been fishing for! "You'd marry just to give him a father?" he asked her incredulously, dropping his hand.

"No. Of course not." She stiffened.

"Then why would you marry?" he asked.

That apparently was easy. "One reason and one reason only," Lainey said softly. "For love."

Chapter Nine

"Mommy, there's a man outside with a great big tow truck. Come and see!"

Lainey went to the window of the guest house. She saw a man in a garage uniform with a clipboard in his hand, studying the license plate number on the bumper of her SUV. "What in the world?" Lainey stepped outside at the same time as Brad came out of the barn and Lewis stepped out the back door of the ranch house.

"May I help you?" Lainey asked.

"I'm Henry Cross from Dallas Motors." He held out his hand. Lainey shook it. "You Mrs. Carrington?"

Lainey nodded, aware the man seemed nice enough. "That's right."

Henry announced pleasantly, "I'm here to pick up your vehicle for its thirty-thousand-mile servicing."

"There must be some mistake. I didn't schedule anything with the dealership." But her SUV had been purchased there.

Henry took off his cap and set it back on his head. "The other Mrs. Carrington said you might say that," he said uncomfortably.

Lots of thoughts came to Lainey's mind—none of them nice. "Bunny asked you to do this?" she asked, as Brad came to stand on one side of Lainey, Lewis on the other.

"Yes, ma'am." Henry lifted his hat again. "She set it up with the service desk yesterday."

Well then, Lainey thought furiously, Bunny was just going to have to undo it. "I'm sorry you came all the way out here, but you can't pick up my SUV. I won't have anything to drive."

Henry shifted from foot to foot. "Ma'am, you should take that up with your sister-in-law."

Believe me, I plan to. Mindful that Petey was standing right beside her, looking every bit as stressed-out as she felt, Lainey put a comforting hand on her son's shoulder. "We'll just have to reschedule," she repeated as cordially as she could.

"I have to take this SUV back to Dallas," Henry repeated.

Brad stepped forward. "Did you not hear the lady?"

Henry looked at Brad, man-to-man. "If I don't do my job, I'll lose it."

And no one wanted that, Lainey thought. "You know what, fellas? It's fine. Go ahead and do the servicing. When will I get my vehicle back?"

Henry looked back down at his clipboard. "Next week."

"Next week!" Lainey, Lewis and Brad repeated all at once. Petey looked up at Lainey.

Henry shrugged. "Vehicle pickups of this distance aren't easy to arrange," he explained.

"So why don't you just reschedule?" Brad asked again.

"I'd really like to do that," Lainey asserted. "I'll be back in Dallas in another week or two."

Petey's face fell. Lainey had an instinctive feeling that his disappointment had more to do with having to leave the ranch than the missed opportunity of seeing the SUV put up on the flatbed tow truck that would haul it back to Dallas Motors.

Henry paused, really looking like he did not want to be here now. "You'll have to take that up with Bart and Bunny Carrington, since their names are on the purchase papers for this vehicle."

Silence fell.

Lainey felt humiliated. And Petey tensed even more. The boy might not understand the complicated nature of the trust Chip had set up to take care of Lainey and Petey in the event of Chip's death, but Petey knew when his mother was unnecessarily embarrassed.

Seeing no reason to prolong the agony, Lainey forced a smile and swept a hand through her hair. "I guess I knew about this," she murmured awkwardly after a moment, in an effort to comfort her son, who, like everyone else present, was looking more and more upset about the situation.

"I've just been so busy and so interested in everything going on around here I had just forgotten about this," she fibbed, picking up steam as she went. "In fact, now that I think about it, I'm sure Bunny and Bart mentioned it to me last time we spoke."

Lainey felt her son beginning to relax. Hence, Lainey relaxed, too.

They all watched as Lainey's SUV was loaded onto the tow truck. When both had disappeared down the drive and had turned onto the farm-market road that ran past the ranch, Lewis turned to Petey. "Ready to spend another day at the testing facility, playing computer games?" He looked as eager to get out of there as Petey.

Her son's face broke into a broad grin. "You bet!" He high-fived Lewis.

"Then we better get a move on."

IT WAS CLEAR LAINEY DID NOT want to talk about what had just happened, so Brad went back to work, as did Lainey. But when Brad walked into the ranch house an hour later and found her in the family room tearfully organizing boxes of videotapes and DVDs, he knew the time for being circumspect was at an end.

"If this is going to upset you so much, maybe you should have a third party deal with Bart and Bunny for you," he said.

Lainey straightened and swung toward him. Despite the tumultuous events of the morning, she was as lovely as ever. Her honey-blond hair was disheveled, her pretty cheeks glistening wetly. The tip of her elegant nose was red from crying, her green eyes still misty with tears. "It's not Bart, it's Bunny."

Brad crossed the distance between them; he had never been more aware of the differences between them. He was clad in the usual jeans, boots and work shirt. Lainey was wearing a slim black cotton skirt and matching black shoes that had the toe and heel cut out, exposing her cute painted toenails. Her blue summer turtleneck sweater had cutaway sleeves that left her shoulders, and a great deal of her skin toward her collarbone, bare. It was made out of some sort of stretchy lightweight cotton that molded to her figure smoothly and hinted at voluptuous breasts and a slender waist, yet still managed to look classy and refined in that city-sophisticate way. Missing were the pearls and earrings she had worn to the ranch the first day.

"And I can handle Bunny," Lainey insisted, stubborn as ever.

Could she now. Brad sauntered closer, drinking in the floral scent of her perfume. He wished he could just take her to bed and make love to her until all the sadness and uncertainty in her eyes went away. He slid a hand beneath her chin and lifted her face to his. "I don't see how," he told her gruffly, "with Bunny pulling stuff like this."

Lainey's shoulders stiffened. Her back ramrod straight, she moved away from him and went back to sorting DVDs. "She's never done anything like this before. Well, anything this insufferable," she said as she put a stack of them in the bookcase.

Brad glanced at her curiously, trying hard not to notice how seductively her hips moved beneath the trim black skirt as she knelt, stood, sorted, reached. He moved closer to lend a hand. "So what prompted this latest shot across the bow?"

Lainey's pouty lower lip curled ruefully as she sorted movies into categories of science fiction, Westerns and action-adventure. "Me being out here with Petey, instead of in Dallas." She paused, sighing deeply. "Bunny asked us to move in with her and Bart, and I refused. Obviously, she is still angry with me over that."

No joke. Brad studied the unhappiness in her eyes. "Is there anything in your finances you control?"

Embarrassed, she shook her head.

"I still don't understand how your husband could have left you in such an untenable situation," he said, not bothering to hide his frustration.

Lainey ran a hand through her hair and continued to regard Brad warily. "Like I mentioned the last time we discussed this, Chip thought he was doing what was best for Petey and me."

It rankled to hear her continue to make excuses for her late husband. Another silence fell between them, this one fraught with tension. "Now who's kidding themselves?" he demanded. "You're always talking about being truthful and letting the chips fall where they may." He paused, then decided the heck with it—in for a penny, in for a pound. "Your marriage must have had some serious chinks in it if Chip could do something like this to you."

LEAVE IT TO THE BLUNT-SPOKEN BRAD to hit the nail on the head, Lainey thought. She swallowed hard around the knot of emotion in her throat. "You want the truth?"

He lifted a skeptical brow. "Are you ready to tell it?"

Knowing it was past time she talked honestly about this with someone she could trust, and that that person was Brad, she plunged on ruthlessly. "I am angry at Chip for this—and I have been for months now—but I'm angrier at myself for letting it happen because, the truth is, I could have fought the various stipulations and the way everything was set up at the time the trust was established."

Brad took her into the curve of his arm and held her against him. "Why didn't you?" he asked quietly.

Relishing the warmth and comfort of him, so tall and strong beside her, she tipped her face up to his and searched his eyes. "Because I didn't want to face the possibility that anything might ever happen to my husband." She paused and drew in a bolstering breath. "I never imagined he would die in an accident. So, like it or not…this is my fault as much as Chip's."

Brad sat down on the edge of the sofa and pulled her onto his lap. "You could still do something about the way things are set up if you want to." He stroked her hair gently.

Lainey shook her head. "It isn't going to be necessary."

He looked frustrated again, and tapped her tenderly on the nose. "Now who isn't being realistic?"

Aware the tables had changed, and that she was the one running from a difficult situation, Lainey looked at him, her tears gone. "You saw how what happened this morning upset Petey."

Brad nodded, looking unhappy about that, too.

She said frankly, "If he sees me fight with Bunny and Bart over this, he'll be even more distressed."

He didn't argue with that. "So don't let him see it. Have your showdown with your sister-in-law when Petey isn't around."

Lainey rolled her eyes. "A little hard to do now."

"I'll drive you into Dallas right now. We can go see your sister-in-law, tell her you want your car back, and we drive back. By the time Petey comes home tonight from the testing facility, everything will be as it should be. Then you can have your car serviced when *you* want it serviced."

Silence fell between them. "You don't think I'm going to take you up on your offer, do you?" Lainey challenged finally.

Brad shrugged. The look he gave her was more understanding than judgmental. "It's a lot easier to pretend all the bad stuff will go away on its own. I know." His lips twisted ruefully. "I'm an expert on that. At least, lately."

"I'D BE HAPPY TO DISCUSS this with you, Lainey," Bunny said, two hours later when Lainey met with her at Bunny's Dallas home. "But not—" Bunny glared at Brad "—with him here."

Lainey was braced for this and more. "Brad can hear anything we have to say to each other."

Brad smiled casually as he sat down on the elegant sofa beside Lainey. "I promised to be referee or witness, whatever is needed."

Bunny returned the warning with a condescending smile.

With effort, Lainey spoke in a calm, even tone. "These power plays have got to stop."

"Believe me," Bunny promised in a smooth, cultured tone, "I'd like nothing better than that."

"So do it," Brad advised, as Bunny handed out glasses of mint iced tea.

"I can't," she returned with a condescending smile. Her eyes narrowed. "As long as you continue to act so irresponsibly."

Lainey was holding on to her composure—and her temper—by mere threads. "Getting a job is irresponsible?"

"Getting a job Chip would never have approved of certainly is," Bunny shot back disparagingly, her resentment obvious. "And the same goes for dragging Petey out to the country to live in intimate proximity to two young, single men."

Brad gave Bunny a lethal look on Lainey's behalf, saving her the trouble.

"What are you saying?" Lainey demanded coldly.

Bunny lifted her hands. "Simply that a family court judge might very well agree with me that such living arrangements are not appropriate for a widow with a child."

"Unless I'm mistaken," Brad drawled, "I think your sister-in-law just threatened to sue you for custody of Petey."

"I wouldn't *want* to do that," Bunny continued sweetly.

"You would just have no choice," Lainey guessed bitterly.

"I see we finally understand each other." Her sister-in-law offered a chilly smile.

Lainey knew Bunny was never happy unless Bunny was calling the shots, and that her sister-in-law always felt she knew what was best for everyone else. But this was downright ridiculous. Lainey stood and picked up her shoulder bag. Her fingers tightened on the strap until they turned white. "You were right," she said to Brad, never taking her eyes from Bunny's face. Her blood ran hot and cold simultaneously. "This is pointless."

"Now what?" Brad asked as the two of them got back in his pickup. He started the engine.

Doing her best not to appear as if she had been run over by a steamroller, Lainey said, "I need to drop by my house to pick up some more clothes for Petey." Then she wanted to return to the Lazy M. To safe haven. She wanted to be with Brad and Petey and the rest of the McCabes and forget all this.

Brad shot her a concerned glance. "What about your SUV?"

"I'll make do without it," she said wearily, as she paused to direct Brad to her home, located just a few short blocks away. "Maybe when Bunny sees I am not going to be bullied or threatened into toeing her line, she'll stop all this nonsense," she hoped out loud.

But that was before Brad turned into the driveway of the imposing pink-brick Tudor with the gray shutters and white trim, and Lainey saw what else Bunny had done.

"ARE YOU OKAY?" Brad asked, some thirty minutes later, as they stowed the belongings Lainey had collected into the storage area behind the bench seat of the cab. It had been quite a shock to find a For Sale sign in the front yard, a lockbox on the front door and a Realtor inside, already taking a client through. A half-dozen business cards lined up on the kitchen counter indicated others were interested in the property, too.

"Yes."

She didn't look it. She was pale as a ghost. And he understood why. Her sister-in-law was trying her hardest to pull the rug out from under Lainey. He reached over and squeezed her hand. "You were very cordial in there." Brad began to drive in the direction of the freeway that would take them back to Laramie. He didn't know how she had kept her composure. She certainly would have been entitled to lose her temper.

Lainey shrugged, looking very much in need of a hug, a kiss. From him. She forced a vulnerable smile.

"Chip trained me well."

Chip had been a lousy husband, leaving her in a mess like this, Brad thought. Lainey deserved so much better. So did Petey. Silence descended. As they drove through the neighborhood, Lainey drew a deep, bolstering breath.

"I think you may be right about getting a third party in to deal with Bunny," she said eventually. "Your cousin in Laramie— Claire McCabe Taylor—is a family-law attorney, isn't she?"

Brad nodded. "One of the best."

"You wouldn't happen to have her number?"

"I can get it." Figuring the sooner Lainey took a proactive approach, the sooner she'd feel better, Brad pulled over to the curb and called Lewis at work. Lewis looked up the number and gave it to him. Brad wrote it down for Lainey and she made an appointment to see Claire later that very afternoon. "Claire will be able to help you," Brad said quietly, after Lainey had cut the connection with his cousin.

He was vaguely aware of Lainey nodding as he concentrated on the traffic.

"You don't have to worry," he continued. "We'll get this worked out."

More silence. Wishing he could do more to comfort her, Brad glanced over. Lainey had her head turned away from him, but he could tell by the way her shoulders were shaking that she was crying, silent, wrenching sobs that shook her whole body. He was almost to the entrance ramp to the freeway that would take them back to Laramie, but Brad turned into the first parking lot available. It happened to belong to a hotel. He eased his truck into a spot just beneath the neon sign, released his seat belt and slid across the bench seat.

He undid the clasp of her seat belt, too. She turned, tears streaking down her pretty face. Not caring that it was broad daylight and that they could easily be seen by anyone driving by, he took her wordlessly into his arms and held her close. She rested her head on his shoulder, and he bent his head, burying his face in the soft, fragrant softness of her hair and breathing in the sweet feminine essence that was her. "There, there, now," he found himself saying, as he stroked a calming hand down her back and shifted her closer. "It's going to be okay," he said thickly. "I promise."

Lainey cried all the harder. He felt her despair and it tore him apart like nothing ever had. He wove his fingers through her hair and tipped her head up to his. "Listen to me. I'm not going to let anything happen to you or to Petey."

The need on her face intensified. The next thing Brad knew, they were kissing. And kissing. And kissing. Who knew what might have happened had there not been a gaggle of female voices just outside his truck.

"I told you! It is him!"

"Brad McCabe!"

"Well, that sure as heck isn't Yvonne Rathbone."

Lainey jerked away from Brad at the same time he broke away from her. A chorus of swearwords sounded in his head as he faced their teenage hecklers.

"Hey!" one of the young girls shouted at Brad. The heckler couldn't have been more than nineteen or twenty. "We saw what you did to Yvonne on *Bachelor Bliss* and we're not ever going to forgive you!"

"Yeah! You had no right to go breaking her heart!"

"And now you're making another woman cry! What kind of louse are you, anyway?"

"Guys like you give all men a bad name!"

Brad looked at Lainey. She was white as a sheet, more distraught than ever. He swore. He'd never meant to hurt Lainey. Especially like this, after all she'd just been through.

Brad swore again, more heatedly this time. He put the truck into reverse and eased out of the parking space—not exactly easy to do given the proximity of the hecklers. He drove toward the exit while the girls chased after them. A soda can landed on his bumper and rattled to the ground as he turned back onto the access road running parallel to the freeway. "Sorry," he muttered.

Lainey wiped her eyes. "For kissing me," she asked softly, cautiously, "or for getting caught?"

BRAD FROWNED, a dark shadow crossing his face. "I'm sorry we got interrupted." He glanced at her briefly. "Sorry you were crying. Sorry about, well, just about damn everything."

His disillusionment was painful to see, but Lainey knew that ignoring it and pretending what just happened hadn't, would not make things better. "This won't help your reputation." She plucked the bottle of water out of her bag and took a drink. She hadn't meant to cry on Brad's shoulder, but her minimeltdown had been cathartic. She did feel better. Lots better. Though maybe that had more to do with the way his arms had felt around her, so strong and sure and comforting, and the hot, sexy way his lips had moved on hers. Had those girls not come along, had they been somewhere—any-where—else, well, who knew what might have happened? she thought, as shocked by her wanton, reckless behavior as by his.

Lainey hadn't expected Brad to want to get involved with anyone else for a good long time, after what had happened to him. And she certainly hadn't expected he would want to get involved with her.

But he obviously did....

And despite all the reasons she knew she should be keeping her distance from the sexy cowboy right now, she realized she wanted to get involved, too.

"It's just a few girls." Brad dismissed the incident in the parking lot with a shake of his head. "Even if they tell all their friends…" He frowned again. "I mean, at this point, with half of America hating me, what does it matter?"

He was exaggerating. Half of America hadn't watched *Bachelor Bliss*, or any reality TV show for that matter. But beneath Brad's deprecating sentiment was a lot of pain. Lainey reached over and touched his arm.

"You should tell your side of the story," she said.

Abruptly, Brad's biceps was as tense as the rest of him. He glared straight ahead as he drove in the increasingly heavy traffic. "Back to that again?"

Lainey swallowed and dropped her hand as swiftly as if she had been burned. She felt pushed away again, the same way she always had when she tried to offer advice to Chip and was rejected for "not knowing what she was talking about." But this time she did, even if she couldn't yet explain to Brad how and why she knew the way the press operated as well as she did.

"I mean it. It's not fair." She continued to look at Brad steadily, glad they were talking about someone's problems other than her own. She wanted to offer Brad the same kind of support he had offered her. "You're such a good guy."

Despite the gentleness of her words, Brad looked even more provoked. "You don't know that."

Aware he had never looked more mesmerizing than he did at that moment, Lainey countered, just as resolutely, "Yes. I do. A bad guy wouldn't do all the things you are doing for me today."

Brad gave a short, humorless laugh. "That's not what the tabloids would say," he told her, looking as if he expected her to argue with him about that, too. His eyes glinted wickedly. "The tabloids would say I just want to get into your pants."

And maybe, Lainey thought, aware it was getting very hot in that truck, that wasn't an assumption very far from the truth. She pulled the neck of her sweater away from her collarbone in an effort to get more air. Still feeling a little breathless, she acknowledged she certainly wanted to get into Brad's pants. Although she doubted she ever would have put it in those terms. But maybe that was the point. Maybe Brad just thought he was bad for her and was trying to scare her off so she wouldn't get hurt.

Had Bunny been right? Was it bad for her to be staying out at the ranch with Brad and Lewis, when every second she was with Brad clouded her perspective more and more, and made her want to be with him—not for the story she was trying to write, but just because she wanted to be with him. And not as his friend. As his woman. She drew a stabilizing breath.

"Perhaps we should move this conversation to safer territory?"

Brad inhaled deeply, too. He reached over to turn the air conditioner to its coolest setting. "Good idea."

Lainey settled back in the passenger seat, determined to get her mind off sex—and that kiss—once and for all. "Tell me your plans for the ranch," she encouraged in the soberest voice she could manage.

"Well," Brad quipped, "first up, is getting all the virgin heifers in heat."

Lainey groaned in mock dismay and real embarrassment and covered her face with her hands. Brad laughed, his old devilry coming back as swiftly as it had fled. He relaxed and went back to teasing her again. "If you're going to hang out on the ranch, you have to get used to the idea that making babies is what we're all about."

Lainey thought about making babies…with Brad.

Another shock.

She really was going to have to calm down.

Brad glanced at her, probably noting the color flooding her cheeks. "What?"

Lainey stammered. No social lie would come to mind. "I—I was just, um, just thinking…" And not very quickly, either.

He reached over and briefly touched her knee. "That you want another baby?"

Her skin tingled where his hand had rested. "How did you know that?" Lainey asked him, serious now.

Brad shrugged, his mood turning contemplative as he continued to drive. "You're such a good mother to Petey," he said, obviously understanding. "You clearly love being a mother. It makes sense you would want more than one child."

Lainey looked out the window wistfully, at the Texas countryside. "I did."

"Then why didn't you have one?" Brad exited the freeway and turned onto the farm-market road that would lead them, first to Laramie, and then to the Lazy M.

"Chip felt one child was enough, particularly since Petey was a boy."

"And you didn't argue with him," Brad guessed, seeming to realize how much that had hurt and disappointed Lainey.

Lainey brushed at an imaginary piece of lint on her skirt. "I tried to persuade him for a while, but when I saw it wasn't working, when I realized how little time he had to spend with Petey, I concluded being mother and father to one child was probably enough of a job for me."

"That was honest."

"Yes, I know. Surprisingly so." Honesty hadn't really been a trademark of her marriage to Chip. The emphasis had been on polite accommodation. Too late, she saw that treating a marriage partner like a guest in your life wasn't the best path to take. She and Chip might have had a better marriage had they stopped being so careful and let their passion…and their feelings…flow. But they hadn't. And now it was too late to rectify that. But she still had a full life ahead of her, Lainey was beginning to see. And room in her heart for love to grow.

Brad gave her a curious glance.

"As you said, I'm always persuading everyone else to be honest and realistic about their particular situation, but not doing it myself." She smiled, for the first time feeling ready to deal with life's thornier issues head-on. "Maybe it's time that changed."

Chapter Ten

"Thanks for seeing me on such short notice," Lainey told Claire McCabe Taylor.

Claire's intelligent, green eyes radiated sympathy. "We attorneys understand family emergencies." Looking every bit the polished business professional in a discreetly tailored suit, Claire took a seat behind her desk. "Why don't you bring me up to date with everything?"

Claire listened intently while Lainey talked. "Sounds like Bunny is really trying hard to get your attention—taking your car, putting your house up for sale, emptying your bank account, and canceling your debit and credit cards."

"Well, she certainly has it now," Lainey lamented with a beleaguered sigh. She reached over and took Brad's hand, glad he had come with her.

Claire paused thoughtfully. The sunlight streaming in through the window blinds illuminated her neatly brushed auburn hair. "What do you think it would take to get Bunny to back off, aside from legal action on your part?" she asked.

Lainey let go of Brad's hand, clasped hers together in her lap. "I think if Petey and I moved in with Bunny and Bart that Bunny would ease up immediately, in a financial sense."

"And personally?" Claire persisted.

"I think it would be unbearable," Lainey admitted honestly. "Bunny means well…"

Brad gave her a look that urged her not to hold back. She knew he was right so she tried again. "Bunny thinks she is doing the right thing."

Claire continued making notes on the legal pad in front of her, then looked up. "And what do *you* think?" she asked bluntly.

"I think," Lainey said, "my sister-in-law needs to get a life and stop trying to live mine."

Lainey's heartfelt exasperation brought commiserating smiles to Claire's and Brad's faces.

"Who set up the trust, do you know?" Claire asked.

"Deloche, Nussbaum and Riker."

"Good firm. They're known for their mastery of estate law. I'll have to take a look at the papers, but I have to warn you—" Claire looked up over the rim of her reading glasses "—the terms may not be able to be overturned. And even if they are, it will be a long, prohibitively costly fight. I'm talking years here, Lainey. Legal fees that go well into the six figures."

"I thought as much," Lainey said, depressed.

"And then there is the emotional damage to Petey and your family," Claire continued practically.

Brad interrupted his cousin. "I thought you were supposed to be helping here!"

"I am," Claire responded with the ease of a respected family-law attorney. "I'm letting Lainey know what's ahead, depending on what path she takes. And it is always best to avoid familial estrangements if you can." She turned back to Lainey. "Have you thought about supporting yourself and Petey on your own? At least during a cooling-off period?"

Lainey nodded. "I've already taken steps in that regard." She knew it was her surest path to freedom, and the best example she could set for her son. Money didn't buy happiness—independence did.

Brad looked at her. "Does that mean you're thinking of staying on at the ranch, as housekeeper?"

"Not exactly," she said. Here it was. The moment of truth. Her chance to come clean with Brad, at least part of the way.

Claire continued taking notes. "Did you work before your son was born?"

Lainey flushed. "No. I wanted to, but we didn't need the money and my husband wanted me to stay home, and so…I did." *I'm not going to be married to a reporter, Lainey. I need a wife with elegance and style, who devotes her life only to me. And in return, I'll provide you and any children we have with everything you've ever dreamed of….* And at that time of her life, Lainey had so wanted to be rescued. Loved. Cared for. Too bad none of it had turned out as she dreamed. Chip had been gone much more than he was ever home. And nothing she had ever done, on her own, had been good enough to really please him….

"So, in other words, you have no practical work experience," Claire concluded.

"Right," Lainey said, feeling a little embarrassed about that. As fulfilling as the roles of wife and mother were, she had always wanted satisfying work of her own, too. Was that wrong of her?

"Except for the professional organizing you're doing out at the ranch," Brad cut in admiringly. "Lainey's a whiz at that."

Guilt flooded Lainey as she realized she had just passed up her chance to confess all to Brad about why she was really there.

Claire perked up. "Maybe you could turn your organizing skill into a moneymaking operation. I know we don't have anyone doing that sort of work in Laramie."

AT SIX O'CLOCK, LEWIS AND PETEY arrived home from the game-testing facility in Laramie. By seven, Lewis was showered and dressed and headed to Austin for business meetings the following day. Travis was on their doorstep with his two younger sons, to pick up Petey for a backyard all-male camp-out on their ranch.

"We'll keep a good eye on the boys, I promise," Travis told Lainey as he herded Kurt, Kyle and Petey toward his Suburban.

Lainey smiled. "What time should I—" She was going to say *pick Petey up*, then she remembered she didn't have a vehicle of her own to drive at the moment, and she didn't know if Brad's pickup would be available for her to use.

Travis smiled. Seeming to understand how much her predicament had humiliated and embarrassed her—Lainey had already explained it to Annie when Annie called with the overnight invitation an hour earlier—he offered gently, "Annie will bring Petey home around nine-thirty tomorrow morning."

"Sounds great." Lainey smiled her relief. "Thanks, Travis."

"You bet." Travis paused to make sure all the boys were safely strapped in, then climbed behind the wheel. "See you tomorrow!"

Petey waved excitedly.

The Suburban disappeared down the drive.

Brad, who had been tending to the herd, emerged from the barn. Aware they were going to be alone together for the entire night, she smiled at him officiously. "Did you want me to make you some dinner?" she asked, aware cooking had become part of the deal. "Or were you planning to go out?"

There was a flicker of concern in his eyes, as if he had something on his mind. Then he shifted gears and said, "How about we make something together?"

Lainey found his casual tone disturbing. Was she reading more into his sympathy—and his passionate kisses of just hours earlier—than there was? This was, after all, a man with a string of abruptly started and abruptly ended romances behind him. Pretending she wasn't the least bit unnerved by her growing feelings for him, she stuck her hands in the pockets of her trim black skirt. "I didn't know you could cook."

"Can't, really. But I can grill. And as you'll note—" he pointed to the box sitting next to the back steps "—Lewis brought home charcoal and a grill for me to put together. So if you can wait for me to get a shower, I'll assemble that and we can cook some steaks out here tonight."

"You don't have to go to all that trouble," she said.

Brad flashed her a crooked smile. "It's no trouble." Without waiting for her to comment further, he disappeared inside the house and up the back staircase.

He returned fifteen minutes later as Lainey was sliding a prepared salad into the fridge. She had two potatoes ready to go into the oven, broccoli ready to steam. And not nearly enough to do given how handsome and sexy he looked in jeans, boots and a navy button-up shirt. His hair was still damp from the shower, his jaw freshly shaven. As he neared her she caught the whiff of his aftershave lotion and her heart skipped a beat.

Brad grinned as awareness roiled inside her. "Don't you look as jumpy as a long-tailed cat around a rocking chair."

Lainey rolled her eyes but did not bother to dispute the truth. She *was* nervous.

Brad plucked the screwdriver out of the toolbox in the pantry, then paused and gave her a hard look. His dark brow arched in surprise. He put down the tool needed to assemble the grill and crossed to her side. "Hey, you're not worried about Petey, are you?"

She felt breathless and confused. *No, I'm worried about being alone with you. Worried that if we spend more time together on an intimate level, I'll end up forgetting why I'm here, get in even deeper.* Assuming she wasn't already in much too deep....

When Brad had kissed her this afternoon, she had moved

from impulsively accepting comfort to wanton need in no time flat. Had they not been where they were—in his truck in broad daylight—she knew they would have ended up making love. And once would not have been enough.

"Because I guarantee Travis will keep a good eye on them," he enthused.

He stepped closer, and her skin registered the heat. Hands on her shoulders, he grinned at her in a way that sent her pulse skyrocketing.

"The triplets are going to be out there in the tent with them, camping cowboy-style, too, so…everything will be fine. Petey will have a great time."

"I know and I'm glad." Maybe this was the time to get it out in the open. Talk about what happened earlier.

"But just because Petey's gone, and Lewis is gone… doesn't mean that…"

He drew closer, all six foot three inches of him brimming with a curiosity that was distinctly male. And distinctly disturbing. His gaze traveled over her, the desire in his eyes unmistakable as he gathered her in his arms, aligning her soft body against the harder length of his.

"Doesn't mean what?" he asked playfully, as if knowing what she was going to say.

Lainey mocked him with a toss of her hair and planted both hands on the width of his chest. "That we…" She lost her train of thought as he pressed his lower body against hers. Her hips were lodged against the kitchen counter, making escape impossible, but she angled her head and chest back as best she could. Unfortunately, her evasive movement only served to plant her hips more firmly against his.

"…have to pick up where we left off this afternoon?" He pretended not to notice the traitorous weakening of her knees and the heavy thudding of her heart. Just as she pretended not to notice the strength and heat of his desire.

His eyes lit up as he removed her forearms from his chest,

draped them over his shoulders, then brought his head down to hers. Their warm breaths met and blended. "Okay. I'm willing to go back to the beginning. Start over…"

"Brad…"

Lainey never finished the sentence. His lips were on hers in a kiss that exuded tenderness and caring, his sweet yearning to simply be with her. Just that simply, all the blossoming emotion she'd felt for Brad, all the passion, came flooding back. Her reservations receded as she was kissed into silence, seduced by the magnetism that made her want to be his. In that instant, the world fell away, and it was only the two of them, this moment in time. Lainey knew, more than anything, what she wanted from Brad. Closeness and love. The unconditional admiration and acceptance that had always eluded her. The desire only Brad could give her. With Brad, she felt she had the potential to be a whole person. Not just a wife or a mother or a woman who never quite measured up in the eyes of those around her.

"Alone at last," Brad murmured contentedly, kissing his way from her lips to her ear to the slope of her neck.

No kidding, Lainey thought.

He drew back. His gaze turned gentle. He traced the curve of her mouth with his fingertip, the fragile caress heating her blood. "I'm about to make a move on you," he told her softly.

A move she had been waiting for forever, it seemed. Although, it had only been a matter of days since their paths had crossed again, this time in an intimate and meaningful way.

"So…" He framed her face with his hands, the raw vulnerability in his expression giving her the courage to acknowledge what had been in her heart all along. Flashing her a sexy grin, he teased as he tunneled his hands through her hair. "Speak now, or forever hold your peace."

Experience had taught Lainey that moments like this were fleeting, at best. As complicated as their situation was—even if he didn't yet know it!—she wasn't going to bypass the chance at love. "I'm not going to resist," she told him, aware she wanted to make love with him so badly she ached. "I want this, too." *More than you'll ever know....*

"Now we're talking." Grinning, he lowered his head and delivered a breath-stealing kiss that had her middle fluttering weightlessly and her nipples tingling. "Let's get comfortable, woman." He swept her up in his arms in a manner that was all the more possessive and carried her toward the stairs—not stopping until he had reached his bed.

He lowered her to the floor and kissed her again, shattering whatever caution she had left. She surged against him, moaning, her arms coming up to wreathe his neck. He deepened the kiss, his tongue sweeping her mouth, tasting, stroking, teasing, until her whole body was alive, quivering with sensations unlike any she had ever felt. It felt so good to be wanted, so right to be held against him this way. She melted against him helplessly. She could feel his arousal pressing, hot and urgent, through their clothing and yearned for closer contact.

She stepped out of her shoes, then reached for the belt buckle, the zipper on his jeans. "And speaking of getting comfortable," she teased as she eased him out of pants and shirt, shoes and shorts.

His manhood sprang free and proud. The rest of him was just as masculine and beautiful. Rippling muscles. Smooth, satiny skin. Whorls of sable-brown hair. Lainey could have stood there admiring him forever.

Brad had other ideas.

"That, darlin', works both ways." Wanting her "more comfortable," too, he reached for the hem of her knit top, drew it gently over her head. The zipper on her skirt was next. She trembled beneath his questing fingers as he divested her of bra and panties.

Her whole body was quaking as he paused to admire her, before slipping those off, too.

"You are so beautiful, so sexy," he murmured.

Wanting to savor everything about this night, Brad let his glance sift slowly over Lainey, then lowered her gently to his bed. She was stunning, any time of any day or night, but she had never looked more radiant than she did at that moment— her cheeks flushed, her silky cap of hair fanning out across his pillow, framing her beautiful face. His gaze moved over her full breasts, her supple waist, the inches of fair silky skin, before dropping to the shadowy vee. He knew it was way too soon for this to be happening, but he didn't care. He couldn't wait any longer. He had to make her his. He kissed her breasts, the hollow of her stomach, softly stroked the insides of her thighs. Their lovemaking was wonderfully sensual, hot and wild. He took the lead. Lainey responded. Savoring the sweetness of her unexpected acquiescence to him, he stroked and licked and nibbled until perspiration beaded her body and she could barely breathe. She gasped, the whimper of sensation turning into a flood of ever-escalating need. Feeling her tremble uncontrollably, he slid up her body. Hard as a rock, he fit his lips over hers once again, demanding, coaxing, tempting, pleasing. Until there was no holding back, no denying the blistering need. Sensations ran riot through him as she arched her back, opened her knees and wrapped her arms around his back, her legs around his waist. He entered her with a long stroke. Her body closed around him, cloaking him in warmth. Savoring the intimacy and the wonder of it all, Brad moved inside her, slowly at first, then with more and more urgency. Lainey moaned against his mouth, her tongue twining urgently with his, taking up the same demanding rhythm as their bodies. The insides of her thighs rubbed the outsides of his. And then there was no more holding back, no more clinging to control, and Brad joined Lainey at the edge of ecstasy and beyond.

"You REALIZE WHAT JUST HAPPENED is exactly what Bunny thinks has been happening all along," Lainey murmured as they lay together in Brad's bed.

"Smart woman, that sister-in-law of yours," he dead-panned, running a hand down her arm, eliciting delicious tingles everywhere he touched, as well as where he didn't.

"I'm serious."

His expression shifted from playful to compassionate. "I know you are," he said gently. He moved so he was on top of her once again. The possessive look in his eyes made her catch her breath. "But Bunny's not right about everything."

"She isn't," Lainey repeated, knowing if they made love again the way Brad clearly wanted to make love to her, she would not be able to blame their encounter solely on passion and a yearning for intimacy, for connection with someone that went soul-deep. Instead, she would be forced to admit their coming together this way—this soon—meant much more. Joining bodies again would be joining hearts and souls, and she would fall all the way in love with him. The vulnerability of a move like that scared her. Not sure she was ready to let him all the way into her heart, when he had yet to learn everything about her and the terrible fix she found herself in, she tensed.

"No, she isn't," he replied firmly. Mistaking the reason behind her unease, he looked at her with all the gentleness she had ever wanted. "You can trust me, Lainey. This isn't a fling. It isn't a one-night stand or a temporary thing. What I feel for you is going to last."

Forever sounded pretty good to Lainey, too. But she knew it was too soon to be making such promises to each other, even if she was sure her feelings for Brad weren't ever going to change, either. She let out a slow breath.

"Things happen, Brad."

He continued to watch her in that unsettling way. "What are you talking about?" he asked in a low voice.

I'm going to have to tell you the truth eventually, about the article I'm writing and researching for Personalities. *Heck, I should have already done so,* Lainey thought.

Aware he was still waiting for her to continue, but too selfish to ruin what had been the most wonderful night of her entire life by confessing everything to him now, she merely said, "I'm not sure either of us can know how we're going to feel one, two weeks from now, never mind six months down the line."

"Well, I do," he told her confidently. He framed her face with his hands, his weight on her as soothing as a warm blanket on a winter's night. "I've never felt this way about a woman before." He looked at her lovingly as he traced her lip with the tip of his finger. "I've never trusted anyone the way I trust you." He pushed aside the ends of her hair and kissed his way down the exposed line of her throat to the U of her collarbone. "Never wanted anyone the way I want you."

His heartfelt words only made her feel worse. Lainey splayed her hands across his chest, her fingers sliding through the thick mat of chest hair to the warm smooth muscle beneath. "Brad—"

But it was too late, he was already claiming her body with his hands. Tendrils of white heat swept through her as his mouth moved sensually on the hollow between her breasts, then returned with devastating slowness to her mouth. She gulped in air, aware of the tantalizing warmth spreading through hard muscle and satiny skin, and lower still, the stirrings of his renewed desire. She'd never known such power as a woman. Never felt such an immediate, intense connection. When she was with him like this, the future shone hot and bright as the Texas sun.

"I know my rep as a ladies' man and a heartbreaker," he said, pausing to kiss her full on the mouth again, "but all that's behind me now. I want you, and only you. But if you want me to stop," he murmured, arousing her as he kissed her once. And then again. And again. "I will."

Lainey moaned as his hand cupped the weight of her breast, his fingers closed over the nipple, massaging it into a point. The pleasure was almost as unbearably erotic as his kiss, and everything around her went hot and fuzzy except the seductive pressure of his mouth on hers.

"No. Don't stop." She sighed her pleasure as Brad rolled so that she was lying on top of him.

He brushed the hair from her face. "Sure now?"

She let her lips come down on his, firm and sure. "Very," she whispered back, knowing she was betting everything on the two of them and their ability to meet the very difficult challenges that lay ahead. "I want you," she whispered, aware her heart was beating double-time as she gazed into his eyes. Lower still, where their bodies touched, there was an altogether too-familiar warmth pooling. Need, burning deep inside.

He kissed her back, forcing her lips apart. "Show me how."

Determined to show him she could be as bold and exciting a lover as he was, Lainey kissed him leisurely, then knelt astride his thighs, letting the sheet that had been covering her fall away. Swallowing the rest of her inhibitions, she let him look his fill, then slid lower down his body. Her hands skimmed over his skin, touching, learning, loving, exploring. Aware she had never felt sexier in her life, Lainey shifted once again, using lips and teeth and tongue, taking him to the spontaneous combustion stage. More than anything she wanted this to be a mutual giving of pleasure.

"Lainey," he groaned, his eyes dark with wanting her, dark with need.

He'd driven her mad with desire the first time they'd made love. Now she took him to the brink, until he could stand it no more, until he was reaching for her, insisting, then she was moving astride him once again. Slowly, she lowered herself, taking the hard, hot length of him deep inside. Then she drew herself up, so that she was once again on her knees. He brought her down to him, their mouths mating just as their bodies did, in one long, hot, delicious kiss. Then Brad shifted and she was beneath him once again. Moments later, as their bodies merged, it felt as if he was a part of her...heart and soul. And for the first time Lainey discovered what it meant to come together, as equals. She hadn't known she could want a man like this. She hadn't known she could give and take like this. But she did, she thought, as the passion overtook them once again.

Chapter Eleven

"What do you mean I'm in one of the New York City newspapers?" Brad asked the person on the other end of the telephone the following morning as he and Lainey lingered over breakfast in the ranch house kitchen. They had been up most of the night making love, yet both were still filled with adrenaline and energy. Until now, they hadn't been able to stop smiling or kissing or touching.

Whatever Brad was hearing from the person on the other end of the connection was putting a damper on his spirits, fast.

He grimaced. "I'll check the Internet. Thanks." He hung up the phone.

"What's going on?" Lainey asked, surveying the haunted look in his eyes.

"Come with me and we'll find out." Brad headed for his office, where he fired up his computer. Seconds later, he was on the Web site he'd been told to read. Sure enough, there was a publicity picture of Brad taken during one of the Heart Ceremonies on *Bachelor Bliss*. He was handing a woman an engraved invitation to stay on for future episodes, but where the contestant had stood was a blacked-out silhouette of a woman and a large white question mark, under the caption *His cheating heart*.

Lainey scanned the accompanying article along with Brad.

Who would have guessed heartbreaking bachelor Brad McCabe would be caught in the arms of a mystery woman in a Dallas motel parking lot yesterday afternoon. Witnesses said the beautiful, blond mystery woman was as distressed as the handsome hunk to be caught canoodling in broad daylight, by a bunch of teenage girls. A check with the motel in question noted Brad McCabe had not checked in yet, nor did he have a reservation under his own name, so no telling what his original plans were for the hot summer afternoon. When contacted, ex-flame Yvonne Rathbone was quoted as saying tearfully, "The secret's out. I think he was involved with her all along!"

"What?" Brad erupted, as he finished reading the nationally syndicated gossip column the same time as Lainey. "I don't believe that witch!"

"Why would Yvonne say you were cheating on her?" she asked, her brain already going into reporter mode.

"Because she doesn't want people to know what really—"

"What?" she demanded, frustrated he hadn't finished. Darn it all, she wanted to be able to clear his name! Get his reputation back for him.

"Never mind," he muttered, his expression becoming closed and unreadable once again.

To her consternation, before she could ask anything else, her cell phone rang. She plucked it out of her pocket, noted the identification of the caller flashing on the tiny screen, and swore silently to herself. Knowing she couldn't possibly take this call in front of Brad, she pointed to the exit. "It's a girl-friend. I'm going to take this over at the guest house, okay?"

"Fine. Whatever." He was still glaring at the computer monitor, as disgruntled as if they had never made love.

Lainey walked quickly through the house and went outside. "Hello?"

Sybil's voice came over the line in a near screech that Brad surely would have been able to hear if they had still been in the same room. "Tell me we are not being scooped!" Sybil said.

Lainey swallowed. She was courting disaster here on so many levels.

"Do you know who the mystery blonde is?" the editor demanded irately.

"I think I have an idea," Lainey muttered, knowing she had done the unthinkable for a reporter—she had become part of the story she was covering.

"Was Brad cheating on Yvonne with this woman while they were on the show?"

Lainey glanced out the window and saw Brad striding toward the barn. "I'm sure he wasn't."

"You have proof? Or you're just guessing?"

"Proof." *Sort of.*

Lainey watched as Brad led one of the virgin heifers out to a pasture located well away from the one where Tabasco Red was grazing.

Silence. "You want to share those facts with me?" Sybil asked tensely.

"When I turn my article in." Lainey hoped by then she would have Brad's cooperation in what she was trying to do for him.

"I'm counting on you to get this story for me, Lainey. Our future career success depends on it."

"I know." Lainey just wished she weren't in such an impossible situation.

"In the meantime, you asked me to see what I could do to get you access to the producers. Well, I couldn't get you that, but I did manage to get you an interview with the show's creator, Gil Hewitt, on behalf of the magazine."

Lainey reached for paper and pen, elated by the coup. Sybil was really helping her out here. "When and where?" she asked.

"Sunday afternoon. You're to talk with Gil, half an hour before you talk with Yvonne. Same hotel."

Well, that was easy. Almost too easy. Lainey wrinkled her brow. "They're going to be there together?"

Sybil paused to say something to her editorial assistant, then returned to Lainey. Paper rustled. "Apparently, Gil and his staff are doing taped interviews of potential contestants for the next season. They have set up some publicity with local newspapers for past stars—apparently Brad was asked but declined to participate."

No surprise there, either, Lainey thought.

"Apparently, the show is attempting to do a little damage control. High ratings of the finale have given way to skepticism about whether people can really find love on a reality TV show. Anyway, Yvonne's going to tell everyone that despite the way things turned out, she would do it all over again, because falling in love…just the hope of a real and lasting romance…is worth it. Blah, blah, blah."

Yes, Lainey thought, true love was worth it. Even if she didn't quite believe that was the case for Miss Yvonne Rathbone.

"I'M JUST GOING TO GO GET the computer games Lewis said I could borrow for the weekend," Petey told Lainey on Saturday afternoon.

Lainey knew once Lewis and Petey started talking software they'd lose all track of time. "I want to be on the road in ten minutes," she warned. "Tell Lewis that."

"Okay." Petey rushed into the house to find the computer-game whiz.

Lainey and Brad were left alone in the guest house as Lainey continued packing up the items she wanted to take back to Dallas. "You're sure you don't want me to go with you?" Brad asked as he watched her fill a wicker basket with laundry that needed to be done.

Wishing she weren't already head over heels in love with

Brad—and she suspected that he felt the same about her—
Lainey shook her head. In addition to the fact that she knew
Brad had a lot to do on the ranch, she needed a little distance
to be able to research the story properly. He drove her to dis-
traction when they were in such close proximity.

She still didn't have her car back, but Annie McCabe was
letting her borrow one of their ranch vehicles. "Petey and I
need to be home for a night or two. I've already asked Bunny
to inform the Realtor not to bring anyone through while
we're in Dallas this weekend, and I'm taking Petey over to
see his cousins tomorrow and spend the day with Bart and
Bunny."

"Are you sure that's wise—under the circumstances?"
Brad asked.

Touched by his concern for her, Lainey nodded. She'd
been thinking about what Claire McCabe Taylor had told her
about the emotional and financial costs of lawsuits, and knew
she had to give the situation more time to resolve on its own.
She wasn't sure yet whether that made her naive or wise, but
she knew they would find out by the summer's end, if not before.

Lainey was glad she had Brad on her side. She felt safe
and secure and protected by him. He made her feel she had
someone to turn to in the storms of life, and that made all the
difference. It was helping her regain her serenity.

"I don't want Petey to feel caught in the middle of this conflict between his aunt, uncle and me," she explained, taking
Brad's hand in hers and holding it tightly. "We might not be
getting along all that well at the moment, but we're still family and always will be. Petey needs to know that with time and
patience—and a willingness to compromise—families can
work out their problems." She was sure it would be worth
it in the end, no matter how much grief she endured in the
process.

He looked down at her admiringly. "You have a lot of grace. You know that, don't you?"

"I'm trying to do the right thing—for everyone," she said, knowing it was what her late husband would want her to do. And she was trying to do right by Brad, too. She just wished she hadn't gone about it the wrong way. But Lainey had given her word to follow through on this story. And somehow, some way, she had to carry through on those promises, and discover and make public the truth. And when the time was right, either just before or just after Brad had his reputation back, she had to muster all her courage and come clean with him. Knowing all the while that he might never forgive her if she confessed what had brought her to the ranch in the first place.

If he weren't so darn mule-headed and full of the McCabe pride, of course, her job would be a lot easier. But no one ever said life was trouble-free.

Lainey smiled, knowing that soon Brad would have his good name cleared of all wrongdoing. Despite his efforts to the contrary. "We'll be back first thing Monday morning."

"Hurry home." He brought her to him for a slow, sensual kiss before she could head out the door.

Home? Lainey thought with wonder as she melted into the warm shelter of his body and kissed him back, as thoroughly and tenderly as he was kissing her. Was that what the Lazy M was to her now? She only knew she wanted it to be.

"Lainey Carrington, here to see Gil Hewitt," Lainey told the clerk at the Fairmont Dallas hotel the following day.

"We're expecting you." The clerk handed over a pass. "You'll need this to get past the security guards on the fourth floor."

"Thanks." Lainey walked past the groups of beautiful young women congregated in the lobby. It was obvious they were here to interview for the new episodes of *Bachelor Bliss*. They looked nervous and on edge. Knowing what the experience had done to Brad McCabe, Lainey was tempted to stop and tell them all not to do it, but realizing she was already in too deep as it was, she kept right on going.

The fourth floor was also a beehive of activity. Lainey got past security, and made her way toward Gil Hewitt's suite. She was almost there when a short, thick-waisted man garbed in clothing fit for a tropical safari stepped out to greet her. He had a scarf around his neck and a ridiculous hat on his head. She recognized him instantly. "Mr. Hewitt? I'm—"

"I know who you are and you're late."

No, she wasn't. She was fifteen minutes early.

"Do you think we have all day to get through these auditions?"

Lainey swallowed. "I…"

Gil shut the door behind them. Lainey realized for all the attention the other staffers were paying, they might as well have been alone. "You're very beautiful." Gil's gaze roved her face, hair, moved slowly over the tailored linen pantsuit she had on. "But if you want to get anywhere with a bachelor, you should wear a sexy dress. Cleavage is always nice."

Pig. Aware she was learning firsthand how future contestants auditioned, Lainey merely smiled and said, "I'll remember that."

Gil steered her toward a stool set up in front of a photographer's backdrop. "Take her picture and get her basics."

Again, Lainey tried to set the record straight. Gil Hewitt cut her off before she could say a word. "Honey, I already told you, we're behind enough as it is. So just do what you're told and we'll get along fine."

Was this the treatment all potential contestants received? Lainey wondered. Two minutes later, she was up off the stool and headed toward the door with Gil at her side.

"Mr. Hewitt…" Lainey began again.

"Call me Gil."

"Gil. I'm here to—"

"Don't worry, honey-buns. It's a lock. You're in."

Lainey blinked. "I am?"

He whispered in her ear, "I knew the moment I saw you that you were my type. Sophisticated, pretty."

And not at all interested in you. Lainey did her best not to recoil as she caught a whiff of his garlic breath. "Did I mention I'm also the widowed mother of an eight-year-old son?"

He blinked. Thought it over briefly. Shrugged. "Fantastic. Viewers will love it."

He looked at her with obvious interest. Too smart to actually touch her in an inappropriate way, but telegraphing his rather creepy intentions nevertheless. A shudder went through Lainey. So this was what it was like to be sexually harassed on a casting couch. Not pretty.

"And I'm not here to audition for the show," Lainey continued, suppressing her desire to knock Gil Hewitt flat on his keister. She smiled. "I'm here to interview you for *Personalities Magazine.*"

Gil stiffened. "Well, why didn't you say so?" He looked irked.

"I tried."

"You have five minutes." He guided her through another doorway, to a small sitting room with desk and chair.

Lainey set her tape recorder on the table and switched it on. She wanted audio backup for anything she wrote down. "I want to talk to you about Brad McCabe and Yvonne Rathbone."

A second passed. Gil assumed a beleaguered expression. "Poor Yvonne. He really did her wrong."

Lainey looked at her list of prepared questions. "Rumor has it that it's the other way around. Yvonne did Brad wrong."

For a second Gil didn't move at all. "Who told you that?" he asked finally.

Aware she had hit a nerve, Lainey shot back playfully, "Now, Mr. Hewitt, you know I can't tell you that."

He dismissed her theory with a frown. "It's rumor."

Lainey leaned forward. "How can you be sure? Did you see everything that went on between the two of them?"

"Yes. Cameras are on one hundred percent of the time."

Not according to Brad. Which meant Gil Hewitt was lying. And if he was lying about this, what else was he lying about? Lainey was about to ask another question, when Gil abruptly declared the interview over.

"So you talked to Gil Hewitt, too," Yvonne Rathbone said, when Lainey caught up with her. The red-haired beauty looked stunning in a white eyelet-lace sundress.

Lainey smiled, admitted this was so. She put her tape recorder on the table between them in full view and asked a few softball questions as warm-up. Yvonne told her everything she had already said countless times to reporters.

"Did you know anything about Brad before the night you all met him?" Lainey asked.

Yvonne shook her head. "They wouldn't tell us anything! We didn't even see a picture of him."

Lainey looked at her questions. "The first moment you said hello and kissed Brad McCabe's cheek, it looked like you whispered something in his ear, and Brad laughed in response. Care to tell *Personalities* readers what that was?"

"Oh, I just said, 'This is so stupid!'"

Okay, Lainey thought, that was the generic flirtatious response. Except... "Weren't you afraid Brad would be offended by that, given that he was there to find a wife?" she asked curiously.

"Well, everyone knew Brad wasn't the kind of guy to tolerate such foolishness."

"But I thought you said none of you knew anything about him, at that point."

"We didn't. But we—I—could just tell that was what kind of guy he was by looking at him," Yvonne amended hastily.

Lainey pretended to accept her answer as truthful, even

though she knew there was no way anyone could have leaped to that conclusion in the fifteen seconds it took for Brad and Yvonne to lay eyes on each other and walk toward each other for the first time. "Can you tell me what happened the day Brad broke up with you—on camera?" Lainey asked, turning to the next page of her notes.

In front of her she had the transcript of Yvonne's retelling of the event on a network show.

"Well." Yvonne sniffed. Her chin trembled and tears appeared in her eyes.

Lainey watched, spellbound, as Yvonne recounted, word for word, pause for pause, sniff for sniff, even eye dab for eye dab, how Brad had come in, snarled at her and left. It was a verbatim account of everything Yvonne had said before. Which could mean it was all a lie, as Brad said, and Yvonne had memorized it in order to keep her story straight. It could also be that she had told it so many times to so many people and reporters that she had unwittingly memorized her recounting. Bottom line, it was all very dramatic and damning, and if Lainey didn't know a lot more had gone on than what was currently being reported, she would have believed Yvonne and loathed Brad, too.

Lainey moved on determinedly. "Back to Gil Hewitt, the show's creator, and the producers. Did you all get along?"

"Oh, yes." Big smile. "Famously, as a matter of fact. They were very nice to all of us."

"No one got special treatment?"

Yvonne paused, looking like a deer in the headlights. "Not that I saw," she said finally.

"I like Gil, too." Lainey followed a hunch to see where it would lead. "He's very, um, friendly, isn't he."

For the first time that afternoon, Yvonne's smile faltered, then faded all the way. "What do you mean?"

Lainey leaned confidentially close. "I heard he propositioned a number of the girls on the show."

Emotion flared in Yvonne's eyes. Jealousy? "That's not true!"

Lainey sat back in mock surprise. "So he didn't proposition you?"

"He—of course not. Nor did he proposition anyone else," Yvonne reiterated stiffly.

"My mistake," Lainey said. "Now, about your background. I understand you went to San Diego State. And you were interested in theater there?" Another hunch that would be easy enough to follow through on.

"I did a few plays," Yvonne admitted proudly.

"So you wanted to be an actress!" Lainey pretended to be deeply impressed. "How did you end up in marketing and sales instead?"

Yvonne sighed, lowered her guard. "Do you have any idea how hard it is to get an agent…?"

By the time Lainey left the hotel, she thought she had a pretty good idea what had happened. But having an inkling wasn't the same as having the facts. She needed a firsthand account from someone she could trust. The question was, would Brad give it to her?

"I DIDN'T THINK you were coming back until tomorrow morning," Brad said Sunday evening when Lainey arrived at the ranch, a sleepy Petey in tow.

"I thought there would be less traffic this evening," Lainey replied.

"I wanted to come back," Petey said, yawning as he got out of the car Lainey had borrowed from Annie McCabe.

"I'm glad." Brad smiled, looking very happy to have them there.

Lainey's heart skipped a beat as she opened the guest house door and turned on the lights. She gazed down at her drowsy son. "Run on in and brush your teeth and get ready for bed, honey. I'll be in to say good-night in a minute."

"Okay." Petey turned and went back to Brad. He wrapped his arms around Brad's middle. "Night."

Brad hugged Petey back with a warmth that filled Lainey's heart.

"Night, son." He turned to Lainey. "Want me to carry your belongings in?" he asked as Petey disappeared into the bathroom down the hall.

Lainey glanced at the car. "No. That's okay," she said hastily. "I don't have much. I'll get it later."

Brad grinned, teasingly. "If I didn't know better, I'd think you were hiding something in there."

She was. Her notes on the interview work she had done earlier in the day were tucked beneath the clean laundry in the wicker basket. "Ha-ha," she said, wishing she didn't want to forget everything else that was going on, throw herself in Brad's arms and kiss him madly.

"It was lonely around here without you and Petey," he said.

Lainey had been lonely, too. Conflicted. Guilty. Torn between her need to see justice done and have a career, and her need to cater only to Brad, to heck with what anyone else thought. But that wouldn't serve Brad or her need to put the truth about the goings on at the *Bachelor Bliss* show out there.

"Well, we're back now," she said. The amount of uneasiness and guilt she was feeling told her she had no future as a double agent. But then she had never wanted to be a spy. She wanted a future as a reporter.

Chip had once outlawed that.

Would Brad, too?

"Mom!" Petey called from his bedroom.

Deciding this was no time to be thinking about such complex questions, Lainey practically pushed Brad toward the door. "I've got to go."

He stepped out onto the porch, and she hurried back to tuck Petey in. The boy was already under the covers.

"Mom," Petey said sleepily, "can I ask you something?"

"Always." Lainey perched on the side of the bed.

"Is Aunt Bunny upset with you and me?"

Lainey forged ahead carefully. "Why would you think that?"

"I tried to tell her about all the cowboy stuff I'm learning from Brad and Travis, how grown-up I already am, and she acted like she didn't want to hear it."

Lainey imagined that was true. Bunny was losing both her daughters to college this fall. Now, she thought she was losing her nephew, too. Lainey had hoped taking Petey to see Bunny would reassure Bunny that she would have plenty of time with the child no matter where Lainey lived or worked. Obviously, that wasn't the case. Yet, anyway.

"I think she just misses seeing you every day," she said gently, doing her best to maintain a charitable attitude where her sister-in-law was concerned.

"Yeah—" Petey thrust his jaw out stubbornly "—but I'm not her son, Mom…I'm yours."

Lainey smoothed her son's blond hair away from his forehead. "She loves you as much as if you were. You're family to her, Petey. And all she has left of your dad. So, if she's holding on a little too tight, I think that's why."

Petey fell silent once again, seeming to understand better. After a moment, he looked up at her earnestly. "I like it out here, Mom. I want to stay even after you finish all your organizing stuff. Can we?"

Lainey wished that would happen, too, but given what she still had to do, she did not know if that was going to be possible.

"What are you doing back so soon?" Lewis asked Brad.

Brad stood in the kitchen, watching Lainey carry her belongings in from the car.

"A gentleman would be out there helping her lug that stuff inside."

Brad did not need to be told that by his nerdy brother or

anyone else. He reached into the refrigerator and took out a bottle of beer. "Already asked and was refused."

Lewis lifted a brow as he helped himself to a brew, too. "What'd you do to tick her off?"

"Nothing," Brad admitted in frustration. "That I know, anyway."

Lewis took the bottle opener his brother handed to him. "Not going to go after her?"

Brad shook his head.

"Why not?" Lewis persisted.

Wishing his younger brother would shut up, Brad lifted the bottle to his lips. "Because she obviously needs her space," he explained.

Lewis looked at him, reminding Brad that of all his brothers, Lewis was the most sensitive to others' feelings.

"Sure that's all it is?" Lewis asked.

No. That was the hell of it. Brad wasn't.

Lewis lounged against the counter. "Maybe she heard about that blonde you were supposedly seen kissing in Dallas. Or maybe that blonde you were supposedly seen kissing in Dallas was Lainey," he suggested slyly.

Brad hadn't told anyone he and Lainey had become involved with each other in a romantic sense. To his aggravation, everyone who had seen them interacting together in even the most mundane way seemed to know anyway. Which meant he was wearing his heart on his sleeve. Not smart, he knew. Especially given the fact that Lainey was obviously having second thoughts about making love with him.

"And maybe she didn't like showing up in the papers," Lewis persisted helpfully.

Brad wasn't about to take advice on how to handle a woman from his only brother whose track record with the ladies was worse than Brad's. "Will you shut up?" he growled.

The smirk on Lewis's face indicated he knew what the truth was. "Guess I better be quiet if I don't want to eat a knuckle sandwich." He lifted his bottle to Brad in silent toast. "If you need me, I'll be in my study."

Brad grunted in response and Lewis disappeared.

The lights were on in the guest house. Lainey hadn't closed her blinds. Through the window, Brad watched as she sat down on the sofa, opened up her laptop and got out a sheaf of papers. Then she abruptly stood, went to the windows and closed the blinds. Because she felt herself being watched? he wondered. Or because she had something to hide?

The second thought caught him unaware. He hadn't expected to be suspicious of Lainey. But, deep in his gut, he was. Why? Was it the way Lainey had refused to meet his eyes this evening, when she returned? The way she hurried him out the door and on his way? Or the way she seemed suddenly conflicted and uneasy around him? As if something had happened…something she didn't really want him to know.

All Brad knew for certain was that he was having the same feeling about Lainey he'd once had about Yvonne.

He didn't like it. Not at all.

Chapter Twelve

"Ready to go test some more computer games?" Lewis asked Petey on Monday morning.

"I sure am!" Petey hopped up from the breakfast table, where he had been hanging out while Lainey did the dishes from the morning meal.

"We'll probably be home about six," Lewis said.

Lainey nodded. "Don't forget—Annie and Travis and all their boys are coming for dinner."

Lewis had invited them the day before, and Lainey thought it was a great idea. She'd been wanting to return their hospitality.

"Can we play after dinner?" Petey asked.

Lainey smiled. "We'll have to ask Annie and Travis, but I'm sure it'll be okay." Since the "ranchers and rustlers" incident, Petey and his two sweet but mischievous cohorts hadn't gotten into any trouble. "Have fun." Lainey hugged Petey goodbye.

"We will!" Petey beamed as he raced out the door.

Brad walked in, coffee cup in hand, as Lewis's car disappeared down the driveway. As always, the sight of him took Lainey's breath away. He hadn't yet shaved this morning and the hint of beard on his jaw gave him a rugged appeal. He was wearing a pair of worn jeans, boots and a clean but rumpled tan cotton work shirt. As he neared her, she could see the hair curling damply against his nape and smell soap and toothpaste. Desire drifted through her, more potent than any shot of caffeine. His broad shoulder nudged hers as he opened the cupboard and lifted out a mug with a rodeo emblem on the front.

"Any more coffee left?"

Lainey flashed a smile. "I just emptied out what little was left and washed the pot. I'll make some fresh."

He leaned against the counter, making absolutely no move to get out of her way. Letting her realize exactly what he wanted and that he was just waiting for the right moment. His gaze drifted over the clip that held back her blond hair. She hadn't had time that morning to carefully blow it out with her hair dryer, so wispy curls framed her face and the back of her neck. "Did I do something to annoy you?"

"What are you talking about?" Lainey asked, as she filled the water reservoir in the coffeemaker.

Brad backed her against the kitchen counter and clamped a hand on either side of her. "Last night you barely had five minutes for me. This morning you're as jumpy as a frog on a lily pad."

Lainey felt herself blush, embarrassed. He wasn't touching her but she could feel the warmth emanating from his body. It beckoned her like a port in the storm. "I just have a lot on my mind," she said finally.

Brad lifted a brow.

"Well, I do!" Lainey protested.

He leaned closer and looked deep into her eyes. "Somehow I don't think that's all it is."

Lainey gulped as her heartbeat sped up. If only she could tell him everything here, now, and be guaranteed of the outcome....

"And I made myself a promise a while back not to ignore my gut anymore, when it comes to suspecting things are amiss." He paused, letting his words sink in. "So, Lainey, I am asking you, what has changed?"

His low persuasive voice melted Lainey's resistance all the more. He searched her face and caressed her cheek with the pad of his thumb as her guilt increased by leaps and bounds.

"Are you acting this way because we made love?"

"WELL, NOW THAT YOU b-brought it up…" Lainey stammered.

Brad had the impression he was not just being pushed away momentarily, but for good. The thought was damn disturbing. And yet here he was following her around like a lovesick pup. What kind of spell had she put on him? It wasn't like him to pursue someone who did not want to be pursued. "Yes?" he prodded, wishing she would cut straight to the chase.

"I'm not sure that was the wisest course of action, under the circumstances," she recited in a low, battle-weary voice.

Frustrated she was not more talkative—didn't women usually enjoy delving into their feelings?—he dropped his hand and settled against the counter. "I didn't hear you complaining at the time."

Lainey crossed her arms. In the soft light of the kitchen, her classically beautiful features were more pronounced. "Well, maybe I should have protested," she said as her eyes met, then veered away, from his. "We hardly know each other."

"A fact I am trying hard to remedy," he countered softly, "by spending more time with you."

Lainey leaned a slender hip against the counter. "Even so—"

"We know everything there is to know about each other where it counts, Lainey." Brad moved closer yet, until he was inundated with the sweet softness of her once again. He inhaled the intoxicating blend of perfume and woman. Determined to prove they did know enough about each other to become intimately involved, he put his arms around her. "For instance, I know you love your son and you're one of the best mothers I've ever seen." She lifted her face up to his, gazing into his eyes, and he continued seriously. "I know you have a kind heart and a generous soul…and a sweetness of spirit I can't even begin to find words to describe. I know you make me want to be a better man than I've ever been. I know you're the woman I've been waiting for, the only woman for me," he confessed in a husky voice, feeling as astonished as she appeared to be by the way he was putting himself out there. "And I know when you finally let your guard down, which isn't nearly often enough to please either of us, you're feeling as connected to me as I am to you." Feeling her melt against him, he kissed her cheek, her temple, the delicate skin just behind her ear. "So what else do we need to know?"

Again, something flared in her eyes. She looked as if she had the weight of the world on her slender shoulders. "Brad—"

Resolved they would not lose ground here, he brought her closer yet. "Stop pushing me away, Lainey. Take down those barriers that surround your heart."

He gathered her against him, bent his head and kissed her the way he had been longing to kiss her since she'd come back last night. Determined to make her see what they could have if she would just let her reservations go, he deepened the sweet caress. Then all pretense, all reserve, was gone as she met him, kiss for kiss. Desire thundering through him in waves, he flattened the hard length of his body against the soft pliability of hers. Able to feel how much Lainey wanted and needed him, no matter what she said, he swept her mouth with his tongue, kissing her until she gave him back everything he had ever wanted, everything he had ever expected. Before long, the blood was pooling hot and urgent in his body, and he wanted her more than he had wanted any woman in his life.

When she sagged against him, signaling she felt the same, he broke off the embrace just long enough to slip an arm beneath her knees and lift her against his chest. Her eyes were misty with longing and love as he carried her up the back staircase, and down the hall, to the rumpled covers of his bed. The need to make her his—not just for this moment in time, or next month or next week, but forever—was stronger than ever.

"You've got to promise me something," he whispered as he tugged off his boots and hers and joined her on the bed.

"What?" She watched as he unbuttoned her blouse.

He eased it off her shoulders and away from her body, enjoying the way the uppermost curves of her breasts spilled out of the white lace bra. Beneath the thin fabric, he could see the jutting nipples. "To stop running from me, from us."

She trembled as he slipped a strap off her shoulder and down her arm. "Is that what you think I've been doing?" she murmured as he drew the fabric away.

Brad traced the delicate pink-and-white flesh, luxuriating in the soft, silky feel of her. "I know you're scared." He stared into the turbulent, forest green of her eyes, eyes that were still vulnerable and full of need. Eyes that maybe believed a little of what had been written and said about his allegedly fickle heart. "You don't have to be. This leap of faith we're taking has success written all over it."

She looked like she wanted to trust him, trust the two of them and their impetuous involvement, so much. And he set about showing her that she could, as he removed her bra and kissed her neck, shoulders, collarbone and breasts. They continued kissing—hard, soft, and every way in between—caressing each other until they lay together naked on the bed.

"And I thought I'd given up all my wild ways," Lainey sighed.

Brad grinned as he thought about the sexy dress he had missed seeing her in. He'd have to get her in one again. One he'd purchase for her. "Wild can be good," he whispered, holding her so close they were almost one. His own body throbbing, he moved down the length of her, exploring as he went.

Lainey arched up off the bed. "You certainly make me believe that," she murmured, whimpering and moaning her pleasure in a way that drove him crazy with desire.

"Good."

"In fact—" she turned and draped her body over his "—being wild with you is downright fun."

"Is that so?" Brad drawled.

"Something about letting go…"

Her lips drifted over his skin. "Doing whatever I please… no longer caring about what people think…."

Brad's breath hitched as her lips wooed and seduced. Wondering if he would ever be able to get enough of her, he moved to switch places with her again, so she was beneath him. Parting her knees with his, he braced a hand on either side of her and situated himself between her thighs. "Take it from me— a person's reputation can only go so far in revealing who that person is deep inside."

Lainey ran her hands over the muscles of his back. "You're a good man, Brad McCabe."

Insistent he be the one to set the pace, Brad took her wrists in hand and anchored them above her head. "And you, Lainey Carrington, are not only a good woman, but the only woman for me."

"So what does that mean?" Lainey teased softly, as they locked eyes, playfully and pleasurably delaying the moment when they would come together completely. "We're going steady?"

"Too high school." Brad lowered his mouth to hers once again, lifted her against him and surged into her slick, wet heat, slowly and deliberately. "I prefer something more grown-up."

So did Lainey. "Exclusive?"

"Permanently exclusive," he told her, all the love she had ever wanted to see shining in his eyes, as he entered and withdrew in shallow strokes that soon had her moaning and trembling, wanting, needing. Straining against him, she took up the rhythm he had started, until there was no more delaying, and their hearts thundered in unison. He was surging deeper, harder, claiming her as his. Holding fast to him, she claimed him, too, and then there was nothing…save one secret…standing between them. Their passion was so strong and so right and so filled with tenderness that it didn't feel quite real. But it was, Lainey thought, as she took everything he offered, gave him everything back in return, and soared into the sweet, hot abyss right along with him.

They clung together afterward, bodies humming with pleasure, hearts content. Except for that one thing.

The fact that he did not know she was working as a reporter, investigating him.

She wanted to tell him. She was going to inform him. She should have already done so. Except that if she did, she was pretty sure he would cease all contact with her. And the thought she might lose him when the truth came out about what she had been doing was devastating. So wrenching, in fact, that she burst into tears.

FOR THE LIFE OF HIM, Brad couldn't figure out why Lainey was crying. These didn't look like tears of bliss. They looked like tears engendered by great conflict. "What's wrong?" he asked, unable to understand why she didn't feel as happy as he did, given what had just happened between them.

She just shook her head.

"I can't understand if you won't let me in," he told her tenderly as he stroked a hand down her spine and guided her closer still.

She only sobbed harder.

Frustrated that he wasn't able to comfort her as he wanted, he searched her face and asked, "Do you think I've treated you badly, making love to you so soon?" Damn it, he had known a woman like Lainey needed courting, a lot of it.

She shook her head and avoided his eyes.

"Because I swear, if I thought that was what was hurting you, I'd call a halt to the physical side of our relationship. It'd be hard, but I'd do it—" His voice caught as he realized how vulnerable he'd become to her. "I'd do anything to keep you in my life," he whispered intensely.

She shoved her hands through her cap of tousled hair. She looked more emotionally inaccessible than ever. "You don't understand."

"Then help me," he pleaded. He hated feeling so helpless.

Lainey wiped the tears from her eyes. She sat up against the headboard, pulling the sheet to her chin, holding the fabric against the nakedness of her body with her bare arms. But to his mounting disappointment, as their gazes met and held, all she did was seem to get further away from him. Finally, she swallowed and took a deep breath.

"I don't deserve you," she said thickly. Fresh tears started as she dabbed at the corners of her eyes with the sheet. "And I want so badly to—" She paused, shook her head miserably, seemingly unable, or maybe just unwilling, to go on.

"Is this because of how your husband made you feel?" he asked as he sat up beside her, really wanting to understand. "Because I swear, if it is—"

She drew in another deep, shaky breath. "It has nothing to do with him," she confessed, finally able to talk more calmly. "It has to do with the fact that I am not the sainted person you think I am."

LAINEY SAW THE LOOK on Brad's face and knew he thought the problem was one of damaged self-esteem. If only it were that simple, she thought unhappily. "It's just…I've gone about this all wrong," she tried to explain in a voice still coated with tears. And she didn't know how much longer she could keep up the subterfuge. She was trying to be all things to all people and succeeding at none of it.

Had she started out telling Lewis and then Brad what she had come to the ranch to find out, Brad never would have spoken to her and Lewis certainly never would have hired her or invited her to stay at the Lazy M with Petey.

Instead, she had let Brad goad her into matching wits with him, and once the sparks had started flying between them, well…it had been as impossible for her to stay away from him as it was for Brad to stay away from her.

And once she had started falling in love with him, the stakes had increased even more.

She'd signed a contract…and Lainey did not make promises she did not intend to keep.

And yet writing a story about Brad and Yvonne and why they really broke up was not something she wanted to do without his permission and approval. But how was she going to get that now…after all that had happened? He was going to think she was just like Yvonne. Pretending to be something—someone—she wasn't.

And worse, he would be right.

How in the world had she ever gotten herself in such a mess?

Despite everything, she didn't regret for one minute loving Brad, because he was the best thing that had ever happened to her.

Brad's glance softened. He wrapped an arm around her shoulders and kissed the top of her head. "Your work for Lewis has nothing to do with my relationship with you," he soothed, still completely misunderstanding the reason for the conflict within her.

"I know that. It's just…" She gulped and started as the sound of a pickup truck rumbled through the driveway.

Brad and Lainey exchanged looks as they realized they were no longer alone. He moved to the window, standing buck naked just inside the curtains, and peered out. "What the…?" He cursed.

Lainey, who knew they couldn't get caught in bed together, was already pulling on her clothes. Brad had enough scandal in his life without adding public knowledge of a dalliance with her to the mix. The truth-telling was going to have to wait until later.

"Who is it?" she demanded, aware she was so distressed her hands were shaking and her knees felt wobbly.

"A girl I used to date."

Lainey blinked, not sure she was ready for this. "Recently?"

"In high school," Brad explained with a frown. "Her parents still live in Laramie but she moved to Dallas after she married and I haven't seen her in…years. She's with her husband. I only know him slightly—he's not from around here—I met him at their wedding."

Lainey blinked and momentarily stopped what she was doing. "You're kidding."

Brad gave her a deadpan look and then went back to observing. "They're headed for the front porch and they both look madder than wet hens." He shook his head, as if his life had gotten so crazy post–*Bachelor Bliss* that he almost expected the sky to fall in, too. "This ought to be interesting," he muttered. "'Cause I have a feeling they aren't looking for Lewis."

Downstairs, someone pounded on the front door—rather furiously, Lainey noted.

Brad opened the window a crack and shouted out, "Hold your horses! I'll be right down!"

Lainey finished dressing as hurriedly as she could, pausing to run a brush through her hair. To no avail. Her lipstick had been kissed off. Her cheeks were flushed, eyes bright, nose red from crying. She was, quite frankly, a mess, she noted as she put the clip back in her hair.

"You don't have to go down there," he said, hurriedly tucking his shirttail into his jeans.

Lainey shook her head. "If I hide, it'll be worse. Everyone in town knows I'm working out here, and that includes her parents. Hence, they are going to expect to see me." She slipped on her red cowgirl boots. "Do I look like I've just made love with you?" she whispered as the pounding on the front door resumed, even more furiously.

Brad paused to kiss the tip of her nose and rub his thumb across her lips. He looked as if he wanted to make love to her all over again.

"Only to me." He took her by the hand. "Let's go."

Lainey went to the kitchen to finish making the coffee she had started assembling earlier, while Brad hurried to the front door.

Both tried to act normal as Brad ushered Melinda Farren, née Evans, and her husband Clint Farren inside. Slim, nicely dressed, with shining blunt-cut blond hair, she could have been Lainey's twin—from the back, anyway. Which was the problem, they quickly figured out as Clint thrust what looked to be a tabloid into Brad's hands.

Lainey stood in the front hall, dish towel in hand, aware she was demonstrating remarkable composure given the fact she had just spent half the morning making love with Laramie's resident heartbreaking bad boy. But maybe that was because Brad had a way of making her feel so loved and cherished, despite the fact he had never once said the words to her.

"Hey, Melinda. Hi, Clint," she said pleasantly, resolved she would not add to the scandal sweeping Brad's life. "What's going on?"

"I'm on the cover of a tabloid!" Melinda wailed.

Lainey blinked. "How did that happen?"

Melinda pointed at Brad. "Ask him!"

Lainey looked at the cover. There was a picture of Brad and Melinda back in high school, going to some prom, and then another of two people kissing, presumably now. It was

Brad, all right, in the photo, but all you could see of the woman was the back of a head. The caption above it read, *Yvonne Rathbone tells all! Brad McCabe involved with married high school sweetheart all along!*

"Well, obviously the kissing photo's a fake," Lainey said, studying it closely. "In fact, it looks like one of the publicity photos for *Bachelor Bliss* with another head superimposed where one of the contestants was." She ought to know—she had the picture stored on her computer, along with dozens of others. They were in her "Research" file. "See?" Lainey pointed to the mystery woman in question. "This looks like a wig."

"The whole story's a fake!" Brad growled.

"We know that!" Clint and Melinda said in unison.

"I don't appreciate my wife being dragged into your problems, her reputation ruined," Clint growled. He went chin to chin with Brad.

"I don't, either," Brad said soberly. Sympathy was in his eyes even as he looked at Clint. When Clint relaxed slightly, Brad turned to Melinda. "I'm sorry, Melinda. I'll contact my attorney, Claire McCabe Taylor, and have her demand a retraction and an apology immediately."

"Well, you better do something," Melinda fumed, crossing her arms. "Because I am *not* amused by this. And neither is my family!"

Brad's temper flared. "You think *I* am?" he fired back.

Clint and Melinda stared at Brad. Brad stared back. Then the fight went out of the couple. Brad apologized again, promising to take swift action. The couple, realizing now that Brad had nothing to do with it and was as upset as they were, thanked him and left. But not before Clint Farren offered these parting words: "You better do something to straighten out your life, Brad, or you're liable to drag everyone you know down with you!"

"CLINT'S RIGHT, YOU KNOW," Lainey said as she and Brad retired to the ranch house kitchen for a much-needed cup of coffee. She sat down at the table opposite him. "The situation is only going to get worse unless you come forward and tell your story."

Brad settled more comfortably in his chair. His knees brushed hers beneath the table. "As much as I'd like to, I can't."

She allowed herself a moment to savor the warmth and strength of those denim-clad knees against her own. Aware how close she had come to confessing everything to him in a most ill-thought-out way, she struggled to regain her own equilibrium. Theirs was a situation neither could have predicted. It was going to take careful handling if she didn't want to lose everything—for both of them. And right now, despite how guilty she felt, that was much too high a price to pay.

"Haven't you heard?" she quipped lightly, trying once again to get Brad to do what needed to be done. She looked him straight in the eye. "The truth will set you free."

And that was, after all, why she had first shown up at the ranch. To track down Brad and help him set the record straight once and for all and get his reputation—and his life—back.

Brad's jaw set in that stubborn way she knew so well. "There's no guarantee anyone would believe me, even if I confessed what happened between me and Yvonne."

"You don't know that," she said.

"Haven't you noticed? Yvonne is quite the actress."

Except, Lainey thought uncomfortably, when Yvonne was being interviewed she always appeared to be speaking from her heart.

Which meant, unless Yvonne suddenly was hit with an attack of conscience and confessed all, it would be a "he said, she said" situation. At this late date, it might look as if Brad were trashing Yvonne publicly out of revenge. That wouldn't help him at all. It would only muddy the waters more. And continue to hurt his reputation.

"No," Brad continued, oblivious to Lainey's thoughts. "The safest way is to proceed through my lawyer, demand a retraction and clarification from the tabloid. Threaten to sue if they don't do the right thing."

"That would take weeks or months to resolve, and in the meantime, lies about you will be spread, your reputation further ruined. You started out a cad, Brad. Now you're a cheating cad," she summed up guiltily, feeling more incompetent than ever. If she had been able to keep her emotions in check, she might have been able to convince Brad to cooperate with *Personalities*. Instead, she had painted herself into a moral corner from which there seemed to be no escape.

Crying about it wouldn't help.

Action would.

She had to put her own selfish considerations aside and help him see reason. "What's next for you except more of a downhill slide?"

Brad quaffed the rest of his coffee and got up to roam the kitchen restlessly. "You don't know what you're talking about," he accused.

"Oh, yes, I do." Lainey watched him pour more coffee for both of them. "My father worked as a mechanic in San Angelo when I was a kid." Able to see Brad was listening, albeit reluctantly, she continued talking about what she never discussed.

"Tools and parts were being stolen from the garage where he worked, and my dad was framed. He got fired. The owner agreed not to press criminal charges because he felt sorry for my mom and me, but he put the word out that my dad was not to be trusted, and my dad could not get another job because of the allegations. He went on unemployment compensation and when that ran out, he did odd jobs here and there, some janitorial work. But he never got over it, and his attitude on life soured. My mom and dad ended up splitting up because my mom never understood why my dad wouldn't fight to get back what he had lost. My dad died a bitter, disillusioned man." She took Brad's hand. "I can see the same thing happening to you, Brad. False allegations and assumptions like that wear on a person. They rob you of your spirit and your joy."

"I'm sorry your dad and your family had such a rough time," said Brad. "But our situations are not the same, Lainey. I'm already moving on. I've got work. And I don't give a damn what strangers think of me. The people in Laramie know what's true."

"You're kidding yourself." Lainey had seen the look on his face when confronted with the latest tabloid lies about himself, the hurt it was causing the other people in his life. As long as the mystery remained…as long as Yvonne kept flaming the fires to fuel her own need for publicity, then it was never going to stop. Long after national interest died, the curiosity of the locals would remain. The citizens of Laramie were too kind, too protective, to ask Brad about it. But they would always wonder what had happened to cause such a scandal. And Brad would know they were wondering why he had behaved the ungentlemanly way he had on TV. The stigma would eat him alive, just the way it had her father, whether Brad wanted to admit it or not.

"You can't go on this way," she reiterated firmly. His need for the truth had put her in reporter gear again. If he would let her, Lainey knew that she could help him.

"It's not your decision to make. It's mine."

Despite his bullheadedness, Lainey would be damned if she'd see Brad McCabe end up as bitter and disillusioned and heartbroken as her own father. She had one more ace up her sleeve to get him to tell all. "So you're not going to tell me the truth about what happened between you and Yvonne, either?" she surmised softly. With a confident smile, she sat back in her chair, lifted her chin and continued. "Never mind. I think I can guess."

Brad smirked, not believing her for one red-hot second. "No. You can't," he replied, just as implacably.

"Want to bet?"

Chapter Thirteen

"Here's what I think happened." Lainey leaned forward, looking deep into Brad's eyes. "I think you signed on for *Bachelor Bliss*, expecting everything to be on the up-and-up, and hoping to find the right woman for you. Instead, from the very beginning, things just weren't quite right, and there were subtle but unmistakable signs this was so."

Brad stiffened, letting her know she had struck a nerve, and she pushed on. "Yvonne appeared to have special treatment from the show's creator, Gil Hewitt. Plus, she seemed to know things about you that she would have had no way of knowing. And while you no doubt noted this, you were too caught up in taping the show, and playing all the games the producers of *Bachelor Bliss* had you play, to dwell on it. Until that fateful moment of clarity, when, as you said, you realized Yvonne was not who she was pretending to be. My question is—" she paused to let her words sink in "—what happened to help you connect the dots? Yvonne has been running around accusing you of cheating on her, but I don't think that's true. I think maybe the *reverse* may have been true. So what really happened, Brad? Did you think Yvonne had eyes only for you and then discover she had someone on the side?"

Bull's-eye.

"Worse," he said, finally giving in with a weary sigh. He shoved a hand through his hair, looking ready to confide his troubles to her at long last. Seeming to need her to be not just his lover but his friend. "I caught her in bed with someone."

Lainey could imagine how much that would hurt a man of Brad McCabe's strength and pride. "Gil Hewitt, the show's creator," she guessed, figuring Yvonne was the kind of woman who would gladly hit the casting couch, so to speak, if it meant she emerged the grand-prize winner.

"Yes," Brad admitted reluctantly. Lips pressed together grimly, he continued. "Fifteen minutes before the final taping was to begin, I got a note from Yvonne asking me to meet her in one of the mansion bedrooms. And she was there with Gil Hewitt, in the throes of—well, you can guess."

How awful. Lainey reached across the table and took his hand. She tightened her fingers on his. "Was anyone else around to witness this?"

"Nope, just the three of us." Brad cupped her hand between both of his. He looked at her evenly. "It was obvious they had set me up to get a big emotional reaction from me, although I don't think they were sure what I was going to do during the taping. And that uncertainty added an extra element of excitement." His tone took on a bitter, sarcastic edge.

Lainey's heart went out to him. It was terrible enough to live through something like that, but to have the cameras on him in the immediate aftermath... Rumors swirling. His reputation maligned. "I'm surprised you didn't just walk out," she said sympathetically.

Brad laughed—a short, humorless sound. "I tried, but the producers caught me going out the door and threatened to sue me for five million dollars if I didn't get back in my tuxedo and honor my contract with the show."

Lainey remembered how tense the final Heart Ceremony had been. With Brad staring at Yvonne like he detested her, refusing to deliver the proposal that she—and all the viewers—were expecting. Then simply telling Yvonne it wasn't going to work out, taking off his microphone and walking out.

Under the circumstances, she doubted most men could have been even that gallant. "Did you tell the producers what had happened to make you want to bolt?"

Brad let go of her hand. "No. I didn't tell anyone."

"Why not?" Lainey asked, curious.

He stood, roamed the kitchen restlessly. "Obviously, you've never been cheated on." He stared out the window, at the pasture where Tabasco Red was peacefully grazing.

Lainey hadn't.

Brad ruminated in a voice laced with hurt. "Your first response is disbelief and anger and humiliation, and all you—all I—wanted to do was get the hell out of there. And never see or speak to Yvonne again."

Lainey certainly couldn't blame him for that. "You weren't mad at Gil Hewitt?"

Brad swung around. "Sure, I was ticked off, but I'm not sure, in retrospect, that I was really jealous. The whole time I was paired up with Yvonne, I had this feeling that the situation was more make-believe than real, that things were just a little too perfect. There was nothing concrete that would have made me feel that way. Just a lot of little things that triggered an uneasy feeling in my gut. When I found her with Gil, I finally had confirmation that it wasn't my imagination—there really was some reason why I kept thinking I shouldn't trust her."

Lainey knew about gut reactions to people. Her feminine instincts had told her she could trust and believe in Brad from the first moment they had come face-to-face with each other on the Lazy M.

Brad studied her carefully. "No one else has come close to guessing what happened. How is it you know all this?"

Lainey swallowed. The same instinct that had told her she could trust Brad told her this was not the time to confess she was a reporter. She got up and went to stand beside him at the window. She wanted to deepen—not sever—their intimate emotional connection. "I've puzzled over this a lot—first and foremost, because I want to understand you," she said softly. "And what happened on *Bachelor Bliss* obviously devastated you."

"You're very observant."

Lainey shrugged. "You already know I watched the show while it was airing. Since we met up again here at the ranch, I've been paying even more attention to you, listening to everything you've said about your experiences on *Bachelor Bliss* as well as everything you haven't said."

"I never said anything about the show's creator, Gil Hewitt," Brad pointed out, a tad suspiciously.

But Yvonne had. And Lainey had met and interviewed Gil. Treading carefully—she didn't want to alienate or hurt Brad now—she said, "A lot has been written about the breakup and the show. I know how to use the search engines on the Internet. I've been doing a little research on my own."

Brad narrowed his eyes at her. "You're that curious?"

"I want to help you that badly," she corrected.

Brad slid his hands into the pockets of his jeans. "At least now you must see why I don't want the real story to come out," he stated in a low voice.

"Because you're embarrassed."

He smirked. "As well as humiliated, cuckolded, duped, and made a complete and utter fool of."

Lainey could see where that would severely dent the famous McCabe pride. "So you would rather be portrayed as the villain?"

Brad shrugged, some of the walls going up again. "I would rather not be portrayed as anything at all," he stated irritably.

"But the media *is* portraying you," she pointed out.

He turned and looked her in the eye. "It'll fade. A person's fifteen minutes of fame always does."

And if it didn't, Lainey wondered, then what? "What about the people who are still signing up for the show?" she asked quietly, taking another tack to persuade Brad to do what had to be done if he was ever going to be free to live his life again the way he deserved. "Have you given any thought to future contestants and what they might end up going through, because you're too self-centered and cowardly to own up to the truth?"

Her words stung.

He lifted a brow, echoing, "Self-centered...and cowardly?"

"Sound a little harsh?"

Brad nodded, his expression grim. "And then some."

"But true. Think about those poor young women, Brad, the ones who aren't like Yvonne. Who just want to find some guy to love them."

"Or be on TV," Brad countered.

Lainey stepped closer, persisting. "Think about the guys signing up to find the woman of their dreams and having their reputations ruined. It's a travesty." She took both his hands in hers, gripped them hard. "You could set people straight. Prevent it from ever happening again. Or at least make it so anyone who entered the competition on *Bachelor Bliss* would know exactly what they were getting into."

LAINEY'S WORDS STAYED with Brad throughout the day. He had told her before he'd headed out to do ranch work that he would think about what she had said, and he was still thinking about it when Lewis and Petey arrived home that day. Annie, Travis and their five boys arrived shortly after that. By the time Brad got cleaned up and entered the ranch house kitchen, the adults were congregated around the appetizers on the kitchen table, while the three younger kids played outside on the tire-swings Brad had put up beneath the shade trees next to the house.

Talk, not surprisingly, centered on the erroneous tabloid story about him and Melinda.

"What are you doing about it?" Travis asked Brad.

Brad shrugged. He had hoped to talk to Lainey about his decision privately first. "My attorney fired off a letter to the publishers this morning, threatening a lawsuit."

"And—?" Annie asked, all motherly concern.

"We're still waiting to hear back," he admitted. He helped himself to salsa and tortilla chips.

"Did you speak to Yvonne Rathbone about her comments?" Lewis asked, digging into the bite-size tamales.

Brad shook his head.

"Shouldn't you be suing her, too, if what she said about you wasn't true?" Annie asked.

The last thing Brad wanted to do was get in a legal fight with Yvonne Rathbone. He'd be happy if he never saw or heard from her again.

"I'll tell you what I think," Lewis said. "I think you should tell your side of the story once and for all. And I'll tell you what else—" He gulped some mint-flavored iced tea. "If I knew what had happened, I'd put the information out there, even if you got mad at me temporarily."

"But you don't have the information," Brad said, warning his younger brother with a look. "So don't go messing in my life."

"What do you think, Lainey?" Teddy asked, seeming older than his twenty years.

"Do you think Brad should tell all?" Tyler inquired.

"Or keep whatever happened to himself?" Trevor put in.

Brad glanced at Lainey, curious as to what she was going to say. He knew she wouldn't tell what he had reluctantly confided this morning. She had sworn she would never give out that information without his permission, and thus far, he hadn't given it.

"When I think of Brad's situation, I think of my father's situation, when he was alive," Lainey said quietly, after a moment. "He, too, was a victim of character assassination.

And he, too, chose to hold his own counsel and not fight. He figured the people that knew and loved him would realize the truth, and those that didn't might not ever believe him anyway." She paused and looked at Brad. "I was just a kid then. I didn't have the means to help him, even if I had wanted to do so."

"And if you had possessed the means?" Lewis asked.

Lainey paused again, her gaze still locked fiercely with Brad's. "You never know, but I would hope I'd have the courage to do whatever needed to be done to help the truth come out."

"TRYING TO TELL ME SOMETHING in there?" Brad asked as he helped Lainey put the chicken on the grill. The rest of the adults would join them shortly, but for the moment everyone was still inside, polishing off the array of Tex-Mex appetizers Lainey had prepared.

"Only that I care deeply about you, and what happens to you," she said quietly. "And I hope you will always remember that—" she briefly touched the region of his heart "—in here."

Brad did. And yet…once again he had the feeling that something was wrong. That Lainey was bracing for something bad, and trying to prepare him, as well. Though what that could be…

"Mommy?" Petey ran over to Lainey's side. "How come that guy is taking pictures of us?"

Lainey and Brad looked in the direction Petey was pointing.

Brad scowled. It was the same guy in tourist garb that had been photographing him and Lainey in the grocery store the previous week. Now he had pulled his car to the side of the road and was using a camera with a long telephoto lens.

"Stay here!" Brad ordered Lainey and Petey. He started off at a run.

The interloper put down his camera, jumped in his car and drove off in a cloud of dust.

Brad came back. Fuming.

"Who was that?" Petey demanded in concern.

"No one we know," Lainey said. Although her tone was re-assuring, her expression indicated she was nervous and upset.

"Probably some tourist who wanted a picture of me," Brad explained, doing his best to comfort the frightened little boy. "I'm famous you know, ever since I went on TV."

Petey relaxed, just as Brad had hoped he would. "Yeah. Kurt and Kyle told me about that."

Petey grinned, reminding Brad what big news Brad's stint on TV had been in the extended McCabe family.

"You got to kiss lots of girls!"

"Yuck!" eight-year-old Kyle said, running over to join them, too.

"Yeah, gross!" nine-year-old Kurt agreed.

All three little boys made gagging sounds, and ran off once again.

"Pretty good save," Lainey said.

"Yeah. I just wish I knew who that guy was." Brad didn't recognize him as one of the tabloid paparazzi that had stalked him while he was doing *Bachelor Bliss.* "And who he was tak-ing photos for," he added as two more cars slowed at the en-trance to the Lazy M and turned into the drive. One was Lainey's SUV—driven by Bart Carrington—the other was Bunny's Mercedes, driven by Bunny.

Brad turned to Lainey, who was looking a little pale at the sight of her brother- and sister-in-law. "I didn't know you were getting your vehicle back today," he observed.

"That makes two of us," she said, too lightly.

Bart came toward Lainey, keys in hand. Brad could tell by the expression on the other man's face that Bart had some-thing serious to say.

Petey, Kyle and Kurt were playing along the pasture fence.

All were glancing their way, as if wondering what was going on. Petey started toward them, but Brad shook his head and put up a halting hand, letting them know that now was not a good time to be joining the adults. Petey continued staring at them for a minute longer, then the little boys went back to conferencing, their heads bent together.

"For the record," Bart said, "I did not know anything about your car going in for servicing at such an inopportune time. Nor would I have known had I not just happened to be home when the dealership called, saying the servicing was complete and wanting to know if they should continue to keep your vehicle next week. Naturally, I insisted we drive it back to you right away."

Realizing this was none of their business, Annie and Travis—who appeared to be on their way outside—remained inside the ranch house kitchen with their boys.

"It's just as well we had to come back out here, anyway, given what's been going on," Bunny said stiffly, glaring at Brad, as the aroma of grilling meat filled the air. "We saw the tabloid photo of you and that—that woman! And for everyone's sake, especially Petey's, I feel we must absolutely insist that Lainey and Petey leave here immediately."

Brad shot a look at Petey. Although well out of earshot, the little boy looked concerned. Doing his best to protect the child, Brad moved to block Petey's view of the adults, then turned back to Bunny, who was still ranting on.

"…Petey cannot grow up under that kind of influence!"

"First of all, Bunny," Lainey said angrily, stepping forward and waving her spatula, "Brad is a wonderful role model for Petey. And that photo is a fake."

"You're saying you weren't kissing a blonde in Dallas two days ago?" Bunny demanded, as Lainey swallowed, taken aback. "I read it in the New York City gossip columns, too!"

"No, that's correct," Brad answered calmly, looking Bunny straight in the eye. Maybe now was the time to come clean with his feelings for Lainey. Let everyone—including Lainey—know exactly where they stood.

"Then, if it wasn't that woman…" Bunny's voice trailed off. She looked at Lainey, her blond hair.

"As long as we're being honest," Lainey cut in, going on the offensive before Bunny could conclude anything else, "let's talk about the 'tourist' who was just here photographing us with a telephoto lens." Lainey's eyes darkened. "What do you have to do with that, Bunny? Did you send him to spy on me?"

"Me!" Bunny echoed, sounding outraged.

"You threatened to sue me for custody of Petey. I assume you're not standing around doing nothing about it."

"You did what?" Bart asked, stunned.

Finally, Bunny was embarrassed into silence.

Thankful for the reprieve, however short-lived, Brad turned to check on Petey. And swore mightily at what he saw. The little boy was over the fence and in the pasture with the bull.

"Oh, my God!" Bunny whispered, her hand flying to her mouth.

"Petey!" Lainey broke into a run.

"Don't move, son!" Brad shouted, running, too.

Petey glared at them, then looked at Kyle and Kurt, who were standing on the other side of the fence, for once urging Petey not to do whatever it was Petey was trying to do. Petey ignored them, too, and kept moving toward Tabasco Red.

Behind them, Bunny was screaming hysterically—until someone—probably her husband, Brad figured, clamped a hand over her mouth to shut off the sound.

Tabasco Red had been chewing grass, his back to the ranch house, but at the sound of all the commotion he turned around. Still Petey edged closer.

"Oh, no…oh, no…oh, no!" Lainey whispered as they reached the edge of the fence. Tears were streaming down her face as her son squared off with the nine-hundred-pound animal.

"It's going to be all right. I'll get him," Brad said, already vaulting up and over the fence. He landed lightly on the other side. Petey was too far away to hear anything Brad said unless he shouted it, but Brad did not want to yell. Heart pounding, he kept moving.

Tabasco Red stopped chewing and stared at the little boy approaching him slowly and steadily from the front. Brad could see Petey was shaking in his boots. And for good reason, since Petey had never been near the ranch sire. The bull had sharp horns that measured seventy-three inches tip to tip and outweighed him by a good eight hundred pounds or more. Tabasco Red had to look like a behemoth to Petey.

Ten strides later, Brad was even with Petey.

Not about to make any sudden moves under the circumstances, Brad fell in step beside Petey. "Let's turn around, son," he said, placing a paternal hand on Petey's shoulder.

Petey's chin thrust out. He allowed Brad's touch but ignored the directive and kept moving. "Not until I pet him."

Brad looked down into Petey's face, saw the stubborn set of his chin, so like his mother's. Brad could see this was some kind of test of courage.

And what the hell, the kid had come this far.

BUNNY CARRINGTON WAS CRYING hysterically when Petey reached Tabasco Red, held out his hand, let the bull sniff it and then petted him on the nose. There was a brief conference among the three of them, with Brad standing there as calm as could be while Petey said a few words to the giant animal. Then Tabasco Red turned away in boredom and went back to eating grass while Brad and Petey walked over to the fence where Lainey stood, crying her eyes out, next to Bunny and Bart.

By the time both guys had climbed the pasture fence, they were surrounded by everyone in attendance.

Lainey hugged Petey like he'd just come home from the

war. She wiped the tears streaming down her face with the heels of her hands, then squared off with him. "There better be a darn good explanation for what you just did," she said shakily.

Petey glanced at Bart and Bunny, and then back at Lainey. "I had to prove to you, once and for all, that I was a growned-up man already."

Lainey blinked. "What are you talking about?" she cried.

Petey swallowed. He waved his small arms expansively. "So Aunt Bunny wouldn't take me away from you and make me go live with them, so's Uncle Bart could teach me how to be a man, 'cause she says only a man can teach a boy how to be a man."

A hush came over the group.

Bart stared at his wife for a long time, then back at Petey. He knelt down in front of the boy. "Is this why you've been so unhappy lately?" he asked gently, showing fatherly concern. "Because you were afraid?"

Petey nodded. He grabbed on to Lainey with one hand, and Brad with the other, and held tight. "I don't want to leave my mommy," he told Bart fiercely.

Bart looked Petey in the eye. "You're never going to have to." He straightened and addressed Bunny. "I understand that you're having a hard time with the girls leaving home for college, but this is not the way to refill your nest."

Bart turned back to Lainey and continued sincerely. "I apologize with all my heart for everything that's been going on. I promise you, every bit of trouble stops now, including the snooping P.I."

"But I didn't—" Bunny protested.

"We'll talk about this at home," Bart said sternly. He took his wife's elbow and steered her toward their Mercedes.

Bunny and Bart departed.

Travis and Annie, who'd been silent up to now, turned back to Kyle and Kurt. "I believe it's your turn to do some explaining," Travis said to their two youngest sons.

"I'M SORRY YOU WERE FRIGHTENED about Tabasco Red," Brad said, hours later, after Petey was asleep and all the guests had departed. Lewis was inside the ranch house, working.

Brad and Lainey were sitting on the front porch of the guest house, enjoying what was left of the summer evening.

"There really is such a thing as a gentle bull?" Lainey asked, for the third time.

Brad wrapped his arm around her shoulders and brought her close. He didn't seem to mind reassuring her. Maybe because he knew how shaken up she still was by all the bad things that could have happened had the situation been just a little bit different. Had Tabasco Red been a rancorous animal. Or Brad not been there.

"You better believe it," Brad said.

Lainey relaxed into the warm and welcoming curve of his body as the glider rocked back and forth. "I always thought bulls were scary-mean and dangerous."

"Some are. Travis's aren't, because he breeds them for temperament." Brad pressed a kiss in Lainey's hair. "And Tabasco Red has lived on Annie and Travis's ranch since he was a bull calf. The boys grew up with him, and they know he's as gentle as a kitten and used to being around little kids. I was going to tell you that when we first brought him here to sire my first generation of calves, but you were so freaked out about cattle in general, I just figured I'd wait and show you later when you got used to being around 'em." Brad paused, shook his head. "I never had any idea Petey would try and go near Tabasco Red."

"So he wasn't in any danger?"

"Right." Brad shifted Lainey over onto his lap. "Although, all the boys know better than to go over the fence unless they are in the company of an adult cowboy. That's what the kids were arguing about before Petey scaled the fence. Kyle and Kurt wanted Petey to do it, but in the company of their older cowboy-brothers. Because they knew that was allowed."

Lainey sighed. "But in Petey's view, desperate times called

for desperate measures, and he thought Bart and Bunny were here to take him away and it was the only way he and Kurt and Kyle could think to prove Petey's manhood in the nick of time." Tears welled in Lainey's eyes as she shook her head. "I should have known something was terribly wrong."

"You did." Brad lifted her hand to his lips and kissed the back of it. "You just didn't know what, exactly."

Lainey laced her arms about his neck. "I should have been able to get him to tell me what was going on."

Brad stroked her hair. "You're a good mother, Lainey. The best."

She choked back a sob, and embarrassed she couldn't seem to get ahold of herself, wiped her eyes. "If anything ever happened to him…" she whispered hoarsely.

"I know," Brad said soothingly. He paused, looked deep into her eyes. "I feel the same way. Which is why, Lainey, the two of you have to leave the Lazy M tomorrow morning, first thing."

Chapter Fourteen

"W-what? Why?" Lainey asked.

"Because," Brad retorted heavily, his guilt apparent, "Petey's already been through far too much lately and it's the only way I know to protect you."

Lainey blinked and slid off his lap, onto the seat of the glider. "By sending us away?" she echoed hoarsely. Impossible, how much that hurt.

Brad caught her wrist before she could bolt. His voice was low, intense. "Suppose Bunny is telling the truth and she didn't send that photographer. Then that means he's not after you and whatever dirt he can dig up—he's after me." The haunted look was back in Brad's eyes. "The last thing Petey needs to see is his mother on the cover of a tabloid."

Lainey agreed with that portion of Brad's assessment. Her brief experience as a journalist told her something else about the rest. "I don't think the photographer was from a tabloid. A tabloid would have published the photos of us last week, particularly in light of what that New York City newspaper gossip column published. Tabloids don't necessarily wait to get a whole story—they go with whatever they've got. Speed and scooping all other news outlets via actual photos of whatever is going on is the priority."

Brad frowned. "You think he's freelance?"

"Maybe." Lainey savored the warmth and tenderness of the

hand encircling her wrist. She moved her hand so her fingers were meshed with his. "If that tourist guy had no legitimate connections, he was just trying to get different pictures of us to sell to lots of places…and that might take a little longer."

Brad slouched against the back of the glider as he considered that. "And if he's not?"

"Then I don't know who he is or why he was here unless he's just someone who is plain nosy and wants something to show his friends. In any case, the revelation of our relationship with each other is going to be news…."

He shook his head. "Not if it doesn't come out until interest in me dies down."

Ignoring the feel of his rock-hard thigh pressed up against hers, she looked down at their clasped hands, then back at him. "What are you saying?"

Brad swallowed. He seemed to know she wasn't going to like what came next. "This afternoon I was ready to come clean, go to the press like you suggested, tell my story, and let the dust settle once and for all. But I realize now that speaking out at this point would only generate a whole new wave of public interest in me, and I can't subject Petey—or you—to that, Lainey."

His mind was clearly made up. "So you're breaking up with me?" She did her best to contain her broken heart. Realizing she was suddenly doubting Brad and his feelings for her, when up until now she'd had absolutely no reason to, she stood and moved to the edge of the porch. Her back to him, she looked out at the broad expanse of the Texas night sky. The summer night was clear and warm. A half moon nestled in the stars winking overhead.

"No." He crossed to her side and drew her into his embrace. "Just putting what we feel for each other under wraps for a while." He stroked a soothing hand down her spine. "We'll still see each other."

"Just not in public." She sighed. "Not where anyone can find out about it."

Brad's mood was as pensive as her own. "Right."

Lainey was silent. She knew it wasn't what Brad was saying, but it felt like he was ashamed of her...and that was devastating. Hadn't she promised herself when she was with Chip that she would never put herself in that situation again? She swallowed, did her best to respond with maturity and grace.

"I see."

"Do you?" Brad asked gently, his gaze lovingly roving over her. He slid both hands through her hair, lifting her face up to his. His heated glance drifted lower and he massaged her shoulders tenderly. "'Cause I don't think you do. What I am trying to tell you here—" he paused to reassure her with another long, direct glance "—is that I want us to be together over the long haul. But to make that happen, we're going to have to protect what we have and keep it secret."

THE ONLY GOOD THING about Brad's sending Lainey and Petey back to Dallas was that she had the time—and space necessary—to honor her promise to her old college roommate well within the required publishing deadline.

Sybil called her Tuesday evening. "I got the article you e-mailed me."

Lainey braced herself for what she knew had to be coming next.

"There's nothing in it about Brad McCabe."

Lainey sighed, glad Petey was already in bed. "Right."

"Nor do you tell why Brad dumped Yvonne," Sybil continued, sounding even more displeased.

Lainey winced. "Right again."

Another pause. Sybil, sounding more boss than friend, continued calmly. "Did you misunderstand what I asked you to do?"

No. Lainey hadn't. She had known exactly what kind of

salacious, groundbreaking, cover-level story Sybil wanted out of her. That was the hell of it. Lainey gathered her professionalism around her like a protective cloak. She knew the work she had done on Yvonne—and even Gil Hewitt—was good. She had to concentrate on that and feel proud of it, while at the same time owning up to her own shortcomings. "I can't write about Brad McCabe with any objectivity. I thought I could. But I can't." So she hadn't. Problem solved. Sort of, anyway.

Sybil let out a short, impatient breath. "That sweet-talking Casanova got to you, didn't he."

Lainey told herself Brad's womanizing days were over. Not that they had ever existed beyond his desire not to get emotionally involved with someone he wasn't cut out to be partnered with for life. "What do you mean?"

Sybil scoffed, as blunt and straight-talking as ever. "Brad McCabe has a reputation for making women lose their head, and obviously he's made you lose yours!"

Lainey knew she was in love with Brad. But it wasn't like that. Brad hadn't used her any more than she had used him. It was just a tough situation, that was all. One Lainey was determined to extricate herself from sooner rather than later. "I never should have signed up to write about someone I knew as a kid," she said, excoriating herself honestly. "It's an insurmountable conflict of interest."

"It's also your big chance to catapult yourself into the bigtime. Or have you forgotten how much you've always wanted to be a journalist?" Sybil demanded, practical as ever.

Lainey wanted to be loved and cared for more—her relationship with Brad held the promise of that.

"You've been seeing him, haven't you," Sybil pressed, beginning to sound a little angry now.

Lainey didn't want to lie to her old friend, so she said nothing.

"He found out what you're up to and—"

"He doesn't know anything," Lainey corrected.

Sybil made a low, dissenting sound. "I wouldn't bet on that. From what I've heard, Brad McCabe is one smart cookie."

Lainey ran her hands through her hair. "Smart. Dumb. Who cares?"

"*Personalities* readers care. They want to know what happened to make TV's sexiest bachelor go berserk and dump a very sweet and loving girl!"

"As the article I sent you attests," Lainey countered tightly, "Yvonne is anything but sweet and loving."

"I don't care what the other girls or even Gil Hewitt had to say. I want to know when and how and where did Brad find that out? I'm presuming, of course, that is the reason he broke up with her."

"I can't tell you that," Lainey said. She rubbed at the headache starting in her temples.

"Lainey, as it is," Sybil explained patiently, "I cannot—I will not—publish this article. There is very little in it that hasn't been either printed or speculated about before. We're looking for a great big scoop, not a guessing game and a rehash."

She sighed, beginning to feel like she had the weight of the world on her shoulders once again. "It's the best I can do."

"Well, it's not good enough. You still have another forty-eight hours before deadline. There's still time—"

"I've had all the time I need," Lainey interrupted firmly.

"Please don't do this," her friend begged. "Do I need to remind you that you threw away any chance at a career for yourself when you hooked up with Chip? Lainey, honey, I can't bear to see you doing the same thing again!"

"Bear it or not, it's what I have to do," she said. "I'm sorry, Sybil. I know I let you down. Thank you for the opportunity, anyway." And she hung up the phone.

"I DIDN'T THINK STAYING AWAY from each other was going to be this hard," Brad said, four days later.

Lainey walked into the conference room at McCabe Computer Games testing facility in Laramie. Petey was there to evaluate the latest changes in the computer game he had been testing all summer. Lainey was there to see Brad. She went into his arms, glad Lewis had thoughtfully provided the two of them with a conference room where they could talk privately, without having to worry about being caught by someone with a telephoto lens.

"Although—" Brad drew back after a lengthy hello kiss, then another, and another "—you look like you are faring much better than I am in this situation. You look—" he studied her tenderly "—like a huge burden has been lifted from your shoulders."

"It has been."

Lainey smiled at him, feeling a little less sure now.

Nevertheless, she knew what she had to do—tell him everything and then see where they stood, if he was as capable of forgiving her as she deemed him to be. She couldn't go on hiding something this important from him. It was too much to bear. And she needed to make certain that, unlike Chip, Brad could accept that Lainey was not perfect. She made mistakes. Occasionally took a wrong turn. Or made a wrong choice. That didn't mean she was a bad person. Just human. Fallible. Ready and willing to learn from her mistakes and move on.

Lainey was in the market for unconditional love now.

Not a love that hinged on her looking and behaving a certain way, and only that way.

She wanted a love that let her feel free to be.

She wanted Petey growing up the same way.

"How are things with the in-laws?" Brad asked gently.

"Better than you could imagine." She sat down on the edge of the conference table, braced herself and looked up at him. "Bunny's decided to hand over the dispersing of the trust funds to one of the attorneys who drew it up."

"She can do that?"

Lainey nodded. "Chip had a provision built in, in case something ever happened to Bunny or she felt it was too much to handle. She and Bart talked it over and decided it would be best to have the trust administered by a third party from now on."

"That certainly sounds a lot less stressful for you," he said.

She nodded. "Claire set up a meeting. We all talked at length about my situation yesterday and agreed it would be best to sell our house in Highland Park. I can use the proceeds to resettle in Laramie."

"How does Petey feel about that?"

"He's as ready for change as I am—although," Lainey conceded, smiling ruefully, "he'd prefer to live on a ranch, rather than in town. But I told him he can visit his friends who do live on ranches, so he's happy about that. In the meantime, I'm going to open my own professional organizing business, and probably do some freelance writing on the side, too." She wanted to start living on what she made, and let the money Chip left them be for Petey's education, and any emergencies that came up.

"I didn't know you wanted to be a writer," he said.

She studied the hem of her cotton skirt, where it rode up above her knee. It was time to confess all. Her stomach fluttered with a thousand butterflies as she admitted softly, honestly, "For a long time now."

"Because of what happened to your dad?"

Lainey nodded. "The truth is important. Reporters have the ability to keep things honest and aboveboard."

"When it's done correctly," Brad stipulated.

"Right." Unfortunately, that was a lesson she had learned a little too late when it came to Brad. "Anyway, I studied journalism in college and worked on the Tech newspaper before I dropped out to get married."

Brad looked impressed with her accomplishments, yet wary of her profession. "You know reporters aren't my favorite people these days," he teased, "but I guess I could change my mind about that, if you become one again."

"I hope so," she said. She gripped the table edge on either side of her, her nerves beginning to get the better of her.

"I know so." He smiled and sat down on the edge of the table next to her. "Because you'd never be the kind of vulture that's been after me since I went on TV."

Guilt swept through Lainey, followed by uncertainty. Was this the time to tell him everything? How could she not?

"Lewis and I've been doing some rearranging, too," Brad said.

Lainey winced, recalling the six boxes she had yet to unpack that were stacked up in the utility room, taking up all the available space. "I'm sorry. I know I'm not quite finished organizing everything there yet." She'd left in such a hurry, at Brad's behest, that she hadn't had time to complete her tasks. "But I promise I'll get to it as soon as you think it's okay for me to come back out to the Lazy M."

"Well," Brad drawled, smiling broadly, looking like he had a secret now, "that all depends."

"On?" Lainey queried.

He reached into his pocket and withdrew a small velvet box. "How fast I can get you to say yes to the idea of marrying me."

LAINEY STARED at Brad, stunned speechless. Her reaction wasn't the one he had been hoping for. Brad gulped and rushed on, telling her all that was in his heart.

"I know it sounds sudden," he said softly as he guided her to her feet and into his arms. "And I guess in some respects it is." He paused and looked deep into her eyes. "But I know you're the woman I've been waiting my whole life to meet. And I want you—and Petey—with me. The only way we can do that in a respectful manner is by making a true and lasting commitment and marrying each other. So...Lainey, will you do me the honor of becoming my wife?"

In place of the jubilant "yes" and kiss he had been expecting, tears welled in her eyes. "Oh, Brad..." she murmured, seeming distraught.

To his dismay, she looked like she wished he hadn't asked.

She splayed her fingers across his shirtfront, his only solace the fact that she did not move away. "If you only knew how much I want to say yes. But I—I need to talk to you about something else—something important—before we discuss that."

"Okay," he said slowly, once again bracing for the worst.

Before she could get another word out, the door to the conference room was flung open. Lewis rushed in so quickly he was practically tripping over his own feet. He had a rolled-up magazine in his hand. He looked at Brad, Lainey, then back at Brad again. "Oh, man!" Lewis said.

Brad glared at his younger brother. "You know, Lewis, sometimes your timing really—"

"Bites. I know." Lewis swallowed hard and shut the door behind them. "Listen, I really don't want to be the one to tell you this, but...you know how I set up that search engine on my computer for stuff about you when you first went on *Bachelor Bliss*?"

Like they needed to be talking about the parameters of Lewis's computer now? "Yes," Brad said patiently, knowing it would be faster to just let Lewis say what he had to say than try to shoo him out.

"Well, it still pulls stuff up every time I get on the Internet," Lewis explained.

"Terrific," Brad muttered, even more irritated when he noticed that Lainey looked upset.

The last thing he needed was Lewis spoiling an already going-downhill-fast mood. "I really don't care what they've written about me," he informed his brother tersely. He sent Lewis a look telling him to leave. *Now.*

"You will care," Lewis countered, just as firmly.

Lainey extricated herself from Brad's arms and moved away.

"Especially when you find out who wrote it," Lewis explained.

Doing his best not to deck his frustrating younger brother, Brad grimaced. "What are you talking about?"

Lewis thrust the magazine at him. "This."

Brad unrolled it. He was not pleased to see it was a copy of *Personalities Magazine.* He swiftly became even less thrilled. On the front cover was a photo of Lainey and Brad in the grocery store. Next to it was a photo of Brad and Yvonne. Below that was a grainy photo of Lainey and Brad kissing, at dusk, on the front porch of the Lazy M guest house. Brad swore at the intrusion into his privacy.

"How did the people at *Personalities* know about us?" he wondered out loud.

"I don't know," Lainey retorted, turning ever paler.

For some reason, Brad noted, Lewis was now staring at Lainey with a peculiar mixture of disbelief and pity.

Which made Brad hope and pray like crazy that the photographer hadn't gotten a picture of him and Lainey in his bed. Brad wouldn't put Lainey through that kind of embarrassment for the world. One thing was certain: Lewis was acting very peculiar. So was Lainey. It was almost as if they already knew something he didn't.

"The story's on page sixty-seven," Lewis said, already making his way to the exit. Hand on the doorknob, Lewis looked at Lainey. "And boy, oh boy, oh boy, do you ever have some explaining to do."

Lewis left the room, shutting the door behind him.

Brad looked at Lainey. She was now trembling.

"What's he talking about?" Brad demanded.

"Only one way to find out." Lainey snatched the magazine out of his hands and thumbed quickly through the glossy pages until she reached the aforementioned page. She opened it up all the way, so they could both see. The title was written in bold red letters: "Yvonne's Secret Tryst!"

Just below that were the names of the coauthors of the article—Lainey Carrington and Sybil Devine.

Brad stared at it. Read it again. And then again.

Lainey was staring as if she had seen a ghost. She looked as if she might faint, and sat down abruptly in the nearest chair.

Wondering if it was possible—if there was another Lainey Carrington other than the woman he'd been trading secrets and kisses with—Brad moved so he could see more of what was on the page. "Tell me you didn't have anything to do with that," he ordered grimly.

Lainey buried her face in her hands. "Unfortunately," she said reluctantly, "I can't."

For the second time in under four months, Brad's world came crashing down around him. "What the hell is that supposed to mean?"

"It means I did. And then—" Lainey shrugged helplessly "—I didn't."

Brad's jaw clenched. "Lewis was right. Boy, do you ever have some explaining to do."

FEELING THE BLOOD DRAINING from her face, Lainey tore her gaze from Brad's angry expression and quickly skimmed the article. To her dismay, it was all there, even the parts about Brad and his rendition of events that she had carefully omitted from the story she had written on Yvonne and the *Bachelor Bliss* reality TV show.

Aware Sybil had obviously finished the job Lainey had set out to do, she grasped the arms of the chair.

She had to stay calm. Brad loved her. Didn't he? Belatedly,

she realized he had never once said the words. He had, however, just asked her to marry him. To commit to a life with him forever. That had to mean something, even under circumstances like these. She swallowed the ache in her throat and met his eyes, determined to do whatever was necessary to make this come out right. "I told you I always wanted to write."

A muscle worked in his jaw. He stared at Lainey, a force not to be denied. Her hot-blooded lover had vanished and in his place appeared a cowboy who always rode away alone.

"You were out at the ranch for two weeks. You never once mentioned you were a reporter."

"That's because I'm not, at least not officially. But when my old friend Sybil called me up and asked me to help locate you, and then do an article for *Personalities*—"

"You agreed."

"No. Not just like that," Lainey said with difficulty, aware he had every right to be angry with her.

"Well, at some point you sold out."

Desperate to salvage their relationship, she defended herself hotly. "I didn't even expect you to be at the Lazy M Ranch when I stopped by!" With effort she lowered her voice to a more manageable level. "I wanted to talk to Lewis about putting Petey in the game-testing program at his company. And then Lewis asked me to help him get organized—and you walked in. And you sort of taunted me, and the next thing I knew, I said I was going to do it."

He looked at her, sadder and even more disillusioned than before. "And then you conveniently spied on me and pumped me for info, all the while knowing you were going to betray me in the end," he said bitterly.

"I couldn't go back—I had given my word and already signed a contract!"

"So you betrayed me, without batting an eye."

Lainey went toward him, arms outstretched. "Listen to

me, Brad. I agonized over the situation I put us both in, and I didn't write anything about you in the article I turned in."

He pivoted away from her. "And what about the rest of it— the tourist with the telephoto lens on his camera?" He gave her a hard, assessing look.

"I swear to you that I did not know the two of us were being photographed by *Personalities*." But that was, Lainey admitted to herself, obviously what had happened. Lainey's sister-in-law hadn't been having her spied on—her editor had!

"Kind of damages your rep, doesn't it, becoming part of the story like that," he observed.

Lainey didn't care about that. She only cared about Brad and how this was likely to affect him. Obviously, it had made him even more cynical and bitter, which was the last thing she had ever wanted. "I didn't tell anyone Yvonne cheated on you," she reiterated evenly.

Brad folded his arms and looked her up and down contemptuously. "Then how did they know I found Yvonne in bed with Gil Hewitt fifteen minutes before the final show was taped?"

Lainey took a careful look at the quotes in the magazine article. Quickly, she put it all together. "Obviously, Sybil got it out of Yvonne. Probably by pretending you had already told all and asking Yvonne if she wanted to tell her side of things." Lainey tapped the pages of the magazine. "Look, it says right here that Yvonne readily admits she only got involved with Gil Hewitt because she knew you weren't really in love with her. She even confesses there was no other woman for you, at that time, that she knew about." Bless Sybil for that much, Lainey thought. "So at least your name has finally been cleared."

Unfortunately, Brad did not look nearly as relieved about that as Lainey had hoped. "Yours, on the other hand, is mud," he pointed out sarcastically. "Since it says here the reason you had to recuse yourself from the article mid-writing was that you became personally involved with me."

Lainey took another look at the photos, of herself and Brad. No denying the intimacy between them.

"I never told anyone that," she said emotionally. She gazed at Brad, embarrassed, miserable. "Sybil must have figured it out on her own."

Brad stood. "So how does it feel to be betrayed by someone you thought was your friend?"

Lainey swallowed at the sick feeling in the pit of her stomach. "Not good."

"At least we're clear on that much." Brad pushed past her and headed for the door.

Lainey moved quickly, barring his way. The happiness they'd once shared now seemed a million miles away. "I'm so sorry. I tried to tell you…"

He scorched her with a look. "Not hard enough, obviously."

Lainey swallowed as her knees began to shake. If only she had leveled with him much sooner! Shoring up her courage, she tried again. "I know I made a mistake, even agreeing to write the article about Yvonne, but once I had signed the contract I had to follow through."

Brad grunted in contempt. "Your responsibility to tell me or Lewis what you were up to be damned?"

Lainey drew another breath, searched his face. There was so much more she wanted to say but she could see it was pointless. She had wounded his already badly damaged McCabe pride. "You're not going to forgive me for this, are you," she said sadly.

The old cynicism was back in Brad's eyes, more potent than ever before. He leaned in closer, until they stood toe to toe, nose to nose. "Now you've got a clue."

Chapter Fifteen

Several weeks later, Brad signed on the dotted line his attorney Claire McCabe Taylor indicated. Claire smiled as she collected the papers.

"That should about do it. You're all set. Although, given the fact you have just agreed to do two million dollars' worth of endorsements for everything from your favorite saddle soap to pickup truck, I'd expect that you'd be looking a lot happier."

Hard to be happy, Brad thought, when he had lost the only woman he'd ever dreamed was the one for him.

"This is enough to buy into the Lazy M as a full partner and get the cattle operation up and running the way you wanted to, before all your previous endorsements fell through."

Brad nodded, acknowledging the fact he was a much richer man. "Thanks for doing such a fine job negotiating on my behalf."

"My pleasure." Claire's expression gentled. She'd been married for fifteen years, had two adopted children of her own and knew the value of family. "Have you spoken to Lainey?"

Brad stretched his legs out in front of him. "Not since the issue of *Personalities* with us on the cover hit the newsstands." That was a day that would live on in memory as one of the unhappiest of his entire life.

Claire tossed down her pen and leaned back in her swivel chair. "She cleared your name."

"And muddied her own." To the point Brad figured Lainey's chances of getting a magazine job—at least anytime in the near future—were nil.

Claire shrugged. "True love is selfless."

Beginning to feel increasingly annoyed—Lewis, Annie and Travis were lobbying for reconciliation, too—Brad shot back, "She should have told me what she was up to from the very beginning."

"Right." Claire shot him a telling look. "And you'd have given her the time of day?"

Brad shifted uncomfortably in his chair. Guilt flowed through him. "Well, no…"

"She was a reporter on a story. She had a job to do. Getting involved with you was not in her plans."

Brad knew that much was true. He had seen her struggling with something the entire time they were together. Suddenly it all made sense why she had cried the last time they'd made love and said they never should have gotten involved.

"She still should have stayed away from me," he said.

Lifting a brow, Claire said dryly, "I'm sure you made that easy." Claire leaned across her desk, determined to make her point. "Come on, Brad, who pursued whom here? Who initiated the first kiss? Or teased her into paying attention to you in that distinctly man-woman way?"

Okay, Claire had him there. Brad had pursued her with everything he'd had; he had wanted to make her his woman that badly.

"Had it been anyone else but you putting the moves on her, I'm sure Lainey would have easily kept her distance. But she didn't keep the walls around her heart up because what was going on between the two of you was stronger than any ambition she might have had for herself. So she sacrificed her long-held goal of becoming a reporter, to do the best she could in this impossible situation she found herself in."

Brad slowly released the breath he'd been holding. For the first time since they'd split, he felt a flare of hope. "How do you know all this?" he demanded testily.

"I talked to her last week when I represented her and Petey's interests in a meeting with Bunny, Bart and the lawyer for the trust her late husband left." Claire paused, making sure she had his full attention. "Lainey regrets what happened more than you will ever know. But the two things she is *not* unhappy about are that, thanks to her, the truth is now out there and all future contestants of *Bachelor Bliss* know exactly what they are signing up for—and risking. And, most importantly, that your name and reputation have been cleared."

"CONGRATULATIONS on your promotion," Lainey told Sybil over her cell phone as she drove.

"Thanks." Her friend paused, then continued awkwardly. "I wasn't sure you were ever going to speak to me again."

For a while, Lainey hadn't been sure whether that would happen, either. Then she'd thought about everything that had occurred, and decided this was a rite of passage that—however painful and instructional—she had been destined to work her way through. It was great, she knew, when someone did everything right the first time out of the gate. But a person didn't necessarily learn anything from doing everything right.

When someone made a mistake, on the other hand, especially a big one, and then found a way to rebound, a tremendous amount was always gained. Those kinds of lessons were the ones a person never forgot. She knew she would be remembering her time with Brad McCabe for the rest of her life.

"I understand why you did what you did," she said finally as she bypassed the road to Laramie and continued driving through the Texas countryside. She knew she and her old friend needed to have an open and honest discussion about what had occurred, and why. "I let you down. You still had a job to do."

Sybil confessed miserably, "I had a feeling you were going to back out on me."

"And you were right." Lainey knew she would do the same thing again. She would always choose to protect the people she loved, even if it meant she had to forfeit—at least temporarily—career success.

"Are we ever going to be friends again?" Sybil asked finally.

Lainey smiled as she drove past Annie and Travis McCabe's ranch. "We never stopped," she said quietly, thinking about a friendship that had spanned twelve years and gotten Lainey through some rough times. She and Sybil were on different life paths now, but they were still connected and always would be. "You gave me a chance you probably shouldn't have. I kept things from you I had no right—as a reporter under your direction—to suppress. You then did what you had to do and managed to uncover the rest of the story in very little time…and gave me partial credit, to boot." Lainey smiled again at the end of her recitation of events. "I'd say we're even when it comes to mistakes made and lessons learned."

Sybil sighed, relieved. "You are something, you know that?"

Lainey just wished Brad thought so, too.

She ended her conversation with her old friend with promises to be in touch soon, and turned her SUV into the Lazy M.

Lewis had assured her, when she had agreed to come out and unpack the last five boxes at the ranch house, that Brad would be in town meeting with their mutual lawyer, Claire McCabe Taylor. However, when Lainey walked into the ranch house, she saw Brad McCabe slouched on the stairs.

For a moment her heart seemed to stall. He was just so

handsome, so ruggedly male. So obviously waiting for her. She eyed him cautiously, unsure of his mood. And suddenly, Lainey couldn't risk another encounter that ended badly. She had barely survived the last.

She took several steps backward, reached blindly for the doorknob behind her. "I'll come back later."

He unfolded himself and stood with a lazy, determined grace that jumbled her emotions all the more. "Don't go."

Lainey stared at him, not sure whether to laugh in joy or burst into tears. She only knew that she had never felt more worried or uncertain or full of bittersweet anticipation in her life. And Brad, darn his stubborn, unforgiving heart, was to blame. As their eyes met she drew a deep, bolstering breath, pretended an insouciance she couldn't begin to feel. "I'm not up for another browbeating, so…if you're planning to tell me what a lousy woman-friend I was to you…" *Or an even lousier reporter…*

He swaggered toward her. As he closed the distance, she could smell the spicy scent of his aftershave lotion and the cool mint toothpaste he favored.

His brown eyes were shrewdly direct as they locked on hers. Triumphant, almost. "You were more than that to me."

Had she been? Lainey lifted a brow, realizing in that instant that he wasn't the only person who had changed. She had, too. No longer was she going to allow herself to have expectations put on her that could not possibly be met. She dropped her shoulder bag on the floor beside her and folded her arms across her chest, more than ready to do battle with him if that was what he wanted. "You didn't seem to have any trouble ditching me," she pointed out.

"I was a fool," he stated matter-of-factly.

"And now you're not?" she asked, a little sadly, aware her throat ached and her knees were shaky and she'd never had so much at stake in her life.

"Only if I lose you." His eyes darkened with sensual intent. His voice dropped a notch. "I don't intend to lose you."

She wanted this. But she had to make sure it would work this time before she leaped in heart-first. "I'm not perfect, Brad."

"I know—" he told her gruffly, his voice catching. "Neither am I."

Tears gathered behind her eyes. She drew a tremulous breath, forced herself to go on. "I have to know…if we ever…resume—"

"I'm looking for a lot more than a resumption, Lainey," he interrupted hoarsely. He stroked her face, cheek, lower lip, until she trembled from his tenderness.

"I need to know that I don't have to be perfect," Lainey continued with a gulp, forcing herself to find the courage to go on despite the fact he obviously was ready and willing to continue their romance. She looked deep into his eyes, knowing this was all-important if they were ever going to be truly happy together. "I need to know that I've got room to make mistakes." She needed reassurance that if she screwed up, he would still love her and want her. That their life together wouldn't be bordered by endless conditions and rigid expectations.

He regarded her soberly, and she saw the love she felt reflected back. "As far as I'm concerned, the only person who needs forgiveness in this situation is me," he told her in a low voice laced with love and hope. "Lainey, you were—are—everything to me. I'm the fool for taking so long to realize that I love you just the way you are, and I always will." His mouth lowered to take hers in a possessive kiss.

"Oh, Brad." She wrapped her arms about his neck and kissed him back sweetly. The warmth and strength of him cured everything that ailed her. "I love you, too. So very, very much."

Contented moments passed as they simply held each other.

He stroked her hair. "I'm sorry it took me so long to forgive you."

She cuddled closer and drew aimless patterns on his chest. "I understand. What I did was…unforgivable."

"No," he corrected, lifting her face to his, "you did what had to be done. You helped put the truth out there—about everything. And you were right, the truth does set you free."

"You really do understand," Lainey marveled. Better yet, he understood—and admired—her determination to set the record straight.

They shared another longer, more leisurely kiss. Relief flowed through her in great, calming waves.

"So, speaking of the facts…you promised me several weeks ago you were going to give me an answer to the question I popped." Brad took a familiar velvet box from his pocket.

Lainey grinned with the promise of the future as he showed her a beautiful diamond ring. "The answer, cowboy, is yes!"

Epilogue

"This is going to be the best-est wedding ever," Petey said as he paced the room where Annie was putting the finishing touches on Lainey's veil. He had been able to come in, as soon as Lainey was in her dress, and was now waiting to escort her down the aisle and give her away.

"You think so?" Lainey smiled at her son. He looked so handsome and grown up in his wedding attire.

"Brad is even wearing cowboy boots with his tuxedo."

Lainey reached out to give his cummerbund and suspenders a playful tug. "So are you."

Petey grinned proudly. "Aunt Bunny isn't feeling too well, though," he said, continuing his recitation of events.

Aunt Bunny was pregnant. And she and Bart couldn't be happier about the late-in-life pregnancy. Lainey smiled and said reassuringly, "That'll pass, honey."

Petey's eyes widened curiously. "Are you and Brad gonna have more babies, too? 'Cause it would be okay with me if you did. Kurt and Kyle and Teddy, Trevor and Tyler say it's lots of fun to have brothers…and I'd really like to have a brother. Even a sister would be okay."

Lainey grinned. She brought her son to her for a hug. "You are one special guy, you know that?"

Petey smiled back as the music started.

"Are you ready to walk me down the aisle and give me away?" Lainey asked.

Petey nodded, held up his arm to her. "Let's do it."

As they left the anteroom, she saw Brad's whole family gathered on the Lazy M lawn. Lainey's friends from Dallas were there, too. Sybil had even talked them into allowing a photographer from the magazine to take photos.

The sight of everyone close to them filled Lainey with gratitude and peace, but it was Brad, looking so determined and so full of love for her, standing next to the minister at the other end of the aisle, that made her heart race. The joy in his eyes matched her own.

The ceremony itself was a wonderful, happy blur. *"...to have and to hold...from this day forward...forevermore..."*

When the minister announced, "You may kiss the bride," Brad grinned and said, "It's about time!"

The crowd erupted around them and their lips met. Basking in their joy, Lainey and Brad's life together, as husband and wife, began.

Welcome to the world of American Romance!
Turn the page for excerpts from our
September 2005 titles.
We're sure you'll enjoy every one
of these books!

It's time for some BLOND JUSTICE!
*DOWNTOWN DEBUTANTE is Kara Lennox's
second book in her series about
three women who were duped by the same
con man and vow to get revenge.
We know you're going to love this
fast-paced, humorous story!*

Brenna Thompson drew herself deeper into the down comforter, trying to reclaim the blessed relief of sleep. But instead of drifting off again, she awoke with a jolt and smacked into hard reality. She was stranded in Cottonwood, Texas, without a dime to her name, her entire future hanging by a thread.

And someone was banging on her door at the Kountry Kozy Bed & Breakfast.

Wearing only a teddy, she slid out of bed and stumbled to the door. "I told you to take the key," she said grumpily, opening the door, expecting to see Cindy, her new roommate. "What time is it, any—" She stopped as her bleary eyes struggled to focus. Standing in the hallway was a broad-shouldered man in a dark suit, a blindingly white shirt and a shimmering blue silk tie. He was a foot taller than Brenna's own five-foot-three, and she had to strain her neck to meet his cool, blue-eyed gaze.

In a purely instinctual gesture, she slammed the door closed. My God, she was almost naked. A stranger in a suit had seen her almost naked. Her whole body flushed, then broke out in goose bumps.

The knock came again, louder this time.

"Uh, just a minute!" She didn't have a robe. She wasn't a robe-wearing sort of person. But she spied one belonging to Sonya, her other roommate, lying at the foot of her bed. The white silk garment trailed the floor, the sleeves hanging almost to Brenna's fingertips—Sonya was tall—but at least it covered her, sort of.

Taking a deep breath, she opened the door again. "Yes?"

Still there. Still just as tall, just as imposing, just as handsome. Not her type, she thought quickly. But there was a certain commanding presence about this stranger that made her stomach swoop and her palms itch.

"Brenna Thompson?"

Deep voice. It made all her hair follicles stand at attention.

"Yes, that's me." He didn't smile, and a frisson of alarm zapped through her. "Is something wrong? Oh, my God, did something happen to someone in my family?"

He hesitated. "No. I'm Special Agent Heath Packer with the FBI. This is Special Agent Pete LaJolla."

Brenna saw a second man lurking in the shadows. He stepped closer and grunted a greeting. Both men looked as if they expected to enter.

Brenna glanced over her shoulder. The room was a complete wreck. Every available surface was covered with clothes and girlie stuff, not to mention baby things belonging to Cindy's little boy. Even fastidious Sonya's bed was unmade. Sonya was used to servants doing that sort of thing for her.

Special Agent No. 1 didn't wait for her consent. He eased past her into the room, his observant gaze taking everything in.

"If you'd given me some warning, I could have tidied up," she groused, pulling the robe more tightly around her. She hadn't realized how thin the fabric was.

Mustering her manners, Brenna cleared off a cosmetics case and a pair of shoes from the room's only chair. "Here, sit down. You're making me nervous. And...Agent LaJolla, was it?" She brushed some clothes off Sonya's twin bed. La-Jolla nodded and sat gingerly on the bed while Brenna retreated to her own bed. She sat cross-legged on it, drawing the covers over her legs both for warmth and modesty.

"I assume you know why we're here," Packer said.

*If you enjoyed Penny McCusker's first book
for American Romance,
MAD ABOUT MAX (April 2005),
you'll be happy to hear that her second book,
NOAH AND THE STORK, has arrived!
And if you haven't read her before,
you'll be delighted by Penny's warmhearted
humor in this charming story set in the
town of Erskine, Montana.*

Men were generally a pain in the neck, Janey Walters thought, but there were times when they came in handy. Like when your house needed a paint job, or your kitchen floor needed refinishing or your car was being powered by what sounded like a drunk tap dancer with a thirst for motor oil.

Or when you woke in the middle of the night, alone and aching for something that went way beyond physical, into realms best left to Hallmark and American Greetings. Whoever wrote those cards managed to say everything about love in a line or two. Janey didn't even like to think about the subject anymore. Thinking about it made her yearn, yearning made her hopeful, and hope, considering her track record with the opposite sex, was a waste of energy.

She set her paintbrush on top of the can and climbed to her feet. She'd been sitting on the front porch for the past hour, slapping paint on the railings, wondering if the petty violence of it might help exorcise the sense of futility that had settled over her of late. All she'd managed to do was polka-dot everything in the vicinity—the lawn and rosebushes, the porch floor and herself—which only made more work for her and did nothing to solve the real problems.

And boy, did she have problems. No more than any other single mom who lived in a house that was a century old, with barely enough money to keep up with what absolutely had to be fixed, never mind preventative maintenance. And thankfully, Jessie was a normal nine-year-old girl—at least she seemed well-adjusted, despite the fact that her father had never been, and probably would never be, a part of her life.

It only seemed worse to Janey now that her best friend had gotten married. But then, Sara had been waiting for six years for Max to figure out he loved her, and Janey would never have wished for a different outcome. She and Sara still worked together, and talked nearly every day, so it wasn't as if anything had really changed in Janey's life. It just felt… emptier somehow.

She put both hands on the small of her aching back and stretched, letting her head fall back and breathing deeply, in and out, until she felt some of the frustration and loneliness begin to fade away.

"Now there's a sight for sore eyes."

Janey gasped, straightening so fast she all but gave herself whiplash. That voice… Heat moved through her, but the cold chill that snaked down her spine won hands down. It couldn't be him, she told herself. He couldn't simply show up at her house with no warning, no time to prepare.

"The best scenery in town was always on this street."

She peeked over her shoulder, and the snappy comebacks she was famous for deserted her. So did the unsnappy comebacks and all the questions she should've been asking. She couldn't have strung a coherent sentence together if the moment had come with subtitles. She was too busy staring at the man standing on the other side of her wrought-iron fence.

His voice had changed some; it was deeper, with a gravelly edge that seemed to rasp along her nerve endings. But there was no mistaking that face, not when it had haunted her memories—good and bad—for more than a decade. "Noah Bryant," Janey muttered, giving him a nice, slow once-over.

Tina Leonard continues her popular
COWBOYS BY THE DOZEN *series*
with CROCKETT'S SEDUCTION.
These books are wonderfully entertaining and exciting.
If you've never read Tina Leonard,
you're in for a treat. After all,
who can resist a cowboy—let alone twelve of them!
Meet the brothers of Malfunction Junction
and let the roundup of those
Jefferson bad boys begin!

Even now, at his brother Bandera's wedding, Crockett Jefferson wondered if Valentine Cakes—the mother of his brother Last's child—realized how much time he spent staring at her. His deepest, darkest secret was that she evoked fantasies in his mind, fantasies of the two of them—

"Well, that's that," his eldest brother, Mason, said to Hawk and Jellyfish, the amateur detectives and family friends who'd come to the Malfunction Junction ranch to deliver news about Maverick Jefferson, the Jefferson brothers' missing father.

Before he heard anything else, Crockett once again found his eyes glued to Valentine and her tiny daughter, Annette. Watching her was a habit he didn't want to give up, no matter how much family drama flowed around him.

Hawk looked at Mason. "Do you want to know what we learned about your father before or after you eat your piece of wedding cake?"

Crockett sighed, and took a last look at the fiery little redhead as he heard the pronouncement about Maverick. She was holding her daughter and a box of heart-shaped petits fours she'd made for Bandera's wedding reception. She smiled at him, her pretty blue eyes encouraging, her mouth bowing sweetly, and his heart turned over. With regret he looked away.

She could never know how he felt about her.

He really didn't *want* to feel the way he did about the mother of his brother's child. So, to get away from the temptation to keep staring, he followed Hawk, Jellyfish and Mason under a tree so they could talk.

"We were able to confirm that Maverick was in Alaska, for a very long time," Hawk said.

Crockett thought Mason surely had to be feeling the same excitement and relief that filled him; finally some trace of Maverick had been found.

"But we felt it was important to come back and tell you the news, then let you decide what more you need to learn," Hawk said.

Crockett felt a deep tug in his chest. Now they would hold a family council to decide what to do. It was good they'd found out now, since all the brothers were at the ranch for the annual Fourth of July gathering and Bandera's wedding.

Now that so many of the Jefferson brothers had married and moved away, Mason wanted to hold a family reunion at least twice a year—Christmas in the winter and Fourth of July in the summer. Christmas was a natural choice, but Independence Day was a time when the pond was warm enough for the children to swim, Mason had said. But Crockett knew his request really had nothing to do with pond water. Mason just wanted the brothers and their families together, on the so-called Malfunction Junction ranch, their home.

Crockett had to admit there was something to the power of family bonding as he turned to again watch Valentine with her tiny daughter.

*HIS WEDDING, by Muriel Jensen,
is Muriel's fourth book in the saga of the Abbotts,
a northeastern U.S. family whose
wealth and privilege could not shield them from
the harsher realities of life,
including a kidnapping. At last the mystery
of the kidnapping is solved—
by the missing Abigail herself,
with the help of Brian Girard, himself an Abbott
child who will soon be planning his wedding!*

Brian Girard sat on the top porch step of his shop at just after 6:00 a.m., drinking a cup of coffee while reading the *Losthampton Leader*. The ham-and-cheese bagel he'd bought tasted like sawdust when he saw the front-page article about Janet Grant-Abbott's move to Losthampton, and he'd thrown the bagel into the garbage.

"Long-lost heiress home again," said the caption under a photo of Janet that must have been taken on her return from Los Angeles.

From the small plane visible some distance behind her, the setting was obviously the airport. Her hair was short and fluffy, and she was squinting against the sun.

At a glance she resembled any other young woman on a casual afternoon. It was the second look that made you realize she was someone special. Her good breeding showed in the tilt of her head and the set of her shoulders; the intellect in her eyes elevated a simple prettiness to fascinating beauty.

The article revealed all the known details of her kidnap, the Abbott family's position in the world of business, her brothers' accomplishments then her own history as a successful stockbroker.

It went on to say that her adopted sister had come to Losthampton thinking she might be the missing Abbott sister,

Abigail, but that a DNA test had proven she wasn't. And that had brought Janet onto the scene.

He was just about to give the reporter credit for a job not-too-badly done, when he got to the part about himself:

"Brian Girard, the illegitimate son of Susannah Steward Abbott, Nathan Abbott's first wife, and Corbin Girard, the Abbotts' neighbor, has been welcomed into the bosom of the family." It continued in praise of their generosity, considering that Corbin Girard was responsible for the fire in their home and the vandalism to the business Brian owned. It explained in detail that Brian had been legally disowned for defecting to the Abbott camp by giving the Abbotts information that stopped them from making a business deal they would have regretted. Brian has no idea how the paper had gotten that information, unless one of the family had told them.

Annoyed, he threw the newspaper in the trash, on top of the bagel, and strode, coffee cup in hand, down his dock. The two dozen boats he'd worked so hard to repair bobbed at the ends of their lines, a testament to his determination to start over at something he enjoyed.

The refinished shop was restocked with the old standbys people came in for day after day, plus a few new gourmet products, a line of sophisticated souvenirs and shirts and hats with his logo on them—a rowboat with a grocery bag in the bow—visible proof of his spirit to survive in the face of his father's continued hatred.

He could fight all the roadblocks in his path, he thought, gazing out at the sun rising to embroider the water with light, but how could he fight the truth? No matter what he did, he would always be the son of a woman who'd thrown away her husband and other two sons like so much outdated material, and of a man who'd rejected him since the day he was born.

The sorry fact was that Brian couldn't fight it. He could do his best to be honest and honorable, but he would never inspire a favorable newspaper article. Every time his name came up, it would be as the son of his reprehensible parents.

He didn't know what to do about it.

Then again, Janet Grant-Abbott wasn't sure what to do, either.

HARLEQUIN®

AMERICAN *Romance*®

Catch the latest story
in the bestselling miniseries
by

Tina Leonard

Cowboys BY THE DOZEN!

Artist, rancher and bull rider Crockett Jefferson
has always been a man of strong passions. So
when he finds himself thinking passionately
about the one woman he can't have—
Valentine Cakes, the mother of his brother's
child—this sensitive cowboy knows
he's in trouble!

CROCKETT'S SEDUCTION
Harlequin American Romance #1083

Available September 2005

HARLEQUIN®

AMERICAN *Romance*®

BLOND JUSTICE

Betrayed…and betting on each other.

DOWNTOWN DEBUTANTE
by Kara Lennox
(September 2005)

All jewelry designer Brenna Thompson wants
is to get back the priceless gems stolen by
her thieving ex-fiancé. FBI agent Heath Packer
thinks he can help—but he has an ulterior
motive, one he can't share with her. Being
with Brenna makes Heath appreciate life…
but what will she say when she learns the
truth about his investigation?

Also look for:
HOMETOWN HONEY
(May 2005)

OUT OF TOWN BRIDE
(December 2005)

Available wherever Harlequin Books are sold.

If you enjoyed what you just read,
then we've got an offer you can't resist!

Take 2 bestselling love stories FREE!

Plus get a FREE surprise gift!